I0584732

MASS TRANSIT

A BIRDIE KELLEY MYSTERY

ROBERT L. JOSWICK

Black Rose Writing | Texas

©2022 by Robert L. Joswick
All rights reserved. No part of this book may be reproduced, stored in a retrieval system or transmitted in any form or by any means without the prior written permission of the publishers, except by a reviewer who may quote brief passages in a review to be printed in a newspaper, magazine or journal.

The author grants the final approval for this literary material.

First printing

This is a work of fiction. Names, characters, businesses, places, events, and incidents are either the products of the author's imagination or used in a fictitious manner. Any resemblance to actual persons, living or dead, or actual events is purely coincidental.

ISBN: 978-1-68513-071-8
PUBLISHED BY BLACK ROSE WRITING
www.blackrosewriting.com

Printed in the United States of America
Suggested Retail Price (SRP) $22.95

Mass Transit is printed in Chaparral Pro

*As a planet-friendly publisher, Black Rose Writing does its best to eliminate unnecessary waste to reduce paper usage and energy costs, while never compromising the reading experience. As a result, the final word count vs. page count may not meet common expectations.

My deepest thanks to Kirstein Schuder of Apex Literary Management, Steve Amos of Crossroads Writers, my writers group, and my wife Janie and daughter Katie who jointly inspired Birdie Kelley, my super sleuth.

MASS TRANSIT

CHAPTER ONE

November, 1957

Blemished by thin clouds and haze, the muted moon hung above the island of Manhattan. Victor Gregory shut his eyes and inhaled. Life had taken a wrong turn; he'd lost Malda to the empty promises of Broadway lights. His beloved Dodgers fled west, abandoning Flatbush, and Communists were taking over Brooklyn. On top of that, a Russian satellite, *Sputnik*, threatened America, circling overhead every ninety-six minutes.

Stepping to the sidewalk, leaving the subway's scarred, graffiti-covered tunnels, his pulse rushed, anticipating their last performance. Years of sacrifice and study squandered because of her.

Close to the buildings, he melded into the familiar blackness of aged brick and concrete. Victor ran his gloved hand over a brown, worn satchel slung over his shoulder. Heavy rubber soles quieted his step. Despite the late hour, New Yorkers rushed from cramped apartments, filling streets, searching for success and love in a city enthusiastic to crush dreams. Temporary reprieves came in clubs and bars. Victor understood rejection and how the night's darkness hid the flaws of Gotham. Knowing Malda's unwavering habits and religiously sticking to her schedule, he pulled a pocket watch from his slacks using a long chain draped over his belt. He remained on time, as always.

Chilling wind pushed across the Hudson River, driving cold night air past high rise tenements lining the West Side. The late hour brought quiet, enough to hear cries of seagulls and the polluted river slapping against rotting wood docks, keeping time with the heavy pounding in his chest.

At Fifty-Seventh and Ninth, nearing the Windermere Apartments, he slowed, spotting a lone woman step from the Flying Horse Lounge.

She pulled her cape, draping it around her shoulders, letting the shapeless red cloak drag on the cracked and lifted sidewalk. Head bowed, buried inside the oversized hood, she marched ahead through gray shafts of light reaching from the lounge's shuttered windows.

Victor closed his eyes. The voice in his head forced him to listen. He stepped from the shadow of an abandoned record store, moving past lines of iron framed tree guards. Moving toward her, he shifted as the voice instructed. He stepped near the curbstone, knowing she'd trust him—everyone did.

She walked toward him on a collision course. The cape's hood shrouded her head and face.

At the last moment, he stepped aside. She passed. Her cloak brushed his arm. Its touch rekindled a memory flash of time together, both wrapped in the garment, warm, enjoying one another.

She didn't bother to look at his face. It wouldn't matter. He'd changed. Victor Gregory stopped, scanning the empty street.

They were alone.

From the satchel, he pulled his treasured collector's piece, an iron tomahawk forged with a unique pipe bowl opposite a long, slender, sharpened blade. The handle's well-honed wood and brass inlaid haft felt a part of him. He sensed the mighty hand that a century ago gripped the tool of war and peace.

With the swiftness of a hunting warrior, he rushed the caped passerby, slashing the tapered blade into her throat. Bursts of blood shot from her limp head, at the same time a blaring surge of air escaped her severed trachea as she collapsed. She laid in a growing pool of blood as Victor struggled to pull the hatchet free, wiping it clean on the wool cape. For a moment, he stood over her, enveloped in quiet.

He stepped around her twisted body, bending low near the dark hood drooped over her face. Final gasps of air released and stopped. Satisfied, he smiled and used the blade, cutting a silver button from her cloak.

His feet remained within the spreading puddle of blood. Victor removed a black rubber overshoe and straddled his clean shoe to dry concrete and repeated the maneuver, pulling the remaining overshoe off. From his shoulder bag came a large square oilcloth, wrapping the blood-covered overshoes. His hands trembled, tugging off tight-fitting bloody gloves which he stuffed into the rubber overshoes.

He inhaled several times to control his pulsing veins and pounding in his temples. He must seek forgiveness. Life had taken another path, one which he could not restrain.

Music from the distant nightclub carried toward them. The same tune continued to play from when she exited—Chuck Berry's, "Roll over Beethoven."

Passing a line of darkened storefronts, a sudden flash of lights from a window display startled him. From the other side of the glass, a red-haired woman stepped onto the elevated platform. She arranged red and green shoes set in a display of candy canes and elves. Victor rushed past, jerking his face away, pulling a white silk shawl close to his bearded chin. It carried Malda's scent.

At the end of the short block, he turned into an alley littered with crates of rotting vegetables and swarming rats. Flames jumped from a trash barrel, shooting fiery sparks airborne. Rushes of warm air comforted Victor, relaxing him, quieting the voice inside. Jagged flames engulfed the oilcloth, wrapping the rubber-soled overshoes and gloves, dropped inside the can. He stepped closer, watching them melt, dissolving to ash, feeling the calming heat against his face. Mission accomplished. He must give thanks.

On the far side of the street, between Ninth and Tenth Street, nested between tenements and run-down flats, his answer came. Terra Cotta spires of a bell tower jutted from both sides of a steep gabled roof. Inside, Victor Gregory removed his cap and dipped his fingers into a font of clear water, blessing himself. The solitude at once freed his mind. Dim lights kept the house of worship in shadows while votive candles flickered from beside a gothic, multi-leveled altar. Aromatic incense, a church aphrodisiac, lingered, luring underprivileged patrons into generous giving, promising a better life. Inhaling, he enjoyed the heavy fragrance, reminding him of Malda's apartment. He stepped into the sanctuary, hoping it was vacant.

Through the light haze, he spotted a pair of babushka-covered heads, synchronized, bobbing as one in a wooden pew next to the gold trimmed altar.

He wanted to be alone. Two shapeless women in dowdy winter coats knelt, gripping rosaries, repeating murmured prayers.

Standing in the church vestibule, sweat beaded the ridge of his forehead, trickling down his cheeks and neck, dampening his tight, stiff collar. He needed to meditate; thankful the damaging hold she'd held over him vanished.

His hand pressed over the leather satchel hanging at his side, touching the form of the axe handle and blade, reassured him. He reached inside, taking a step toward the praying women, but abruptly stopped and returned to the font of holy water, pressing his back against a marble column.

A black-robed priest marched from the sacristy, hidden behind heavy ornate curtains, genuflected and stepped to a gold-plated box encased beneath the giant crucifix. After removing the silver chalice, he stepped back, bowing toward the altar and exited.

Victor blew out a deep breath, releasing his grip from the hatchet. Both hands reached into the cool basin of holy water, scooping and splashing his face with absolving water, liberating mortal sin from his soul. He backed his way to the doors, stopped and genuflected, not bothering to wipe his soaked face. The elderly women continued their hushed prayers as the door's metal latches snapped shut.

Cold night air off the Hudson chilled him. Somewhere, a bell clanged—a river buoy. The ringing faded into a harsh scream of an ambulance siren. Victor stepped back into the arched doorway, stumbling over a sleeping hobo who blended into the tunnel-like blackness. Something about the tramp unsettled Victor. Their eyes met, and he sensed a foreign, unearthly presence, something which no longer surprised him.

Red and amber orbs of roof lights flashed at the corner and sped along Tenth, braked and turned against a traffic light onto West Fifty-Seventh. Green and white patrol cars blocked the street at both ends. The crowd of onlookers stepped back as the Saint Luke's ambulance slowed and inched its wheels, backing over the high curb, onto the sidewalk.

Zipping his brown leather jacket, Victor regretted failing to take additional mementos from the body. He'd have a last chance to admire his work. Maybe *The Villager*, a city tabloid, would cover the grizzly death. Perhaps a photo?

From behind rickety sawhorse barricades, blue-coated patrolmen cast long shadows into the street as they secured the stark scene. Clots of thick, dry blood surrounded a sprawled corpse. Gathered onlookers hovered near the body while a photographer's flash burst. A few gawkers turned away, while others strained for a closer view of the garish death of the nearly beheaded victim. Two cops, one stocky, the other tall, both in dark wool suits, paced around the corpse. Victor smiled, asking why cops buy low-end suits and wear cheap, heavy-soled shoes after becoming detectives.

He lingered in the crowd, confident of not attracting attention, pushing close to a wide open ambulance door, watching the morbid scene of another New York violent killing.

Could he take another souvenir?

Victor Gregory remained next to the ambulance, aroused, viewing the results of his well-executed plan. Within the growing crowd, they'd keep him unnoticed, a face in a mob of eager faces reveling in each detail of the investigation. Afterward, the lookie-Lew's would catch a late bus or subway home to retell the experience, expounding the details of a life ended on a dirty street in Hell's Kitchen. Times Square and the Great White Way of the Theater District were only blocks away from where his dreams had been laid to rest.

The attendants slid the ambulance cot under the body, still clad in the blood red cape. Her face remained hidden, wrapped in a black, heavy rubber sheet. A medic shouted for onlookers to step away as the cart approached. Turret lights continued to revolve, throwing a red and amber cast across the hellish scene. Nearing the swung-open door, the cart's wheels folded and before being pushed inside, an attendant stumbled and fell to the curb.

Victor jumped in, grabbing the stretcher's side rail. The fallen medical worker regained his footing and rushed back into position, assisting Victor to slide the body inside. Victor smiled at the worker, letting his hand drag across the corpse, yanking away an earring. He merged again into the gathering as they broke-up after the embarrassed medic slammed the rear door. In twos and threes, the audience vanished with the closing stage curtain.

Satisfied, he strode toward Fordham University and the Columbus Circle Station. Inside his coat pocket, Victor Gregory fingered his remembrances and smiled. Malda Boddy had spent her last and final hour in the stage's bright spotlight.

There would be no encore.

CHAPTER TWO

The R train rocked to a stop, arriving at the deserted Brooklyn, 59th Street station. Nearly home and exhausted, Victor Gregory had never experienced the madness or raw excitement as he did tonight. Its sound and fury stimulated a new evolving awareness.

Reaching for his pocket watch, he lifted the waistband of his coat, touching the narrow slit below his belt. A broken silver chain dangled free from his pants. Alarmed, he raced to where he had relaxed in the vacant rail car. He pulled a bus token and a hatpin which pricked his finger from between creases of the padded seats. Licking his wound, he flung the items against a window.

Victor jumped from the subway car as the door slid shut. Patches of sweat covered his face. Where in hell was it? He fingered the empty watch pocket again. Had he lost it in the church he'd visited?

The last passenger car rumbled by, its dull, fading red eyes watching him, vanishing in the blackness of the slow curving tunnel. The vacant set of rails would be clear, all green, returning the train to where he'd boarded at Columbus Circle station.

Why did he go back to Malda's corpse? Had revisiting the scene been necessary? The pleasure of a curtain call? A final bow?

Careless, he was not. Each step rehearsed—flawless, a performance no audience would witness.

He needed to think of his safe refuge, to escape the city and its flaws. With few riders at the late hour, the conductor or transit officer could find the time piece on nightly inspections. Tomorrow, in Penn Station's lost and found, the missing pocket watch would be there among the misplaced items.

Few dim lights illuminated the underground platform. With his heavy-duty flashlight, Victor peeked into locked and empty token booths. All secure for the night. The tunnels and stations, although considered sanitary by city standards, smelled like sewage and soured trash. Despite that, their warmth on wintery nights attracted vagrants and tramps, believing the transit facility a guesthouse.

Inside his jacket pocket, he touched the heavy silver lobes of the button cut from her cape. A frayed thread hung from its loop. The shamrock's four leaflets felt cold in his fingers. The red cape and its unique buttons were her good luck charm. Malda wore it to her last audition. She had worn it tonight. Eve, according to folklore, removed a single clover from the biblical Garden of Eden to remember paradise.

He had almost forgotten the other item taken. To his surprise, touching the diamond earring brought no satisfaction. No connection to Malda. Closing his eyes, he saw the flashing amber lights of the ambulance.

Surrounded by the muted crowd, passing through orange and yellow blinking lights, her wrapped body strapped to a gurney rolled near him, cocooned in a sheet of black. The red cape wrapped around her motionless body. Distracted attendants chatted, sharing a vulgar joke at her expense. It was a snap decision. As they prepared to load the body, a white-uniformed medic stumbled. With a magician's misdirection, he'd stepped close, placed one hand on the stretcher, the other reached inside the hood, grabbing and twisting. She lifted from the gurney as it tore from her ear.

The nightmare charged at him, like a rush hour express train, his memory flashing a sickening image. With jolting realism, he saw the watch jerk from his pocket and break free from its long silver chain.

Cold sweat covered his face and forehead.

The watch, a gift from Malda, celebrated their venture into show business. When she walked out, he scratched away their names and inscription. Nothing remained. He once read criminals take and leave behind clues at the scene of their crimes.

The streets were quiet. Victor hummed, walking, welcoming the solitude of the late hour. At 61st Street he headed west, toward the piers and abandoned warehouses of the Brooklyn Army Terminal. The end of World War II doomed the military supply depot. Cutbacks in the jobs it provided left thousands of Polish and Irish families without work in the modest dockside area.

Abandoned, run-down neighborhoods of row houses and apartments multiplied. Bricked-in windows of affluent, large brownstones failed to discourage vagrants and tramps.

In the distance, the cold water of New York Harbor slapped against decaying wood piers. Near Third Avenue, Victor slowed, enjoying the chilly sea mist against his face. He drew in fresh air he missed so much, accepting his destiny, a castaway from the life he craved and deserved on the Upper East Side.

Tall, corroded chain-link fences, crowned by coiled barbed wire, discouraged vandalism of remaining factories and storage depots.

Through the light haze, Victor eyed the Brooklyn Army Terminal, BAT, as natives called the five million square foot facility. It played the role of an ancient medieval citadel guarding New York Harbor. Its warehouses, cargo cranes, and rail yards wasted away, no longer needed in America's war efforts. Nearby, the familiar Liberty ship had returned home moored, at its dock. Owned by World Wide Salvage and Lev Reznik, the tramp steamer made frequent trips in and out of the neglected port for the past year, none on a regular schedule, as far as he could tell.

To Victor, it didn't matter. Reznik paid cold cash to keep an eye on the vessel when in port. He'd become suspicious of the cargo off-loaded from the mysterious ship. As long as the owner paid him, he'd keep his nose clean.

Stepping over a low-hanging chain at the dead-end street, Victor trudged through thin, dormant grasses of an abandoned boat and tug storage yard. At the far corner, two streetlamps illuminated a tattered American flag flapping day and night over the entrance. Heavy steel and wood beams sunk into hard, crusty ground, supporting dozens of houseboats and out of service tugs.

Victor pulled a cluster of keys from his belt, locating the three needed for the gate's lock, deadbolt, and alarm. He planned to add his security system, not trusting the owner he rarely saw, Lev Reznik, a Russian Jew.

Perched six feet above the ground, the derelict vessels were protected against occasional flooding. Shadows of broken-down boats stretched across the yard, creating images in his mind of aged, hulking creatures which had lumbered home into the fenced cage, searching for a final resting spot.

His boots crunched past rows of deteriorating steel and wood hulls, empty of life except.... A small light burned, as always, in his galley. Since childhood, he disliked returning to a dark house.

The forty-eight-foot houseboat came with the part-time job. Lev Reznik insisted on an on-site caretaker, keeping watch over the vacant terminal as well as discouraging vandals and hoboes from the waterfront storage yard.

Nothing sounded better than home and crawling into bed. His visit to the Liberty ship and tonight's rounds were vetoed. A kick opened the narrow gate. Victor noticed the lifted red flag on his mailbox. He hadn't posted anything. No friends or family existed. A brown envelope curled inside, addressed with his boldly typed name, VICTOR GREGORY. The formality brought a laugh. He turned toward his houseboat, jamming the letter into his jacket pocket.

A narrow shaft of light shot from the nearby houseboat. Surprised, Victor stopped, ducking next to a set of stairs leading to his home, "The Dream Catcher." He crouched, inspecting the houseboat three spots away. A rear cabin filled with a soft pink light. He was the boatyard's sole occupant.

A lone power line strung from a utility pole stretched to the boat's stern and attached to a tall wood two by four.

The trespasser was in for a surprise, like the others.

Victor dropped his leather pouch, kicking it past thick laced cobwebs woven corner to corner from cedar and iron beams supporting his home. A steel storage chest, shovel, rake, and small hand tools lay nearby. A wooden box held tear gas grenades. Victor grabbed a canister and tiptoed to the intruding houseboat.

A stepladder leaned against the boat's gunwales, near the recently installed power lines. With light steps, he climbed aboard and stepped along the raw, unfinished wooden deck. At the rear, pinkish light came from a window. He paused, intending to bust down a boarded-up window and launch the tear gas can. In seconds, the vagrant would gag and become helpless. The housewarming gift never failed to convince the unwelcome guest to vacate. Many fell over the side, running blind. While powerless, Victor administered additional greetings, leading the victim to the street.

Something didn't add up, someone had connected electricity. Curious, Victor peeked inside, hoping to see his special trespasser. Balancing on the rail, he leaned near a narrow, open louvered window, enough to see the bare slender back and scarred shoulder of a lady facing a full-length mirror, combing long black hair.

CHAPTER THREE

Detective Joe Nagle tossed the leather shoulder holster on his cluttered desk at the Midtown North Precinct. If he had thought for a moment six months ago and walked away, he would still be part of the city's elite organized crime unit. Homicide was not his cup of tea. Here he was, working daily scenes of shootings, stabbings, and the many creative ways enraged New Yorkers found to kill each other.

"Who the hell is Mary Clary?" he said to an empty squad room.

"You're about to find out," an unexpected voice shouted from the break area.

Owen Roe carried a paper cup of coffee into the deserted detective offices, heading toward two desks pushed against a dirty brick wall. Gooseneck lamps, twisted at odd angles, lit stacks of files scattered over chipped and scarred wood tables.

Joe Nagle forced a tired smile. "It's late for games. What are you driving at, partner?"

Roe swung a leg over the arm of his chair and swiveled, pointing toward distant high-rise apartments and condos visible through the precinct's large, arched windows.

"Some Broadway fat cat wants his daughter's killer hanging from the yardarm of his yacht."

"Mary Clary?" Joe Nagle asked.

Owen Roe blew on his steaming coffee. "Captain wants to know what we're doing."

"It's been what... three hours since she was slashed?"

"This guy has friends downtown."

"That the file?" Joe Nagle asked, pointing to the brown folder in his partner's hand.

"They woke the medical examiner. It's preliminary."

"Where's the body?"

"Saint Luke's was close."

"The doc must like the theater," Nagle said.

Roe flipped the few handwritten pages until reaching notes describing the victim's injuries.

Nagle sat up and read over Roe's broad shoulder. "The wounds weren't from a knife or blade like we guessed."

Roe held his finger on the page and looked at his partner. "I can't read this bullshit scribbling."

"He said it was a chop, judging by the gash. It almost took off her head."

"An axe?" Roe said.

Nagle turned sheets of police forms and photographs fastened to the folder.

"There's a sketch... the blade has an extended, thin taper, longer than a standard hardware store axe," Nagle said. "Killed her quick."

"Other marks?"

"Later today. In the final report."

Nagle knew what came next. Nothing.

He'd suffered a stern dressing-down along with the humiliation of being busted back to junior detective, thanks to botching a search near the Brooklyn Army Terminal. Here he was, filling out reports, fed up with 5's, and knowing before the ink dried, they'd catch another case. Mundane routine would break him. He planned to redeem himself, rebuild his reputation. Without a sponsor in the upper ranks, he had no choice. He'd find a way to solve a major crime.

Roe sat back, rocking in his chair. "Was the attacker behind her or in front?"

"M. E's working on that."

"He usually has a theory."

"Didn't say anything."

"That's hard to believe."

"What are you driving at?" Nagle asked

"You should know."

"What's that?"

"It's obvious," Roe said. "Since you got dumped here, you've been trying to crack these on your own." He waved his hand over the piles of current files. "Get your old job back."

Joe Nagle tossed the file next to his handgun. "I called the M.E. to speed things up."

"He told you something."

"This is it." Joe Nagle nodded to the file.

CHAPTER FOUR

The surprise of a female intruder caused Victor to lose his footing, nearly falling from the houseboat's railing. She had to be deaf. The table radio blared, but not enough to cover the ruckus he made a few feet from her window.

A fog of steam hung in the cramped room. She tapped a barefoot to the beat of Elvis's, "Jailhouse Rock" while brushing long, black hair. Parted in the middle, it fell over her shoulders to a narrow band of white skin crossing her slender back.

Was he mistaken? Did her eyes lift, for an instant, spotting him in the hazy mirror? She shook her head, letting her hair spread flat along her shoulder blades, adding sway to her hips with the beat of the music. Puzzled, he slid the gas canister into his jacket pocket.

Unsure if he had been exposed as a peeping-tom, Victor scrambled from the rail, returning to the deck. The music continued and increased in volume. Wary, this was no ordinary trespasser. He took pride in reading people's motives, which led to the promotion. He'd take it up with the reclusive Russian Jew, Reznik.

As he climbed the splintered stairs, Victor returned to his sanctuary and removed the tear gas can from his pocket. The forgotten crumpled envelope slipped from his jacket and fell to the floor. No return address, his name typed in large bold letters. The little mail received was delivered to a post office box.

Despite fatigue and desperate for sleep, curiosity won. He ripped the taped edge open, pulling out a single white sheet of paper. The memo, on World Wide Salvage's stationery, looked important in spite of spelling errors, scattered commas and, he guessed, the Russian Jew used a pint of correction fluid.

Victor dropped the letter to the table. The quiet boat storage yard was destined for beachfront living. Renovations, restoring the aged vessels to a habitable condition, began within the week. His new neighbor, the on-site leasing agent for the new Seashore Villas, lived three spots away.

Victor re-folded the stiff sheet of paper, sliding it into the brown envelope. At arm's length, he lit the galley's propane stove. In a second, the fiery ball blackened, decomposed, and vanished in the bottom of a trash can.

Satisfied, he returned to the shoulder bag, removing the tomahawk, scrubbing the blade with scalding water and hydrogen peroxide, removing traces of blood. Nice and clean, the antique axe was wiped dry and placed into the satchel. On his knees, he slid it under a sofa bed. His new neighbor came to mind. He circled the room, shutting curtains, wondering if she'd return his visit.

One he looked forward to.

After placing his leather jacket on the wood hanger, he examined it and his dark blue shirt for blood spatter. As a precaution, he attacked from the rear, using a sweeping motion, using Malda as a guard from the spray of blood.

A splash of brownish-red blood dotted his polished metal shield. Victor grabbed the heavy coat, inspecting the sleeve insignia. The round, yellow and black patch with bright gold stitching highlighted the city's skyline and the tail end of a subway car. The emblem, known as "The Lemon", belonged to the tunnel rats of The New York City Transit Police.

It suffered no damage and remained spotless.

His cramped showers, powerful sprays of hot water washed his body, like baptism, freeing sin. Would Malda become a martyr, with her few fans burning candles and placing flowers at the site of her death?

From a cabinet near the galley, Victor removed a copper and gold bowl, along with a small wooden mallet. Cleansing the body brought liberation of the mind and a return to equilibrium. After he wove his legs into a lotus position, Victor sat on a bamboo mat, cradling his meditation bowl in his palm, recalling the calmness preceding birth. Slow, steady breathing induced a mild trance. Muscles from the soles of his feet to his neck relaxed in warmness, melting away hostile feelings he'd harbored against Malda.

He laid the mallet against the bowl's top edge, circling the lip, applying slight pressure, following an ancient tradition of tenth century Tibetan monks.

The soothing song of the bowl radiated a tone. Its peaceful rhythm pulsed within. Tomorrow he'd start his life again.

No, no, a voice shouted in his subconscious.

Malda lives.

CHAPTER FIVE

"No, no," Detective Owen Roe shouted, spilling the paper cup of coffee on the precinct's conference table.

Captain Parnell and Joe Nagle jumped, knocking back thick wooden chairs as hot steaming coffee flooded the green Formica table and dripped to the tiled floor. Parnell brushed his hands against his dry slacks as he backed into the corridor.

Parnell took a deep breath. "You're cleaning this when we're done, Roe."

Roe crumpled the cup and tossed it into the wastebasket. "Go to hell. I'm not the janitor."

As soon as the words flew from Roe's mouth, Parnell marched back into the squad room, stepping through puddles of coffee.

Both cops appreciated the captain stayed out of their way, city politics being his strong suit. Parnell kissed the rings of every power broker in the five boroughs, seldom venturing among the working class cops. Something big blew in the wind.

Parnell stepped close to Roe, pointing a finger at his chest. "Sit and shut up."

Joe Nagle slid between them. "We have a murder. Can we start?"

Parnell dropped a new file folder on a small table near a wall phone. "You caught a hell of a case, Nagle. Don't let your partner's temper push me into tossing you two off."

Roe waved his white handkerchief over his head.

Parnell nodded. "Don't make me the heavy. I'm following orders. What've you got on Mary Clary?"

"An actress," Joe Nagle said. "We don't know much."

"Like it or not, you're gonna have help," Parnell said.

"This is going somewhere I don't like," Roe said. "What the hell you driving at?" Roe laid his palms out in front of him... waiting.

"Something you two should understand—"

"We don't need interference," Roe said.

Parnell held a hand up. "Let me finish."

"By all means." Roe shrugged, lighting a stubby cigar.

"You can bang your thick head against the wall. Nothing will change what's been ordained by the city's higher powers."

"That important?" said Nagle.

"The victim's father, Sidney Tilson Breen, has friends in the mayor's office."

"Big shot Broadway producer," Roe said, circling his index finger in the air.

"Mayor Wagner takes crime and influential people seriously."

"Not necessarily in that order," Roe said, stomping to the window, his back to the room.

"Victim's name is Clary," Nagle said.

"Stage name," Parnell said. "She didn't want favors because of family."

Parnell did an about face and stepped from the room.

Roe shouted. "What kind of help?"

"Birdie Kelly," Parnell shouted back. "... and don't push me."

It was a punch to the gut—hearing her name. Roe rubbed his face, recalling the sting from the slap the day she walked in. It happened on Birdie's birthday. Everyone was loose. They all let their hair down. He helped Hollis find her earring, nothing else.

Roe kicked the table, splattering cold coffee on him and Nagle. "Case could be big. We wouldn't mind seeing our names in the papers."

Parnell returned a slight smile on his face, pointing to the new file, winking. "Share only what we give the public."

"Who's Birdie?" Joe Nagel asked, glancing between Roe and Parnell.

"Former Pinkerton, before that, an actress in the city." Roe closed his eyes, calming himself. Why did he let her control him? What would she do to dominate the investigation? Her acting skills were always in play and impulsive. He never knew what to expect.

Joe Nagel flipped through the file Parnell left behind. The first page, a typed note on the mayor's stationery, gave the address and time to meet Birdie Kelly for lunch. A scrawled message from their boss, at the bottom of the page, instructed to let her pick up the tab.

"Where we dining?" Roe asked.

"Sheffield Plaza, Ninth and West 57th."

"Near the murder scene," Roe said, examining his coffee-stained coat and slacks. There was no point to rush home to Queens for a newer suit.

Joe Nagle snapped his fingers. "I like her already."

CHAPTER SIX

Victor awoke with sticky eyes, opening them with splashes of cold water dipped from day-old dishwater. Noticing thin streaks of dried blood on his palms, he scrubbed them until realizing he'd imagined it.

Change disturbed him. The abandoned boats he watched over were about to become homes to the new long-haired generation populating the city. Till now, he shared the docks with transients, seagulls, the Liberty ship, and today her.

Musty perfume lingered in his thoughts. Discovering the tall, older, but firm female wearing only a sheen of water from a steamy shower stunned him. Her unblemished olive skin, near perfect except for the jagged scar, intrigued him. Victor shuffled his feet, waiting for the kettle to boil.

From the port side window, he hoped to see the sky; instead, the rising sun remained hidden behind dirty, overstuffed clouds which overtook New York Harbor in early winter.

A dim light came from his new neighbor's boat. She was an early riser. The pot's whistle broke his concentration. Without his pocket watch, time got away. Tardiness was not in the genes he'd inherited from unknown parents. He arrived in a shopping basket at the door of a Newark fire station. Orphanages and foster homes conditioned promptness at meal time.

Once dressed, Victor stood at attention facing a full-length mirror inspecting a new, dark-blue shirt and three brand new chevrons on the upper sleeve. Five years of work and study brought the advancement.

As much as he tried, he couldn't silence his doubts.

The meditation bowl's message and his dream pushed him, to be sure. Her face hidden, shadowed inside the hood of her wool cape as she exited The Flying Horse Lounge. It became a religion to Malda after her show's final curtain.

After pulling the silver clover-shaped button, he'd cut from her cape, from a bureau drawer, he examined it, although tarnished, it belonged to her. The pearl and diamond earring, taken as they wheeled her by, puzzled him. The pearl's roughness against his teeth confirmed it genuine. He guessed the same for the single diamond. It couldn't be hers. Malda detested shows of wealth.

To stay undetected by his new neighbor, he rushed from the boatyard, carrying a peanut butter sandwich made days ago, and a Thermos of instant coffee. Everything fit snug inside the satchel, which, at no time, left his side.

Pleased to have avoided crossing paths, he allowed himself to relax. His spirits lifted as the magnificent Manhattan skyline granted him a view. Thick clouds passed, pushed by a chilling wind off the bay, leaving streaks of thin haze smudging a blue sky.

The sullen profile of the gray, four-hundred-foot Liberty ship anchored nearby reminded him of last night's neglected rounds. Tonight, he'd walk its decks, inspecting the empty ship. The vessel slipped in and out of the terminal like a ghost ship. There were times he was sure of hearing dull, hollow sounds from its holds. Lev Reznik had been firm. Those areas were off limits.

A sudden chill hit Victor, forcing him to zip his leather patrol jacket. His hand stopped at the shield of the New York City Transit

Police, perfectly placed and shined. His fingers touched raised brass letters—Sergeant.

As always, he ran ahead of schedule. The N train was due in forty-two minutes. The tower bells rang clear in the crisp air from The Basilica of Our Lady of Perpetual Help. He'd have time to check the paper's coverage of Malda's savage death.

Brooklyn was Brooklyn, not much changed. Gig's was a place you settled for, more from habit than taste. After shooing away flocks of pigeons congregated near trash cans fronting the café, he stepped in, scanning the cramped space for left behind papers. Disappointed, Victor dropped a nickel into a coffee can, grabbing a fresh morning edition from a stack inside the foyer. He favored *The Daily Mirror* for its continuing attack against bureaucrats.

Blue work shirts and pinstripe suits mingled at the counter. He took a stool opposite the door and settled in, opening the paper. The bold headline, "Sputnik Continues Orbit of Earth," almost brought a laugh. More danger existed on the streets than from the Russian spaceship hundreds of miles away.

Victor propped his elbows on the laminated counter, turning the tabloid's pages, hoping to see Malda's mutilated face.

The Hurst paper thrived on New York's violence. Something was wrong. Nothing appeared.

"The usual?" asked the white-aproned waitress.

Startled, Victor ordered coffee, not bothering to look away from the pages.

An ache churned in his stomach. He'd check a later edition, regretting *The Village Voice* published weekly. It was their type of story.

Coffee arrived, steaming hot, along with a bent, smudged spoon resting on a paper napkin quietly slid next to the cup and saucer. He didn't bother to thank her, but refolded the newspaper. Each crease and page exactly as it had been.

Disappointed, Victor worked a quarter from his pocket, pushing it to the counter's edge. He saluted an entering beat cop and slipped past, dropping the paper to its original pile while retrieving his nickel. The feeling of being watched overcame him. After a quick look, he spotted nothing suspicious except for a scruffy, over coated man limping from the diner. He'd not recalled seeing him inside the diner. Maybe an oversight? A carryover of nerves from last night.

Walking toward the Sixth Street Station, the bells of the Basilica chimed, sparking thoughts of the meditation bowl and doubts of Malda's death. At mid-block, Victor stopped at the shabby three-story apartment building near the subway entrance. Leaning against the red painted railing guarding the stairs, he took a deep breath before joining the masses, moving through lines of noisy, ratcheting turnstiles—descending to Dante's hell. Last night, with a surge of primitive power, he'd entered the seventh circle, violence.

The museum's plaque claimed his rescued pipe tomahawk was a prized part of Indian history, presented to Seneca Chief Red Jacket as a symbol of peace and diplomacy, by General George Washington.

He'd swung the ancient weapon with efficiency and accuracy, his skill drawn from the dead warrior.

The MET relegated it to a little-used exhibit in a distant wing of the museum. Not long after, to a crate in its catacombs.

Victor spotted the spindly young man in leather sandals and long hair entering the terminal—a member of the new beat generation. A guitar slung over his shoulder, one of the free spirits taking over the city. Greenwich Village became home to free love, drugs, coffee shops and bad poetry.

The lanky youth stood out among the suburban commuters, lingering near busy token booths, looking for left behind change. As the incoming train stopped, he hopped a turnstile and shoved his way toward a waiting subway car.

With an adrenalin rush, Victor shoved through the crowd, hopping the same turnstile with ease. The beatnik wove through rushing travelers and pushed inside a crowded passenger car. At the far end, he turned his back to the door and gripped an overhead strap. Eager to cuff the lawbreaker, Victor worked his way past seated and stand-up passengers, giving them time to view his sergeant stripes and shield.

The train rattled and swayed around a long curve as Victor shoved the long-haired trespasser. The offender staggered, regained his balance and turned, exposing a transit officer sitting with ticket pad and pen in hand. Undaunted, Victor intended to pull rank, taking the arrest. After a quick glance, he noticed a gold bar on the crisp, white shirt and jacket shoulder. The higher ranking lieutenant looked at him and grinned.

"I got him, sergeant," the officer said, emphasizing Victor's lesser rank, waving the ticket book. "Spotted him in the terminal. We've been looking for this one."

Victor smiled, backing away, tapping his empty watch pocket. He'd forgotten. The transit system's lost and found department had been on his list of rounds.

After squeezing his way through crowded railcars, he climbed into the locomotive. Unlocking the cab door, he took a seat near the motorman.

How can a human do this all day?

He had nothing in his view but a hypnotizing single light, illuminating track and tunnel walls burrowing beneath the streets.

At Penn Station, he glanced down the line of emptying passenger cars and took a position near a metal staircase, hoping the long-haired member of the beat generation would emerge.

As Sergeant, he commanded the day shift's ten patrolmen, protecting the peace of the city's crossroads. The badge allowed freedom to roam the massive hub and the entire city.

Nickels and dimes bounced into the red felt lining of a violin case, rewarding three tuxedoed musicians. A somber-faced harlequin clown played harmonica and tap danced. Had the beatnik exited earlier to strum his guitar somewhere in the city?

He gave up too quickly and once shared their passion. Malda was the cause if she hadn't walked out on him, denying connections. A simple endorsement....

The lost property office, housed in the lower mezzanine, became a burial place for thousands of items left behind in the 450 stations and 6,000 train cars of the mass transit system. Bypassing the counter, Victor waved his way past clerks assisting passengers claiming misplaced belongings. Like tombs, cramped and musty floor to ceiling wood cartons crammed unpainted wood shelves. Victor rushed by row after row of purses and briefcases until reaching stacks of smaller items. With little confidence of success, hoping his vision of losing the pocket watch at the killing had been wrong, he searched the shoe boxes packed with men's and women's watches.

After the last container, he gave up but intended to return. In need of a watch, he grabbed a simple one with a leather band.

He'd calculated his attack carefully. His return to the scene proved careless.

Before being missed, he'd store his lunch sack and coffee in a work locker. He climbed to the station's main concourse, which never failed to impress him.

Immense riveted lattice and webbed girders raised fifteen stories above, shaping tall arches spanning the boisterous mall while throngs of commuters waited to be swept away by the hundreds of trains crisscrossing Penn Station. Vaulted skylights formed a greenhouse over it all, drenching the granite floor with filtered early morning sunlight.

He should be pleased, accomplishing his mission. Why did the voice deep in his head deny her death?

Victor glanced at the terminal's massive clock suspended over the concourse. After a check of the time, he set and wound his new Timex. Television's John Cameron Swayze promised it would take a licking and keep on ticking.

Could Malda have survived?

Holding back from breaking into a sprint, he rushed past congested ticket counters and baggage claim areas. At the far end, a concrete archway opened to Eighth Street. There, stacks of open bundled morning and later edition papers surrounded the kiosk.

He searched several newspapers, finding no news of last night's killing.

"Any early afternoon editions?" he shouted to the newsboy.

"Couple hours, mister."

Victor dropped the papers on a still-tied stack, walking away.

"This ain't a library!" the boy yelled. "You cops never pay."

With those echoing words, he looked at his new wristwatch, deciding to check on his officers, make sure they were squared away, let 'em know he was boss. After inspection, he'd visit Saint Luke's. Malda's body would be in the morgue, waiting for dissection. He didn't care to see the postmortem, only confirm it was her.

What if he'd made a mistake?

Streaks of dried blood again appeared on his palms.

CHAPTER SEVEN

Roe and Nagle arrived at the Sheffield Plaza for a briefing lunch hosted by Birdie Kelly, as arranged by the mayor.

Joe Nagle looked toward the Upper West Side high rise. "Expensive digs for a PI."

"She knows the manager," Owen Roe said, "... and uses the lobby for an office."

"She in there?"

"We'll wait and see," Roe said, pulling a cigar from inside his sports coat while taking a seat on a curved bench fronting the building's gardens.

"We going in?" Nagle asked.

"Note said meet here."

"Plenty of good eating spots. Don't matter to me."

Roe looked at his watch. "If she's late, we're not wasting time."

"You two look hungry," Birdie Kelly shouted, carrying a wicker basket, marching toward the detectives. Behind her, uniformed doormen closed polished metal doors. "Let's get to work." She nodded to a group of park tables.

Not expecting much cooperation, she hoped to get off on the right foot and gain a small bit of respect. Anything they knew beat what she had—nothing. Recognizing her impulsive bent, she planned to relax and be nice.

Spotting him was a jolt. Of all the luck. Why was he back in her life? Working the case with Owen Roe was a bad break.

She marched to a table near a large reflecting pool and plopped the picnic basket in the center. Despite the bad luck, she asked with a smile, "Are you going to let me do all the work?"

"It's chilly," Roe said. "I thought we're meeting for lunch?"

"Owen, have you forgotten what a picnic is? Still like Katz's Pastrami?" She handed him a folded red tablecloth. "Put this, nice and neat, over the table. You'll think you're in one of those swanky places you like."

Nagle stepped forward, helping his partner. "You two know each other."

"Long story," Roe said.

Birdie arranged white butcher paper, wrapped sandwiches, bowls of potato salad and creamed cucumbers on the table.

The task finished, she looked at Roe. "Aren't you going to say anything?"

"You mean bless the food?"

She let her hands run down the sides of her gray wool dress. "I lost weight."

"I knew what you wanted," Roe said. "You look good. You're taller."

"Heels, I can wear 'em again." She looked down at the stilettos and performed a well-practiced pirouette, followed by a curtsy. "With them, I'm six foot."

"Let's get to business," Roe said, opening a file and setting it next to an open sandwich wrapper.

Birdie felt the slight but held back and smiled. "We'll take one glove off."

"What?" Nagle asked.

"Eating while you work," she answered. "It's an old expression."

Nagle placed the crime report in front of Birdie.

"What's this?" she asked.

"We're playing nice and sharing," Roe said, taking a large bite from his pastrami sandwich.

Birdie shook her head, patting Roe on the shoulder. "I got a copy. A messenger delivered it. I want the Medical Examiner's report—not background on the victim."

"Don't have it," Nagle answered.

"Tell me what you have," Birdie said, waving the closed file near Roe's face.

"This is it," Roe said. "This isn't our only case, so—"

She cut him off. "That's why Birdie's here. Tell me what you think, not what's in this bullshit report."

"The killer, we assume, is male, used some kind of axe or hatchet to attack the victim," Roe said. "So far, no witnesses. She left a nearby club alone around midnight."

"The victim has a name, Mary Clary," Birdie said. "Anything taken?"

"Not as far as we can tell."

"That's it?" Birdie asked.

"For now," Nagle answered. "Beat cops are going door-to-door to neighboring shops. Traffic's checking tags of cars parked in the area. We may get lucky. Roe and me, we'll do a routine check with family and friends."

"After that, the file goes in a stack on your desk," Birdie said.

"We'll do what we can," Roe said, walking from the table, puffing his cigar.

"Anything on her clothes?" Birdie asked.

"We're not rookies," Roe said. "We examined everything at the scene—zilch."

Nagle turned to Roe, then back to Birdie. "Check the report. It's all there. Nothing unusual."

Birdie stopped chewing and swallowed, staring at the crime scene photos, knowing the two held something out. Lunch was over, so much for expecting cooperation. She recognized her next step.

"Someone chops off a girl's head, leaves no tracks, even though the damn sidewalks are covered in blood and all you have to say is there is nothing unusual."

Birdie paused, catching her breath. "What have we come to in this city?"

"We'll take a closer look," Roe said.

She regretted the outburst and tossed a half-eaten sandwich to a flock of begging pigeons. An apology would signal weakness. She gathered containers and napkins, along with remains of their lunch, and shoved it into the basket.

"I'm not counting on luck to find the killer."

Roe and Nagle crumbled empty wrappers, tossing them in a street trash can. Roe spoke as he stepped close to Birdie. "You and that Irish temper haven't changed. We're done here."

She closed the basket and smiled. "The M.E's report?"

"Someone will deliver it to you, I'm sure," Roe said. "Same place?"

"Good," Birdie said, pointing toward the high-rise. "Give it to the doorman. If you don't mind, one of us has work to do."

"Wait," Roe said and took her by the arm.

"Wait! I have been since my accident," Birdie answered.

"... and I feel sorry about that. Things got crazy. I should have been there for you."

"The flowers were lovely." Birdie touched Roe's hand. "You could have visited. That would have been wonderful."

"I broke it off with Hollis."

"I'm glad."

"So am I," Roe said and laughed. "I'd hate to waste what we had. I haven't forgotten the ring."

"At Mort's. I nearly forgot." Birdie lied, protecting her pride.

She'd cherished the day they'd selected it and often returned to admire it. Her friend, Mort, promised to hold the engagement ring until she and Roe were ready.

"For now, we have a case to work," Roe said. "I hope you can put aside our history so we can work together?"

She looked at him and tapped his jacket, knowing Owen Roe occasionally sent mixed signals to hide his tactics and motives.

As soon as the two homicide detectives left, she tossed the files into her oversize shoulder purse and whistled for a taxi. She planned to outmaneuver Roe and Nagle.

*****

Birdie Kelly paid the driver and requested a receipt. She noticed the rosary hanging from the rearview mirror and hoped Saint Mary's power would somehow be with her.

Her first stop, the crime scene. She stepped from the cab on 57th, near the Flying Horse lounge. A mix of businesses, depressed low-rise apartments, and a few remaining curbside trees lined the narrow street. The early morning sunshine faded into a grayness brought by a stiff north wind. She spotted the beat up blue sawhorses guarding the scene of Mary Clary's murder. Hell's Kitchen was only a short block from the bright lights of Broadway. Birdie recalled the good times spent in the seedy bars lining the street.

Splotches of dried blood remained on the cracked sidewalk. She crouched over the splatter, pushing her ballpoint pen into small pieces of solid matter suspended in the blood. Looking close, she guessed it to be bits of bone and flesh, supporting the initial police report the killer used a heavy bladed weapon. The size of the blood splatter indicated a fall of five feet, telling her the victim stayed on her feet and had not been knocked to the ground before being bludgeoned. She'd add that fact as a separate note to Roe and Nagle's version, knowing they may have omitted a few observations once the two detectives learned she'd join their case.

Birdie stepped from the sidewalk, crunching into a gutter of dried leaves. In the street she tried to imagine last night's attack, relying on her mind to re-create the scene, hoping to gain insight into the brutal assault.

Nothing stood out on the lonely, dirty street. Blood, which yesterday pulsed through a young woman, today stained the cities' dirty concrete.

Feeling the cold, Birdie saw enough. She wouldn't bother to attempt hailing a cab and instead planned to walk to her next stop. She hoped it would be more productive. Anything found at the scene would have been bagged and recorded as evidence. While she stood in the street, a New York City Traffic Safety van, yellow lights flashing, pulled to the curb. For a moment Birdie watched two men in gray coveralls disassemble sawhorses and crime scene markers. She guessed it a sign of Roe and Nagle's intent not to return. According to the case file, they had no more clues than she had.

Though there had been something her client said. If true, she'd gain the upper hand. Despite the two cop's attempt to stonewall her, she'd learned from their wafer-thin report, and Roe's admission, they hadn't yet obtained the victim's personal property. They had done their inspection of Mary Clary's body and belongings at the scene—not the ideal location. She'd gamble and pay an unauthorized visit to Saint Luke's morgue.

Cheered by this small break, Birdie stepped to the sidewalk. A gust of wind swept away piled leaves, scattering them in a whirlwind beneath her feet. She stopped and stood over the iron storm drain. Blood diluted in morning rainwater dripped down the drainage grate.

* * * * *

Saint Luke's-Roosevelt Hospital had been home for almost a month. Surgery repairing her shoulder and hip brought complications, keeping her bedridden. The old hospital near Columbus Circle gave no fond memories, besides walking out without a cane.

Her life had taken numerous paths. The most severe detour landed her in Saint Luke's, occurred while performing on Broadway. The accident brought down stage lights and rigging, crushing her under a mass of steel and glass. Before her shortened acting career, she worked seven years as a Pinkerton detective. Because of quick thinking and improvising, her revolver never left her purse. Guarding actresses and wives of pampered Wall Street investors had opened doors on the Great White Way.

Birdie stared at the hospital's grimy, worn brick and concrete facade which overlooked the Upper West Side. Solving her first and only case began here. Time worked against her. Chances of solving a murder diminished after the first seventy-two hours. Everything became stagnant and cold, clues, witness memories and, above all, police interest.

There was no plan, only hope for rushed and inattentive morgue attendants. Once passing through the central lobby's revolving doors, she spotted the reception desk and elevators watched over by a familiar security guard. She couldn't afford to be recognized and shielded her face, turning away, moving to a private stairway, taking it to the basements.

During rehabilitation, she searched for diversions to pass time. With no interest in card games or Scrabble, adventure came roaming the building's unfriendly lower bowels, exploring the morgue and hidden areas. The stairs led to the first sub-basement. A wide hallway narrowed, crowded with cartons stacked to her shoulders. One direction led to the morgue and offices used by department pathologists.

Attendants and general staff used the smaller rooms near the lower level entrance. She felt as if she'd descended into hidden passageways of an Egyptian tomb as she walked the gray tiled hallway, arriving at the viewing room and body storage lockers. Disliking cadavers, she planned to avoid the area. Birdie's objective was not the corpse of Mary Clary. There was something else Roe and Nagle missed or held back.

It was all she had, her motive for trespassing; chancing arrest came from a hunch, something Mary Clary's father whispered to her while viewing his daughter. After being told, she'd discounted it. Sid Breen was grieving and in shock, understandably confused.

It wasn't likely Nagle and Roe, despite the mayor's office, would be much help. She needed something, anything. If she had been nicer? She hadn't forgiven Detective Owen Roe. How long had it been?

Tampering with evidence was a bad idea and would land her in jail. Her bank account hovered near a hundred dollars, not enough to make bond.

At twenty-five, Mary Clary had already become a successful actress and had not lived at home for years. Her father could not know her entire wardrobe. Most likely, it was nothing but worth making sure.

Roe and Nagle should have been told.

Waiting until the cops returned the personal effects to her client allowed the clues and trail to age. She needed to act quickly; besides, Sid Breen had little patience and considerable power. A speedy resolution would boost her fledgling business and infuse much-needed cash. After settling debts, she'd find an affordable basement office in Greenwich or Soho.

Corpses involved in a murder rested on a trolley, locked in an isolated cold storage area and held as evidence. She planned to search and inspect Mary's clothes and belongings, maybe find a clue overlooked by Roe and Nagle on their inspection at the crime scene. Everything would be boxed, inventoried, and kept in the morgue offices near the bodies.

She heard footsteps coming toward her.

The few doors in the hall were locked. Birdie found herself trapped at a dead end and her last option sat in front of her, a chipped and dented white metal door. A sheet of yellow paper taped to it read, Private Keep Out. The lever handle wouldn't budge. Someone approached. Birdie gripped both hands on the bar, lifted herself off the ground, pushing it down. In a surprise, it swung open.

Her hand fumbled against a smooth concrete wall, finding a junction box and light switch. The long, wide, unfinished room was filled with racks of green metal shelves and massive doses of industrial strength, Pine-Sol. Folded white sheets filling canvas laundry carts cluttered the center of the room. Loud voices continued down the hall.

Birdie put her ear to the door, shut off the lights and waited. Whoever approached must have changed their mind, at least now.

Florescent lights sputtered on again. A light bank at the far end fluttered, giving the old hospital basement an eerie, unsettling appearance and seemed to shrink and bloat. This time Birdie questioned if she'd slipped into an old thirties movie with Boris Karloff lurking in the shadows.

Birdie pulled a large, numbered metal container, the size of a file drawer, from a shelf. It contained a dark suit, shirt, and scuffed men's shoes. On top, a paper bag with a watch, cuff links, and leather belt.

She hunted the room for paperwork matching numbers on the containers with a name.

With luck, Mary Clary's clothes were not in Roe and Nagle's possession.

At first, she missed it; a sullen, drab gray glassed-in office hid behind tall shelves filled with pillows. Pushed against a wall sat a heavy-legged table, void of photos, coffee cups—only a phone and notepad. She guessed the workplace unused.

A quick search found a clipboard sitting on a dusty file cabinet containing outdated telephone directories. The sheets were identical, alphabetized by the victim's last and first name, followed by address and contact phone number. Below that, an itemized list of personal belongings.

Birdie flipped several handwritten yellow pages, spotting—Clary, Mary. In bold red, the number 21 circled at the bottom of the form. Scotch-taped to it, a note.

Hold for NYPD, Roe and Nagle pick up.

She's won a minor victory and smiled, reading the day and time on the pink reminder slip. The two called the morgue after they left her. She had to hurry.

The black phone startled her. Its sharp, high-pitched tone echoed in the tiny room. Looking down at the unwelcome intruder, she spotted a tan purse leaning against the desk leg. Its owner could burst in at any moment.

Trapped, she wouldn't panic, years on a live stage taught improvisation. She'd have a look at box 21 before Roe and Nagle confiscated it. Birdie grabbed the phone from the cradle and held it to her ear.

"Yes," she answered.

"Lobby security. I'm sending down two cops."

Before she could stall their arrival, the line hummed. The voice was gone. How long did she have?

Birdie rushed to the shelves, pulling Mary Clary's clothes from above her head.

A paper bag sat on top a blood-stained, navy blue dress. Inside were stockings and underwear. Birdie then reached inside the crumbled sack, feeling jewelry. Curious, she spilled the contents, a silver watch bracelet, along with a single pearl and diamond earring to the table. After a quick inspection, she grabbed the jewelry and tossed them back into the bag. She needed to get out now. Time worked against her. She may have squandered her escape.

Getting a jump on Roe and Nagle took a back seat to being caught tampering with evidence. Birdie stuffed the bag inside her purse.

Sid Breen's earlier statement of not recognizing his daughter's cape came to mind. The red wool cape lay folded at the bottom of the metal box—she wouldn't leave without it.

Birdie grabbed it and yanked. The silk dress and shoes flipped into the air, falling into the box. Something else appeared. How did she miss it? A pocket watch with a broken chain rested near the dress. Not hesitating, the timepiece went into the bag with the other jewelry. She slung the heavy red cloak over her shoulders, covering her own, coat and was about to make tracks for the entrance. After seeing Mary's purse, she hesitated.

She ran her hand inside, finding a billfold packed with tens, twenties, and fifty's. The money made little sense. It was easy to take, faster than prying rings and jewelry from a dead body. The motive wasn't robbery.

She tossed the purse and billfold next to the dress, needing to escape. Roe would have her behind bars and off the case.

Birdie buttoned the pilfered cape and adjusted the hood, covering much of her face. Her large purse, concealed under the bulky garment, carried additional proof of her crimes. She pulled off her heels and headed toward the rear entrance used by the ambulances, hoping Nagle and Roe took the elevator or stairs from the upstairs lobby. Since security called, she assumed they did.

In the wide hallway, Birdie walked at a fast but not hurried pace. A smile covered her face as she approached the rear entrance and escape. A white and red ambulance rolled slowly under the roofed area, blocking the glass double doors.

Two morgue attendants appeared and marched beside her. Hospital security and coffee drinking staff nodded as she passed. Feeling conspicuous in the stolen blood red cape, she shoved her hands into the long cloak's pockets. If her client was correct, who did the cape belong to?

She picked up her pace—wondering, had she over-stepped? She acted no better than the thieves she arrested as a Pinkerton. Before exiting, she took one last look behind. No sign of the two detectives.

Cold air hit her face. Then a chilling fear forced her to a stop. A uniformed officer approached. The way he stared at her struck her as odd. There was something familiar about him. If not security, or NYPD. Who?

CHAPTER EIGHT

Victor Gregory stepped from the subway near Columbus Circle, blocks from Saint Luke's. Work delayed him, thanks to morning arrest and ticketing reports.

As sergeant, he no longer ran down the crazies plaguing the five boroughs. The city bureaucrats expected reports, detailing commuters jumping turnstiles, counterfeit tokens and aggressive panhandlers. The promotion had not been what he'd anticipated. Being handcuffed to his beat-up desk had become all too frequent.

Maple trees along the street were practically bare; dried leaves swirled past, lodging against entryways of high-rise residences and medical offices. He inhaled, the cold air felt refreshing, giving him confidence. As he walked, he tapped his badge pinned to his heavy coat. Although not officially part of the city police, his rank as transit officer brought professional courtesies.

The stately Upper West Side hospital covered the entire block. Close to the public entrance and purposely hidden, a wide ramp led to its lower level, his destination. Unmarked, it serviced coroner's ambulances and funeral home vehicles. Malda's corpse would be kept in storage here until released to her family. He hoped to confirm the body delivered last night was hers.

He caught a break. The two spots reserved for police cars were vacant. From behind, a red and white ambulance, without lights and siren, came toward him. Victor stopped oncoming cars with a stiff arm while waving it past, watching it turn into the steep drive. Satisfied traffic was in control; he carried on, his authority as a peace officer unchallenged.

Victor rehearsed his lines one last time as he approached the hospital's glass doors, hidden under the ambulance bay, confident he'd be convincing.

His mind drifted back... alone in front of bright lights holding a script. His solitary voice echoed, reading to a darkened theater. A momentary tremble and a missed line spoiled his performance. A distant cough and a cigarette lit signaled his finish. We'll let 'ya know, cued his exit. He rushed off stage, avoiding the entering actor.

The sliding doors opened. As they did, a tall figure wrapped in a shapeless red cape brushed past, nearly walking into him, dodging at the last moment, turned and ran barefoot up the sloping ramp, disappearing. He was caught off guard, stunned by the appearance of Malda's cloak. The face buried in the cape's hood, just as it had been last night.

Had his imagination fooled him? Victor hesitated, looking back to the hospital door shut. No one chased the runaway. He dashed back to the street, hoping to spot the mystery runner. At the sidewalk, he collided with a pedestrian, catching the frail man and grasping him, preventing a fall. Victor's eyes shot in the sprinters direction. Both she and the coat were gone. Bus and subway stops were not far off on 114th Street. She may have hailed a cab, or like many New Yorkers walked, enjoying the cool, crisp late November day.

Two hands pushed his chest. The old man broke free from their near embrace. Victor stumbled back, surprised by the older man's strength. The man turned away, brushing off his frayed coat, and limped into an alley.

Victor suspected he'd previously encountered the vagrant. Tempted to stop him for questioning, he passed, more pressing business waited in the morgue and the person he chased. Angry with himself, his first reaction should have been to stop her. After several deep relaxing breaths, he circled the block, hoping to spot the distinctive cape in the surrounding neighborhoods and parks. Whoever she was vanished for now. He'd return to his search after his visit to the morgue.

Victor caught his reflection in the hospital glass door. He appeared trim in uniform, and his cap sat squarely on well-groomed dark hair. Casual but confident, the mark of a talented actor and police officer— maybe a touch of boredom in his voice? Showing too much interest, as a transit cop, in a homicide would bring unwanted attention in the morgue.

Entering the lobby, he approached a pimple-faced attendant. Victor noticed the metal name tag pinned to the blue lab coat. He spoke to Oscar.

"A murder victim come in last night?"

Oscar nodded. "This is New York City. What do you think?"

Victor looked down at the young man and stepped close. "Her name is Malda Boddy."

"Don't know names. I just get the bodies ready."

"Who can tell me?"

"Got a case number?" Oscar asked, pointing to a beat-up filing cabinet behind an unmanned lobby desk and pay phones.

"Mind if I look?" Victor scanned the room, deciding if he should stay.

"You might get lucky. The new ones are at the bottom."

Oscar rushed away before Victor asked more questions.

Victor waited a moment, no one noticed him, and walked to the files. They did not question the transit badge. The attendant was correct, files used no names, just numbers. He guessed they matched a toe tag in the back room. It appeared hopeless, with so many records to search, he'd become conspicuous.

Heavy footsteps shuffled down a corridor behind him, the same direction Oscar retreated. Two men in thick-soled shoes walked behind a curly-haired man in a white lab coat and black rubber apron. Victor turned back to the files, guessing them to be detectives.

He thought for a second, recalling them from the murder scene. Victor remembered the shorter cop was called Roe by his partner.

Could they have seen his face? He had remained in the shadows, behind the spotlights of the ambulance. Had the detectives assigned a patrolman to watch the crowd on the chance the killer hung around, reveling in the aftermath?

Victor closed the file cabinet with a hard push. From the corner of his eye, he caught the three looking his direction. Victor tapped the cabinet top and turned to face the cops.

"I'm done. I'll get out of the way," he said.

The two cops shouldered by, ignoring him.

Victor doffed his cap, smiled, and stepped aside. He crossed the lobby and took a seat at an open pay phone. After dropping a dime into the slot, he dialed his home number while watching the detectives.

The short, heavyset cop stood over the white-coated coroner as he pulled open the bottom drawer.

"How can you lose her coat?" Roe asked.

"Let's be sure she had it when we checked her in," the coroner said, standing up opening the gray folder on the cabinet.

Not saying a word, the coroner looked at the file, peering over the tops of his glasses. After a moment, he folded it closed.

"There's a problem," he said. "They brought the victim in wearing what they described as a long wool cape."

"You're damn right there is," Roe shouted. "That coat's evidence in a murder. We need to examine it."

Victor watched the two, knowing all too well the battles he fought within his department. No one on the city payroll accepted blame. They passed it around. The taller detective jumped between the two as they stood, sweating noses and foreheads inches apart.

The coroner bent to the lower drawer and slid the file inside the front edge of the cabinet.

Victor kept an eye on the ongoing argument. They had led him to what he searched for. He'd remained patient, no rush, and wait them out and then retrieve the file, confirming his victim.

Tonight, a celebration. A bottle of wine to break the ice between him and his new neighbor. What he'd seen of her so far looked good.

First things first, he waited, sitting in a phone booth, watching the three argue. They shouted at one another as if alone in the small lobby. It ended with the doctor swinging his arms over his head, pushing past the cops and rushing off into the hallway. The Mutt and Jeff detectives chased. Victor paused, waiting before he approached the files. A door slammed, their voices trailed off and disappeared.

All he needed was a minute. Pulling the bottom drawer open, he found the gray folder the coroner and cops argued over. He looked for a name.

Victim: Clary, Mary, Female, 25 Yrs. Caucasian.

Victor stared at the name. There must be a mistake. Had the wrong file been pulled? He dropped to his knees and rifled through each folder in the cabinet, finding nothing. Curious, he returned to the first file. The date of death matched, as did the location and description of the murder scene. An attached page recorded personal property found on the victim. Victor ran a finger down the list and stopped at the last four items. They were all familiar. He'd removed them from Malda's corpse, except the last—the pocket watch he'd left behind.

One long wool cape with hood. Red with large silver buttons, one missing.

One silver wristwatch.

One pearl and diamond earring

One silver pocket watch, badly scratched

There had been a paperwork mix-up, an unfortunate occurrence during the late shift which drew less capable employees. It explained why the two detectives became angry. He'd been careless, losing the engraved watch on his return to view Malda's body. It had been a gift, symbolizing their acting careers, their names etched inside theater masks. Thanks to lady luck, he'd scratched out the inscription, making the timepiece useless to identify him.

The morgue visit had been foolish and a risk he should not have taken. The lost pocket watch would not be useful. He hoped for a small mention of the bloody murder in the late afternoon papers, along with identifying the victim. Malda, an unknown understudy, rarely appeared on stage would receive minimum coverage, nothing like a big star.

The sight of Malda's wool cape worn by someone fleeing the morgue tested his self-control. Nothing made sense since last night. Could there be a higher divine power working in his life? He no longer had Malda as a shining light, preventing his slipping further into the dark place he feared. There had been something else—he sensed being watched.

She wore the red coat, lying dead on the street. If the hospital lost it in error, they could have easily blundered identifying the body. Someone like Oscar may have stapled the wrong papers to a file. Her clothes and eclectic tastes set her apart. She never failed to wear the unique blood red cape and often joked it brought out the devil in her.

Victor replaced the file as found, pushing the door shut with the toe of his polished shoe. There was nothing he could do and exited the building. Could this have been a clever plot by the police to trap Malda's killer? He wouldn't be trapped. He, too, wore a badge.

As a transit cop, he had authority to question city bus drivers. The route near Saint Luke's and Columbus Circle saw many passengers, and he hoped a driver remembered the red cape. Before he drew attention to himself, he had a simpler plan.

The day's unfinished arrest reports waited for him at his Penn Station desk. First, to satisfy his curiosity, he'd take time for a second walk, canvassing the perimeter near the hospital. The runaway may have hidden in a nearby building, waiting out his earlier search. As a cop, he knew the best source of information in New York's well-off silk stocking neighborhoods came from the men in uniform guarding the doors.

Doormen elaborately dressed in styled and fitted wool overcoats stood as sentries, employed by the upscale apartments, did more than open doors, walk pets and whistle down cabs. As unarmed security, the athletic men possessed a keen sense of observation. It would be difficult for anyone in a red cape to go unnoticed.

Victor questioned many he found standing post. With a few, he pounded on doors, pulling them from early dinners. He planned to circle the block until he spoke to each of them.

Most greeted him with a smile, none volunteered information. Their loyalty belonged to generous tenants.

He'd reached a dead end unless a bus driver spotted the red cape.

Nearby, a Chevy step van turned a corner, double parking in front of a small market and deli. A heavyset man hopped from the passenger side and removed the unsold papers from metal racks and inserted fresh copies of *The New York Post*. If the murder made the news, *The Post's* later edition would exploit it, providing readers with graphic photographs.

Bold photos of Martin Luther King and Fidel Castro captured the front page. Victor turned pages and spotted the small headline.

Broadway Producer's Daughter Slain

A smiling headshot of the victim's face ran as a postage stamp-sized insert below the producer's larger image. Victor staggered, stumbling back against a display shelf, knocking long, crusty loaves to the floor. Catching himself, not bothering to replace the sticks of bread, he took a seat at a small counter, sharing it with two long-haired young men.

Details of the murder matched, except the victim. According to the hospital and now the paper, he killed a stranger, the paper identified as Mary Clary, not Malda Boddy. How did he go wrong? The coat belonged to Malda, a gift from a fan, tailor-made, her name stitched into the satin lining. It didn't have a twin, he was sure.

There had to be a mix-up. *The Post* rushed sensational stories to press and later, retracted in small obituary sized print, buried deep in a classified section. The explanation had been simple. It should have occurred to him sooner. The paper would not confirm a victim's name unless they happened to be a celebrity. With ordinary citizens, they took information released by the hospital morgue. The original error transferred itself to the newspaper.

It had been dark. Could he have made a mistake? He'd rushed, failing to see her face. Did he go to the correct street? Could someone besides Malda have worn her cloak?

Who in blazes walked out of Saint Luke's morgue wearing it?

Victor needed to find Malda. He'd prefer to check the morgue again, but he couldn't simply walk in and inspect the body. Her apartment would have to do. She had been lucky to find the cheap one-room flat above a Greenwich Village pizza kitchen. He disliked the surroundings and long hairs that moved into the once quiet area. After that, it would be the theater she worked.

He riffled through the paper, finding the entertainment page and current Broadway productions. Should he pay five dollars for a balcony ticket or wait at the alley's stage door? He'd vowed to never return to the theater. After a few seconds, his finger stopped on the title, *The Tunnel of Love*, playing at the Royal.

CHAPTER NINE

Birdie Kelly paid the cabby with her last four crumpled dollar bills and asked for a receipt. The twenty, she kept for an emergency and pinned to her bra, represented the last of her ready cash until her client's retainer check cleared—with luck tomorrow.

She slipped the receipt into an envelope stored in her leather purse. A small, hammerless Ruger rested in its own pocket, easy to reach. She'd shoot through the purse with nothing to obstruct the .38 caliber bullet. Beside it, a paper bag contained the belongings of her client's daughter. She touched the brown bag, knowing she'd committed a felony, stealing it and the red cape. The contents of the bag would remain a secret—no point letting her client know.

PIs occasionally operated on the jagged edge of the law when working a case. Clients paid her to do things they weren't willing to do on their own. Risks were taken. Police bent rules, planting evidence, coercing confessions, and misleading judges, all in the name of justice. The cops she knew, including Owen Roe, were all about clearing cases, promotions, and bragging rights. Fabricated testimony by a bad cop or one of their informants sent many people to prison. That's how the legal system worked.

She did not excuse herself for what she did. The evidence from the morgue had been degraded, not useable in court. When she brought the killer to justice, she'd need other proof.

She knew all too well the personal items in Mary Clary's morgue box would not be examined. In thirty days, the police would send it to storage to rot, buried the same as Mary Clary. Classified as an active case by the police, Mary's belongings most likely would never be returned. To New York City and the over-worked cops, the murder case was unofficially dead, chalked up as another random street killing and added to the growing list of unsolved killings. She would be a single force keeping the victim's case active. As she became better acquainted with Sid Breen, she'd let him know of her theft.

Instinct told her the cape, along with the contents of the paper bag, would be helpful. She needed to examine it alone.

Living in Brooklyn wasn't the best situation with her current and only job. Rent was free but not convenient. The case required full attention and late hours in Manhattan, leaving little time to commute to her new place. She wanted an office in the Theater district, close to Broadway and bright lights. This is where the crime happened and where it would be solved—by her.

Birdie suspected the bloody attack to be more than a senseless, random killing. The murderer used the dark sidewalk as a stage. He could have used a knife or handgun, both easy to conceal. Instead, the killer sought a grand finale, using a large tool for a gruesome death as the final curtain dropped.

This was her turf, where she belonged. She would solve the murder, establishing a reputation—her mind made up. One of the day's objectives would be a request for a full-time car and driver and use of an office.

The familiar neon sign of Sardis flickered overhead. She wasn't in the mood to eat and hoped her client Sidney Tilson Breen would be in his ninth-floor office above the popular Broadway eatery. Something about Mary Clary's red cape bothered her. It may be nothing, but the cape seemed oversized and much too long for the owner. While riding in the cab, she spread the heavy wool cape across her lap, examining it for the first time, and spotted the dried blood. It wasn't the blood that interested her. Strands of long blonde hair clung to the coat's shoulders, puzzling her. The victim's hair had been naturally black. While folding the cape, she noticed the bottom seam appeared unsoiled and showed little to no wear. During her short time wearing the cloak, it dragged the pavement. Birdie knew the victim to be shorter. For an unknown reason, she reached into the cape's pocket and pulled the puzzling item out. Many things didn't add up, and she hoped her client could help.

A moment ago, she'd had zero leads and now, thanks to her break in, she had two. She hoped there would be more after the police released the final autopsy. Her next task, clarify the coat's ownership with Sid Breen.

Sid Breen Productions was surprisingly busy when Birdie walked into the main entrance of her client's penthouse office. Birdie carried the red cape over her arm as she passed several well-dressed men and women waiting in the crowded lobby. Sid required a daily report in person in his office. His door was open no matter what he was doing.

She had never been shy, and in her new occupation, aggressiveness proved she belonged in the male-dominated world of private investigating. Birdie guessed the men waiting were private detectives hoping to take her case. Conflicted, should she become more like them, suppressing feminine behavior? But could she revert back? Had it been the reason for her enjoyable Gypsy Rose Lee performance with last night's voyeur?

The job came as a stroke of luck. A publicist close to Sid Breen, unknown to her, recommended her because of her ties to Broadway and Sid believed the killer was an actor or someone familiar to the theater district.

Birdie knocked once on the smoked glass door and stepped in, closing it behind her. Sid Breen lowered a thick sandwich to the white wrapping paper and lifted his round face. No pictures of his daughter hung among the many covering an entire wall. His curved antique desk failed to reveal anything personal, lacking photos of family. There could be several reasons.

"Hungry? Something from downstairs?"

She shook her head and smiled. "You said if I find anything..."

He remained at his desk and pointed to a coffee table surrounded by leather chairs and a worn sofa covered by a blanket. A yellowed pillow rested at one end.

Birdie arranged the cape in her lap, folding and refolding it, being sure to hide the dried blood. After taking a seat, she noticed heavy puffiness under his blood-shot eyes. She guessed he hadn't slept and wouldn't for a long time. The loss had taken the drive from Broadway's prolific producer.

Breen pulled a white napkin from his collar.

"Tell me what you've found."

"I did something I shouldn't have," Birdie said.

"My father told me not to invest in show business, but here I am... so tell me."

"This isn't my coat," she said, holding it up. "I took it from the morgue."

Breen pressed his heavy lips together, looking at Birdie and the red cloak in her lap.

She didn't wait for an answer and asked, "Have you seen it before?"

Breen looked at it again, not responding.

"After you identified her body, you told me this coat wasn't hers."

Breen nodded.

"This is the coat she wore when she was killed."

"You took a big chance," Breen said.

"You were correct. It's not your daughter's."

"Mary lived at home until recently," Sid Breen said. "I never saw it before."

He ran his hands over the coat, stopping at the collar. "Button's missing. My daughter would not tolerate that."

Birdie pulled out the silk lining of the oversized pocket, revealing a line of sewn in silver buttons and red hand-embroidered lettering.

She smoothed the fabric. "Do you know this name, Malda Boddy?"

Sid Breen sat back. "I'm not much help."

"This coat belonged to Malda Boddy, but your daughter wore it," Birdie said. "Did she use an alias?"

"My daughter's real name is Mary Breen. Clary was her mother's maiden name."

Birdie smiled. "She wanted to make it on her own."

"She was stubborn."

"Do you know the name?" Birdie repeated.

Sid Breen held the cape close, inspecting the red fine stitched cursive.

"Could be a friend. This happened so fast, and I'm not sure of anything."

"I suspect Malda Boddy was a close friend." Birdie regretted using the past tense and touched the cape, speaking in a soft voice. "Is there any way you could check?"

"My daughter's friends were all actors. They knew her as Mary Clary."

Birdie ran her hand over a black and red label sewn near the collar. "Fritz and Schoultz Company. Know them?"

Sid nodded. "Custom tailors on Lexington."

"They make costumes for the theaters."

"That they do," Sid said.

"Was she working?" Birdie asked, changing the subject.

"Since February. The Tunnel of Love."

"Gene Kelly's directing. The Royale on West 45th?"

He nodded. "She replaced Doris Day in the lead."

Despite the tragedy, Birdie detected pride in Breen's voice and body language.

"It could be someone from the show," Birdie said. "What else was she involved in?"

"The show became her whole life." Sid stood hunched over his desk. "I'll make calls."

Birdie jumped to her feet, putting a hand on his arm, stopping him from lifting the handset. She backed away, returning to her seat. She should not have touched the hallowed producer—not this early in their association. Through gossip, she knew both sides of Sid Breen's reputation. Taking a moment to gather herself, she tugged at the hem of her dress.

"I'd rather visit the theater and talk to the cast."

Breen tapped one of the black phones covering his desk. "I want to do something."

"I'll let you know."

Birdie welcomed the offer, deciding to continue with her findings. The amenities she'd request wouldn't be a problem.

Sid eased his hand off phone. "Someone may be missing a coat? You think?"

"I'll start with the owner." Birdie held the cape up. "Malda Boddy could give me a lead on the motive."

As she spoke, Sid Breen spun a heavily loaded Rolodex. He frowned and pushed it aside. "I keep track of actors who have worked for me."

"And?" Birdie asked.

"No luck. She can be anybody."

"You're sure?"

"I told you, I didn't know her."

The thought hit her. Why hadn't she made the connection sooner when first seeing the stitched name inside the cape?

"I will need your help now."

Sid Breen stayed quiet. He tilted his head back and raised his arms, revealing sweat-stained armpits. "So ask... already."

Birdie refolded the cape, exposing Malda Boddy's name, holding it near his face. "She may have been the intended victim."

The announcement brought Sid Breen from his chair.

"This madman killed my daughter by mistake?"

"It's a hunch," Birdie said. "The coat's owner may know who did this."

Breen lumbered around the desk, taking the coat from Birdie, staring at the name.

"You said all your daughters' friends were in show business?"

"If she's an actress, I'll find her."

"They may have been together last evening," Birdie said. "They had to know one another pretty good to loan a cape like this. It wouldn't have been a mix-up. They knew one another. I'm sure of that."

Birdie felt a great deal more confident about what she planned to ask. She'd earned his respect.

"Sooner the better." Birdie pointed to the phones.

Sid looked at her.

"I have to find her before the killer does."

* * * * *

Birdie sat at the desk of her new office, compliments of Sid Breen, and laughed out loud. How did she get herself into this? Once, she'd been a climbing actress, above even her expectations. Now, here she sat in the cramped, musty room staring at two coffee stained visitors' chairs and a threadbare couch slid into a dark corner. At the rear of the building's ninth floor, not the view of Broadway's bright lights and glory she longed for. At least it offered the prestige of a Manhattan address—temporarily.

It didn't seem that long ago her personal life and acting career headed in exciting directions. In a single second, it altered. She'd moved from the Brooklyn flat shared with Roe after the surprise of spotting him enter a mid-town hotel. He hadn't been alone. Hollis Gail, a city meter maid, wrapped an arm around his waist while the two slipped into a revolving door. She'd been prepared to accept the weakest explanation. He declined and accused her of spying, refusing to discuss the incident.

She packed a suitcase, escaping Roe, and rushed to the theater early for her performance, hoping the empty auditorium offered peace. That same day, her world crumbled again. The stage lighting rig collapsed, crushing her. She wondered if Roe meant anything to her. The eighteen months they'd spent together were tumultuous, both driven in their careers. As a cop, Owen Roe earned a reputation for tenacity, to the point of finding evidence where none existed and forcing confessions at gunpoint. She, as an up-and-coming actress, sacrificed morals, securing roles and slight fame. It ultimately resulted in a clash of two selfish personalities. How had they existed for a year and a half? Between thorny moments, there were roses wrapped in velvet. Did she wish to invest a lifetime with Roe? Could she handle the thorns?

The view of the fire escape and alley below reminded her she was close to living in a cardboard box under a bridge in Queens. For now, this would do.

Although a part-time job at a rundown boat storage yard in Brooklyn gave her free rent, it was not much better than an empty corrugated box. Her present living arrangements in Seashore Villas of Sunset Park offered the thrill of teasing a nosy neighbor.

Results were needed and fast. Despite the cozy charm of Sidney Tilson Breen, Birdie knew his reputation as a producer. He paid generously and expected immediate answers. Enemies and that covered everyone in the theater business, referred to him as make 'em bleed Breen. He demanded his Broadway productions draw sellouts and rave reviews. If not, the show closed before the stage lights cooled. Sid Breen's gentle side showed today and would soon wear off if she didn't find the killer.

She waited for Sid's call, giving her Malda Boddy's address. It would be her next stop. If correct, and she had faith in her hunch, the case was close to being solved. Collecting the hefty payment would be welcome, but solving and closing case ahead of Roe and Nagle would make her feel like a kid on Christmas morning.

The car service she asked for was a throwaway and not expected. Sid Breen didn't flinch. The vehicle came with a full-time driver. Birdie looked at the business card, "Top Hat Limo." She believed locating the coat's owner, Malda Boddy, would be the break needed to close the case. She stood at the threshold of the new life; one forced on her since her accident. She would stop at nothing to solve the murder of Mary Clary.

Birdie kicked the door shut and dumped the contents of the paper bag on her new desk and picked up the pocket watch by its broken chain. She could only read fragments of a few scratched out letters hidden under a scarred silver plating.

Luckily, a friend in the jewelry business owed her a favor.

CHAPTER TEN

Victor walked three blocks from the Port Authority Bus Station, arriving at the poorly lit, narrow alley off West 45th. Ahead, a hooded light illuminated an unmarked stage door recessed in a grimy brick wall of the Royale Theatre.

Knowing actors preferred to show up early before a performance, he planned to catch them before they scattered to dressing rooms to exercise voices or relax, preparing for an eight o'clock curtain.

He was more than an hour early and the stage door, Johnny's and Mary's, were in place, staked out near the heavy metal door. Hordes of fans held Playbills, pens, cameras and gifts—some appeared lavish. It astonished Victor anyone would attach themselves to actors. How well did they know them? They were mere performers, an illusion reciting lines written by someone else.

Did Malda somehow remain alive? He tried to push the thought from his mind, not permit himself to consider it, despite the newspaper's erroneous report. Last night he found her, as expected, leaving her favorite club, wearing the distinctive tailored cape she never failed to wear. Although certain, he'd wait at the stage door to confirm the axe did its job. How would he notify *The New York Post* of their mistake?

An anonymous letter from a concerned reader?

In uniform, he waited at the far edge of the alley, keeping a distant aloofness from the building crowd, hoping no disturbance occurred, requiring his official attention. He was a peace officer, not a star-struck fan. His badge would gain entrance to the theater. He wished to avoid scrutiny from actors and staff on the chance he'd be remembered. He'd remain faceless to the crowd and arriving actors. Many came in cabs, others walked, strolling to the single door guarded by a chain-smoking stagehand.

Thirty minutes passed with no sign of Malda. Victor knew, although she worked as an understudy for several actors, she routinely arrived early, allowing plenty of time, never knowing how she'd be costumed and made up. Lines were read and rehearsed during this period.

Waiting became maddening and difficult, he had become too noticeable in his transit police uniform. Had a break been applied to the passing of time? Torment made it feel that way and, with every minute that passed, lessened his chance of an unwanted reunion.

Victor's confidence grew with each opening and closing of the stage door. She never arrived this late; nothing broke her routine. His conviction strengthened, and he allowed himself to relax, recalling the unexpected raw pleasure of spying on his new neighbor.

The headlights of the black limousine glared into the crowd as it crept into the alley. The black Cadillac crawled between buildings, inching its way, rolling to a stop at the stage door. Streaks of rain, like darts of light, glistened in its bright beams.

Onlookers shaded their eyes and parted, anticipating.

The uniformed driver stepped from the car to open a rear door. Victor recognized the show's star, Darren McGavin, as he exited opening an oversized umbrella. Immediately, Malda rose from the limo, wrapped in a gray wool coat.

A jolt of panic hit Victor. He let himself fall back against the rough stone wall, staring as she walked silently through the onlookers, waving off autograph requests and gifts. Her eyes darted about the crowd as she passed under the dusty haze, framed in the spotlight overhead.

The doorman took a last drag and slammed the door shut. It took less than a minute. He saw her, Malda Boddy, alive. There was no doubt.

Had she glanced his way?

She arrived with the leading man in a limo. During the show's nine-month run, Malda had been an understudy, appearing as the lead a handful of times. That type of stage door reception had been reserved for stars.

Victor pulled his tie and collar loose, straining to breathe. How did this happen? The shuffle of feet near him alerted him to the stage door fans were breaking up. A passing voice asked no one in particular, "Will they keep Boddy as the lead?"

Another spectator responded, "Who knows? Mary Clary could be related to somebody. That's how she got the part after Doris Day."

Alone in the alley, Victor Gregory shook his head at the dispersing crowd. What did he see, an apparition returning to torment him? A year had passed since she walked out. Her pale, drawn complexion unmistakable. Yet doubt lingered. He'd been uncertain, separating visions from the reality of daily life.

He pulled his collar and necktie tight and ran both hands down his blue jacket, brushing off light drizzle and glanced at his wet palms. Blood covered both.

Victor leaned against the stage door, seeing the next newspaper headline, "Show loses second leading actress."

He was invisible to the public, moving about the city acting as a guardian angel. She couldn't hide.

CHAPTER ELEVEN

The contents of the paper bag—comb, lipstick, tissue, the usual things found in a woman's purse gave Birdie a personal feel for the victim, Mary Clary. At the start, she believed the attacker knew and stalked the quarry. The murder of Sid Breen's daughter was a horrible case of mistaken identity. By a quirk of fate, two ladies exchanged coats, altering destinies. How long would it be for the murderer to make that discovery? Birdie was hopeful, bordering on confident, the intended target, Malda Boddy, knew the killer.

She took a deep breath, slowing herself and whispered, "Let evidence lead to the suspect and solution."

The red cape and personal property, stolen from the morgue, gave her a big jump on Roe and Nagle.

The Pinkerton Detective Agency had drilled the simple axiom into her—jumping to conclusions caused errors of judgment. To isolate relevant clues from the noise was her job, as it was initially to consider everyone a suspect.

The personal effects were pushed aside with a quick sweep of her hand. Birdie remembered the slim case of a pocket watch and broken chain and pulled it from her purse. She slid it near the small wristwatch and stared at the two. In a moment, she slipped the watch back into the large pile.

What remained intrigued her.

Although the pocket watch had been part of the victim's possessions, at least according to the morgue's inventory, Birdie had doubts. Why carry it and wear a wristwatch? She studied the case's heavy gashes and scrapes—obviously an attempt to remove an engraving. Cleaned and examined under a powerful magnifying glass, it could make sense. Birdie recalled Sid Breen disclosing his daughter's meticulous care of her belongings. The haphazard scratching didn't fit. If the watch belonged to her, Birdie believed the inscription would have been expertly polished out. The big questions popped into her mind: Who owned it? How did it get to the murder scene, and why did Mary have it?

Was the single pearl earring Mary's? Why only one? She added that to the growing list of questions. Pleased, the case was taking shape. She had a good start and felt confident.

The killer was careless, maybe their first time, making several errors, beginning with misidentifying the victim. Birdie slammed her fist on the desk. Malda Boddy needed to be found for her safety. Why was it taking Sid Breen so long to locate her addresses? Something didn't smell right about the recent meeting with her client. Did he hold back information?

Frustration built, and when it did, she took risks.

Today she broke many laws, putting her new PI license in jeopardy. Not to mention jail time. To return what she found in the morgue to Roe was out of the question. She was sure he'd run to the district attorney. She'd tainted evidence, preventing it from being connected to the attacker, making it useless in court.

It all centered on Malda. With or without her cooperation, she'd become the bait, a lure to capture the murderer. The physical evidence Birdie had spoiled would not go to waste. She'd make sure they would find it in the killer's possessions. Words from her training, again, echoed in her mind. All criminals took something from the scene and left something, no matter how small. Birdie smiled, there were times justice needed a little help.

Except for the pocket watch and earring, Mary's belongings were slipped into the bag and shoved to the back of a bottom drawer. They'd be returned to her client once the case closed.

The office door eased open. Birdie looked up, seeing Breen's secretary, stiff-faced with a complexion-complementing her pale gray dress. She entered, inspecting the barren office. Her hands rested on her hips, avoiding contact with the room's contents. She squinted her long face and stepped around the visitor chairs to the front of Birdie's empty desk, dropping a sheet ripped from a shorthand pad. It floated to the wood desk.

She nodded and blinked false, inch-long eyelashes. "Sid sent this."

Birdie looked up, deciding not to make an enemy. Every business she'd known had a deadly viper lurking, ready to take down new arrivals. This one slithered from her office wearing a gray pinstripe dress.

The door closed as silently as it opened. Clicking high heels echoed down the hall.

Birdie waited until she heard the door to Sid Breen's suite open and shut at the far end of the corridor before reading the handwritten note. She placed her palm on the paper, staring at the addresses.

Sid Breen came through, locating Malda's workplace and apartment. For a moment, she imagined how he felt. No, she stopped; emotion would not find the killer.

She made a call to Top Hat Car Service. The ride to the Royale Theater was short, only a few blocks. For an instant, she thought of walking and then reconsidered. The luxury of the car service wouldn't last much longer.

The pocket watch went into her purse. Her first stop would be a nearby jewelry shop, which stayed open late, catering to the Theater District. Curious, Birdie examined the watch face, looking for anything explaining how it got into Mary Clary's morgue box.

She'd overlooked something so obvious she wanted to scream. The scarred timepiece ticked reading the correct time. The owner, or someone, wound it recently. It didn't belong, yet it sat, ticking in perfect rhythm, nagging her. What did it try to tell her?

Time escaped Birdie. She looked at the clock, picked up the red cape and jumped to her feet, remembering the car service. Her first case was on its way to being solved, along with collecting Sid Breen's promised ten-thousand dollar bonus.

She paced the small lobby, glancing at every passing black Cadillac. When tonight's final curtain fell, she'd be there to greet Malda Boddy, the new Broadway star.

The tap on her shoulder surprised her. "Ma'am."

She jumped and stepped away, thinking a panhandler approached her.

"Miss Kelly?" he asked.

"I'm Birdie Kelly."

"Then I'm your driver, Jark." He half-bowed, offering his hand.

"You?" she asked, looking at a row of parked cars. Nothing resembled the limo expected.

"Top Hat Car Service, that's me."

After adjusting the red cape hanging over her arm, Birdie stuck out a hand. "Pleased to meet you... Jark."

"Where to?"

"Jewelry store around the corner, then The Royale Theater. Know it?"

He smiled, waving toward a double-parked green and white Dodge four-door sedan.

Birdie followed, allowing him to open the rear door and help her enter. Disappointed. However, she was pleased the car was clean and didn't smell like a pool hall ashtray. Jark didn't wear the top hat illustrated on his business card, but his broad, friendly smile matched his plaid wool shirt. He wasn't from New York; perhaps Texas or Oklahoma.

After two blocks, late Manhattan traffic backed up, leaving them at a standstill fronting a row of boutique shops and a brightly lit travel agency.

"This is good," she said, stepping from the car. "Find a place to park."

Birdie spotted "Mort's Gems and Jewels." The small basement level store imitated its reclusive owner, hiding below the street, beneath an "appointment only" Tiffany lamp shop. As she entered, a bulky tabby sauntered past, dragging its dull, yellowed coat and bushy tail against Birdie's legs.

Morts appeared empty, but she knew better. The retail floor was an obstacle course cluttered with well-lit glass showcases crammed with glistening necklaces, rings, and watches. Shelves filled with hand-painted china surrounded the compact room. The air, as always musty, mingled with a cheap cigar, brought an unexpected thought of Owen Roe.

There was a time Birdie pretended Roe loved her. The ring she wanted was in a display case, near the Flora Danica china.

At the rear, Mort hunched over a work table starring through a jeweler's loupe. An unbroken line of smoke rose from a stub of a cigar. Despite the years, their banter never changed.

"It's been a while," he said, not looking up.

"He never asked," she answered.

"Didn't deserve 'ya."

Birdie leaned against a cracked glass counter top next to Mort. She'd swear tufts of moss grew on an ancient floor safe behind his elevated repair table. From habit, she spun a tall wooden case displaying Timex leather banded watches while watching him set a solitaire diamond.

Mort looked up, smiling. "Can't talk. Late on a job."

Birdie held up the pocket watch by its broken chain and placed it on a felt pad near the relic of a cash register.

"Take a look when you can. I need to read the damaged inscription."

Mort grunted and waved a palm over his sock cap covered head.

At the door she threw a kiss and stepped over the same lazy, blond cat which hadn't bothered to notice her. "Can you make it a rush? I owe you."

Through the closed door, she heard, "A few days."

Back at street level, traffic once again moved... slowly. Jark and the Dodge sat in the alley and blocked most of the crowded sidewalk. Happy to see her new driver, she ran toward the car, neon coconut palm trees and surfboards pulled her attention. She couldn't get the travel office off her mind. Did she need a vacation? Except for a rushed business trip to Mexico, Birdie's view of the world had been The City and Jersey. There was more in life. She stared at what her life could be—being anywhere, meeting someone who wasn't a cop or wannabe actor.

Plastered over many of the travel agency's windows were captivating posters, luring affluent New Yorkers to far off vacation spots. Her eyes drifted to a flamboyant matador adorned in sparkling gold and blue attire side-stepping an angry, charging bull. His lavish red cape fully extended, waved over the bull's horns as he plunged a sword into the unsuspecting animal.

The Dodge rolled forward, leaving the rubbish littered alley. Jark signaled out the window, pointing to an open spot at the curb. Birdie rushed, fighting off the pain of her not yet healed hip.

The idea hit her as she hobbled along the trash-can-lined sidewalk.

Inside the car, Birdie looked at the cloak resting beside her. Why hadn't she made the connection earlier? It was obvious, another possibility to the grisly murder, explaining why Mary Clary wore Malda's cape. Perhaps the brutal slaying had not been an accident. Could the killer be a paid accomplice and the blood red cape identified the unknown target?

Malda Boddy now, became a suspect. She was the new star of *Tunnel of Love*, replacing the dead Mary Clary. Broadway actors had killed for less. The part would advance Malda's career.

Ambitious actors were hungry and dangerous—at least some she knew. To land a starring role could be a powerful motive for murder. Birdie planned to approach the newly created leading actress with care.

More rain came, slowing traffic to a near standstill.

"Stop the car," Birdie shouted. "I'll walk,"

Before Jark reacted, Birdie jumped from the back seat and marched toward The Royale Theater.

The red cape lay folded in the rear seat.

CHAPTER TWELVE

Dejected, Victor Gregory returned home late, well after sunset, needing rest and something to distract him.

He'd seen a ghost.

To see someone wearing Malda's cape fleeing the morgue knocked him on his heels. Stunned, he'd allowed them to escape. Her appearance, later at the theater's rear door, brought panic. He stopped, froze, standing among the crowd of onlookers. She remained alive, uninjured. How long did he linger at the stage door, dazed? Malda looked his way. They'd made eye contact. He saw fear on her face despite the alley's dim light.

How did he fail? He closed his eyes, recalling.

Malda's unique red cape had been easy to spot. While they dated, her theater night schedule never varied. She'd exited the Flying Horse Lounge as usual after sipping two glasses of vintage champagne and nibbling on an egg salad sandwich. She referred to it as an orgy of food and booze. Withdrawn, unless on stage, she feared new people and frightened easily. Everything in her life fit a pattern, appearance, clothes, jewelry, no chances taken. Uncompromising in her privacy, drapes and blinds in her Greenwich Village apartment never opened.

Red Jacket's tomahawk would return to battle.

He should have noticed it sooner. The earring taken from the corpse sat on his dresser. A simple pearl and diamond hung from a silver ear wire. Malda resisted piercing her ears, fearing infection.

Now she stepped into the star's role, she belonged to the public. He'd track her using police records. If she fled to a new address, he'd locate her. Day or night, his unlimited travel through the mass transit system allowed quick, undetected movement about the congested city.

For Victor, Reznik had robbed him of his cherished privacy. Boatyard renovations moved quickly. In a short time, the solitude would vanish, overrun with the growing hip generation. At daybreak the chain-link fence and gate were pulled and removed, laying in a jumbled nest of bent pipe and rolled mesh at the far end of the lot. An ivy covered brick wall, according to the picture, would replace it. Carpenters, electricians, and plumbers, laboring under glaring spotlights, showed no signs of stopping.

Victor stepped to the deck of his boathouse. A large flatbed pulled near him, raising its tilted bed, sliding off bundles of framing lumber. Another truck followed. There seemed to be an endless supply. Nothing would be the same.

Restless, he'd become obsessed and walked along the deck,, spotting the home of his new neighbor. The small windows were dark, unlike last night. Something was curious about her. Unsure why— probably cop's instincts.

His appetite lost, Victor sat slumped in the galley, staring at the Russian-owned Liberty ship. Dimly illuminated, it sat alone, appearing abandoned. Why did Lev Reznik pay him to walk the decks three times a week? What did he guard? He walked the same route night after night. Occasionally sounds came from below deck. He guessed rats. They overran the city. The ship rats could have a sizeable nest—one he wouldn't barge in on. Some nights, when the wind remained calm and quiet, he swore he heard voices.

While placing his necktie and badge on the dresser, he glanced through the porthole toward the docks. Would the same car be there tonight? It showed up each time he patrolled. He'd failed to get close to read the tag. Whoever they were, they knew surveillance.

*****

Victor arrived at the waterfront, entering through a steel gate. Relocking, he watched for signs of being followed. Reznik's bayside warehouse and dock were nothing more than rusted sheets of tin siding attached to a decaying pier.

Nearby, a brightly lit and guarded fortress, the Brooklyn Army Terminal never slept. The massive military depot, a complex of concrete buildings, rail lines and docks—five million square feet under roof, covered one hundred football fields. At its peak, during the Second World War, twenty-thousand civilians found work at the base. Still active, the storehouse supplied personnel and equipment to military bases worldwide.

What did the Russian Jew plan for the lonely ship and warehouse? He'd asked Reznik that after taking the part-time watchman job. The little Russian escorted Victor to the door of his Brighton Beach realty office. While slipping a cash pay envelope into Victor's pocket, Reznik reached up and slapped Victor's cheek.

"Do not ask too many questions," he said, flashing a smile of brown teeth.

The money came each week, by private messenger, slid into the mailbox next to his door. He made no further queries, but Victor's curiosity grew each time the ship left and returned to port months later.

With a passkey, he entered the vacant, dilapidated building, using it as a shortcut to the Liberty ship, tracking his heavy-soled shoes through light powdery dust and bird droppings. His flashlight remained on his belt thanks to a full, round moon glowing through a giant skylight—a good sign. He'd draw on its lunar energy.

At the far end of the long warehouse, near the docks, whiffs of the bay and rotting sea life strengthened. A brick wedged in the door frame held a man-door open. Victor looked back inside the empty warehouse. This time he spotted faint depressions. Sets of tire tracks crossed the dead building.

The blast of the horn startled Victor. Large boxcar-sized crates covered the top deck of a passing container ship leaving New York harbor. He recalled Reznik's advice and continued inspecting the wharf. On the dock, below the black hull of the Liberty ship, he walked along a row of roll-up doors connecting the wharf to the warehouse. After close inspection, he found additional traces of tire marks—most had been swept away.

In the distance, to the north, Lady Liberty shined bright in the harbor against the Manhattan skyline. From here the unsleeping metropolis appeared unsoiled, cleansed by darkness which masked The City's sins.

A long tow of passing trash barges heading to sea brought choppiness to the bay, rising and lifting the creaking Russian ship. Heavy hemp mooring lines flexed and tightened, tugging against rusted dock bollards.

Scavenging gray seagulls squawked, taking flight the moment Victor's tired legs stepped on the gangway and climbed alongside the rusty, black, riveted hull to the ship's aft deck. Surprised to find the vessel seaworthy, he wondered what secrets the stoic, unnamed boat kept.

After reaching the ship's stern, he couldn't shake the feeling of being watched. From habit, he paused at the railing, looking back toward its towering bridge. The only movement–a silent red beacon monotonously rotated above the ship's radio tower.

At the starboard side, near the water, he poked a light into a row of lifeboats, not bothering to glance inside. His hand twitched, gripping his flashlight, tapping the butt end against the steel handrail. He grasped the steel pipe guarding a cargo winch. A slight pulsation resonated in his palm and finger tips. He placed his ear against the ship's steel plates hearing the same faint humming as once before.

Massive cargo doors covered most of the main deck. Two mounted guns, forward and aft, appeared normal. At midship, he climbed a ladder to the bridge. In the cramped wheelhouse, compasses, controls, and gauges dominated three walls. At the heavy ship's wheel, he looked over the 360-degree view bow to stern. Inside and out, the ship was austere, an ugly duckling with fire power to out-gun German U boats.

A narrow set of stairs took him to the crew's quarters. Cramped rooms reeked of stale cigarette smoke and body odor. Newspapers, stained mattresses, and Russian girlie magazines littered gritty tile floors. After flipping through several slick pages, Victor tossed them into a corner. At the next level, he found the security log in the galley. Reznik insisted it be signed and dated. The cagy Russian Jew moved the book to a new location from time to time. Today, it hung inside a sour-smelling broom and mop cabinet. He swung open the door, intruding on a family of swarming cockroaches. Victor signed and entered the time, dating it yesterday.

The abrupt sound stopped his search. At first, he thought he had company. After a moment, Victor recognized it as one of the deck's immense cargo winches swinging loose. On still nights, sounds resembling human voices drifted up from ventilation ports along with an odor of cooking cabbage. The ship had no name as far as he knew. Was this the bad luck which supposedly followed unnamed ships?

The only unexplored areas were the massive holds below deck. Lev Reznik made it clear; they were secure and off limits.

An illustrated evacuation plan, in Russian, hung in the galley. Three forward holds and two aft were separated by the ship's boiler and engine room.

To enter the ship's holds required opening a sizeable waterproof hatch cover on the main deck. A steel vertical ladder dropped to the base of the ship's hull. Each of the five holds were, separated by heavy steel plate and resembled canyons sunk deep into the ship. His curiosity grew about the ship he'd protected for almost a year. What did he guard? He was a sworn peace officer in the City of New York and obligated to investigate possible wrongdoing.

Relieved to return to the main deck and breathe fresh air, Victor inspected the rows of covered cargo doors, unsure if he could open the hatches. Flashes of light caught his eye from below.

He spotted his visitor as he arrived, pulling near the entrance gate of the Brooklyn Army Terminal and stop. In a second the lights blinked out, a moment later, a quick flare of a match came from inside the car. The unwelcome visitor showed up as he always did.

Who was it? Victor leaned against the ship's railing, watching the sightseer. A bright ember flew from the shadow. Another flicker immediately followed. The pattern never changed. Did he intend to be seen? What did he want? Victor guessed they were alone. He didn't get a make on the car's model and color. Attempts to make contact with the suspicious vehicle and driver failed: whoever they were sensed his approach.

Victor heard the sound again, coming from a deck vent, it sounded human. He looked at his watch—midnight.

CHAPTER THIRTEEN

Joe Nagle tossed the empty pack of Camels on the dash and struck a match, lighting another bad habit. Nicotine numbed him, helping him endure. Stretching his long legs across the floor of the car, kicking aside coloring books and tissue boxes, he leaned back to wait for his target.

The unauthorized stakeout happened on personal time, using his wife's ten-year-old Ford coupe. He'd clocked out and declined drinks with his partner, Owen Roe. The unnamed ship he watched was part of something illegal—he knew it in the pit of his ulcer-lined gut. Before his demotion from the organized crimes unit, he had tracked a local Brooklyn citizen and Russian immigrant, Lev Reznik, to the ship. For his effort, they had legally prohibited Nagle from stepping on the dock and warehouse area.

He scribbled two words on his notepad over and over during the hearing he underwent. The court had pounded it into his memory. The accusations labeled him a spy—his actions, an act of war. Relations between the two countries were strained by his armed assault on the Soviet ship, aggravating tensions between the two countries.

He had disagreed. His .38 Smith and Wesson side arm remained holstered. The trio, dressed in suits, carried no assault weapons other than a heavy-duty bolt cutter to enter what they thought an empty boat belonging to an international criminal.

His pencil lead snapped, jamming the point into the paper, completing the words.

DIPLOMATIC PROTECTION

Reznik owned a real estate office and a jewelry shop in Brighton Beach. Both legal, profitable, and he paid taxes on time.

The problem with Reznik, according to the state of New York, he made too much money—far higher than similar companies, catching the attention of the state's Department of Taxation and Finance, the Brooklyn District Attorney and the Organized Crime Bureau Joe Nagle had been part of.

An initial inquiry showed Reznik involved in small-time scams and shakedowns of local businesses. Nagle and his unit suspected something bigger: counterfeiting, fraud, protection and more. They'd tolerated Reznik's independent operation, hoping it led to the discovery of larger criminal activity tied back to the Soviet Union, much like the American Mafia families which had already gained a foothold in the United States. New York would not be the entry point, allowing Russian Jews, the Kosher Nostra, as they were called, to do the same.

Despite his demotion to homicide detective, Nagle refused to step away. As captain, he took the brunt of the heat for boarding the vessel. Unknown to him and his unit, the liberty ship was part of the Soviet consulate, enjoying diplomatic protection in foreign waters according to the Vienna convention.

If he'd bothered to see a judge and file for a legal search warrant, he'd have learned of its immune status. Then again, it may not have stopped him. He believed his unit acted for the common good of city and country.

He'd been fortunate to keep his badge and considered himself lucky, despite the dip in pay grade. Notoriety over the international incident gained unexpected support from an aggressive Wisconsin Senator warning of Communism taking control of the United States. Joe McCarthy's personal visit saved his job and police pension.

For many citizens, and to him, the Red Scare represented a threat to America's freedom. Nagle watched waves of Soviet political prisoners, released by an up-and-coming Soviet activist, Nikita Khrushchev, infiltrate New York. Most were honest and blended into the country. Others—common criminals, arrived poised and hungry to lay their hands on money using scams and shakedowns.

Lev Reznik climbed his way to the top, becoming a key figure in the early Red invasion and Brooklyn's rise in crime. With the amount of Russians arriving, it remained only a matter of time before the cancer spread to other boroughs.

Joe Nagle believed his target, Victor Gregory, was not involved in Reznik's criminal plans. Although he had not met the Soviet ship's night watchman, he was confident the guard noticed his nightly presence—yet he hadn't alerted the Russian. If he had, Reznik would have brought in his thugs. He felt a bond to Victor Gregory, cop to cop, after watching him on the ship's deck and bridge for months, the same routine each night. They were on the same side of the law, wearing badges, protecting citizens of New York.

The moment to recruit came. He'd approach Victor without raising the wrath of the Soviet consulate or the attention of Lev Reznik, remaining anonymous until gaining Victor's confidence. Nagle also suspected someone on the ship watched the guard.

Joe Nagle checked his watch—time to return home. He turned the key, kicking over the noisy, big block V8. One additional stop remained in Sunset Park.

The muffler and exhaust pipe rattled and scraped each time the Ford coupe bounced through a pothole on the uneven street. Before Nagle had time to daydream of the sleek lines of a new Ranch Wagon, unaffordable on his current paycheck, he arrived at Harbor Wash and Fold Laundry.

Nagle enjoyed surprising people, catching them off guard, making them uncomfortable. Their reactions often told of their nature. He'd planned to reach Victor Gregory that way—discreetly.

The laundry remained open twenty-four hours. The door stuck on the metal threshold, stubbornly resisting, forcing Nagle to lean his shoulder into it. He stumbled forward, catching himself as it jarred open. A second later, a chime sounded.

Inside the brightly lit area, smelling like soap and bleach, rows of white coin operated dryers and washers lined three walls. An American flag, the size of a car, hung above a bench littered with newspapers and magazines. An aged man wearing an untied, shabby flannel bathrobe pulled clothes from a dryer, folding them at a long table. Nagle headed to a counter at the rear and tapped a finger on a desk bell several times.

The thought of a gray-suited gentleman sporting a British accented voice appearing at the desk of the Waldorf Astoria flashed in his mind.

No one materialized.

The bath-robed man tapped his cigarette into a tin ashtray. "Night manager's in the back listening to Gunsmoke. Doesn't like being bothered."

Nagle knocked on the Formica counter until a grizzled face appeared from behind a curtained wall.

"Police," Nagle flipped open a leather case holding his badge near the manager's face.

The manager walked to the counter, wiping his hands on the seat of his pants.

"I need a favor," Nagle said.

Behind Nagle, the door scraped open. The bath-robed man limped away, wobbling side to side. His clothes basket stayed behind on the worktable.

A pair of barking dogs sprung from an alley, jumping and attacking the cripple In an instant, a bright flash engulfed the two. Two German shepherds vanished. Nothing remained, no fur or collars.

The old man wobbled and walked away into the night.

CHAPTER FOURTEEN

Birdie arrived at the Royal Theater, wet and shivering with no actual plan, only expecting to confront Malda and possibly the hatchet killer. A hunch told her he'd be at the theater either celebrating with the newly crowned star or finishing last night's job. The situation could not be avoided and brought a definite chance she would be caught in the crossfire if they both had conspired to kill Mary Clary.

She'd left the blood red cloak in the rear seat of Jark's Dodge, keeping it out of sight. She resisted an impulse to wear the cape to assess Malda's reaction, but no one could learn she'd stolen it from the morgue; besides, seeing the cape would raise suspicion of a police trap. There was also a chance Owen Roe and his partner Joe Nagle watched the theater.

Birdie's memories returned, seeing the bright lights and show posters. Overhead, a cache of yellow light bulbs snapped and flashed intermittently, chasing around the show's giant marquee. They practically shouted, reminding her she would never walk on the stage again. Her moment in the limelight had been brief and painful. Every actor faces their final curtain. Hers crashed down on her. A glass-covered billboard grabbed her attention.

Role of Isolde Poole played by Miss Malda Boddy.

After a deep breath, she entered the empty lobby. Her skin tingled, and pulse raced, feeling heavy throbbing in her temples. Nothing in her life topped the sensation of walking into a New York Broadway Theater. The hip hooray and ballyhoo of Harry Warren and Al Dubin's music sang in her head. Birdie resisted dancing across the marble foyer.

Her daydream evaporated.

Centered in the foyer, surrounded by maroon velvet ropes, a head and shoulders portrait of Mary Clary rested on a gold easel. Bouquets of roses, lilies, and orchids covered the floor. After a look at her watch, Birdie guessed the show reached the final act. Most likely, many of the ushers had gone, leaving a small staff and a few janitors to clean and secure the theater.

Without a description of Malda Boddy, she'd rely on the show staff. Birdie tried several doors she knew led backstage. All were locked. A sudden burst of laughter came from the theater, startling her.

"Anyone here?" she shouted.

A green coated usher appeared with a cigarette wedged between his fingers. He used the other hand to point to the exit doors.

"I need to go backstage," Birdie said with a smile.

The usher looked at her but said nothing. He stepped from the doorway, shaking his head, and moved toward her.

"Stage door's around the corner. Outside in the alley, sugar."

Birdie wished she had a badge to flash to the stooped shouldered usher. Instead, she held out a business card. He leaned close, squinting to read it.

"Private eye, huh?"

"I need to see Malda Boddy."

"That's easy. Buy a ticket."

Another chorus of laughter came from inside the auditorium. Birdie looked in the door leading backstage and dressing rooms. She resisted the urge to throw a hammerlock on the usher and force him.

An assault charge added to the thefts would make it easier for Roe. While she searched for a new approach, the usher stepped back.

"Who did you say?" He yanked a Playbill from his coat pocket and pointed to the list of performers. "Malda Boddy, you said? She's not here. She took off before the show started."

"What happened?"

"You're the private detective lady. Figure it out."

She smiled and held up her hands in mock defeat.

The usher tapped his palm. "Money talks, sweetheart."

This time Birdie snapped. She grabbed his thumb, bending it toward his wrist, lifting the usher to his toes. His cigarette fell to the carpet. She let it smolder.

Birdie looked him in the eyes. "One more time, what happened?"

He whimpered and danced on tiptoes. She eased the pressure slightly.

"Stage manager said she came in acting spooked. Next thing, she's going out the front door and gets in a cab."

Birdie freed his thumb and mashed the cigarette butt with her shoe.

He rushed from the lobby, looking back as he ran. "I'm calling the cops." The usher stumbled and disappeared into a darkened doorway.

Birdie regretted releasing him. She needed to know what caused Malda to run before the most significant moment of her acting career.

Certain the police would arrive after the assault, she couldn't stay to question the cast and crew. With one last look around the lobby, she glanced at the portrait of Mary Clary and hurried through the double doors, angry at her failure to contain her aggressiveness.

Cars and yellow cabs splashed past. It was no night to be on the street. Taxis became a premium and would become scarcer as theaters let out.

She'd walk in the light drizzle to Sid Breen's office, confident it would calm her and maybe teach her a lesson. After half a block, the green and white Dodge pulled alongside, and the rear door flung open.

Jark leaned across the seat and flashed a wide grin. "I'll run the heater. You'll dry off fast."

Birdie slid across the plastic covered seat as the car pulled from the curb. After fluffing out her hair several times, she'd regained her composure. She'd hoped Sid Breen's note remained stuffed into Malda's cloak.

This time she'd caught a break. The steno sheet remained, folded in the capes inside pocket, nice and safe.

"Where to?" Jark asked.

Birdie unfolded the paper and looked at the Greenwich Village address belonging to Malda Boddy. Something tempted her to call it a day. Not much had gone right, and she had broken enough laws on her first case as a PI. For the first time, she conceded the sound of ships and the rotten smell of garbage scows moving in and out of New York Bay would remain a part of her life longer than intended.

She noticed Jark's blue eyes glancing in the rearview mirror, silently asking for a destination. What harm could it do to stop for the night? It was late. She needed a bath and a warm drink. Perhaps her late night visitor would make another surprise call. Had she turned into Walter Middy? What had become of her dignity, living life as a daydreamer? Is it her destiny to die before a firing squad, or more likely, in her case, arrested and sentenced to Rikers Island as penance?

Her conspiracy idea hadn't crumbled, but weakened. It once made sense. An ambitious actress such as Malda sees a way to advance her career. She uses a lover or pays someone to kill the leading lady she conveniently is backing up. The red cloak simply marked the target. Schemes popped into her mind. Malda's actions tonight, running away before her "grand opening," placed doubt she had been part of such a plot. It caused Birdie to believe the killer may still be hunting Malda Boddy.

Birdie jumped forward in her seat, tapping Jark's shoulder.

"How late do you work?"

"Long as you need me."

Birdie leaned back and read the address, "Waverly and Sixth."

"Greenwich Village. I know it."

"Take Fifth, 'till you hit Washington Square."

"Then a right," Jark said. "It's a tough place to find an address."

Birdie sat back, watching rain splatter against the window, not noticing the passing buildings and stop-and-go traffic. She held the folded red cape in front of her. The murder case appeared to be a simple mistaken identity. The inadvertent loan of Malda Boddy's cloak to Mary Clary saved Malda's life. Or had it been? A question stuck in Birdie's head. Was she rushing to find Malda, knowing someone hunted her, or to learn the name of her stalker and killer of Mary Clary?

Possibilities drifted in and out of her mind. Malda may have spotted her stalker at the theater and ran away frightened—or else it had been a rehearsed act. Caution dictated Birdie's planning. She'd operate as if Malda knew the killer, maybe as an accomplice. Why else would she run? Birdie intended to reach her before the killer. He may be at her home, waiting. If Mary Clary's killing had been a well-planned conspiracy between Malda and the killer, she needed Malda as bait, regardless of her involvement.

The streets narrowed to a congested single lane. Jark inched the car in stop and go traffic and a pedestrian-clogged intersection. Grand old brownstones, bars, coffee, and espresso shops lined both sides of the street. Stores offered army boots to Turkish pipes, all displayed on tables scattered along crowded sidewalks. The Dodge slowed and stopped at a traffic light. Fifth Street narrowed further. Across from them, the bright lit, massive, marble arch stood, centered in the park honoring George Washington, marking the unofficial border of Greenwich Village.

"We're close," Birdie said.

Jark nodded and steered the big Dodge past musicians seated on wood crates and folding chairs near the street playing violins and horns. On the same sidewalk, street preachers shouted to cars and passer-byes, promising eternal damnation while waving Bibles over their heads.

"Look for Arbor Manor Apartments." Birdie rolled down a rear window.

In a moment, the Dodge pulled into a red zone across the street from a painted brick-and wood, four-story building jutting into the street of a five-corner intersection. Faded and curled posters plastered storefronts announcing art shows, poetry readings, and cheap food.

"This is it," Jark said. "Want me to have a look?"

Birdie looked at the folded paper confirming Malda's apartment number, 401. A few lights lit tall, narrow casement windows fronting the building. Rechecking, she didn't want to knock on the wrong apartment at the late hour, but she doubted many of the tenants remained home. If they were, she expected to find them on some kind of drug or alcohol high. For both their sakes, she hoped Malda Boddy slept safe tucked into bed alive and well.

Had the killer arrived first? The papers covered the killing, complete with pictures of the victim. He'd stalk her, knowing her habits. The advantage belonged to him. Birdie had only one. If the killer suspected someone sought him, he wouldn't expect a woman.

Birdie, although a native New Yorker, spent little time in The Village. The tight, compact neighborhood didn't fit with Manhattan's efficient structure of high rise, urban landscape. Centuries ago, it thrived as a rural hamlet. Today, its streets remained narrow and twisted at odd angles, accommodating mid-rise apartments, row houses, shops, and hide-a-ways for anyone wanting to step away from the hurry and stress of big city life.

The late-night rain left behind a damp chill. After a quick massage of her neck and arm from habit, Birdie felt the stiffness build in her injured shoulder. Smell of warm dough and sauce came from the crowded pizza joint reminded her she hadn't eaten since a small lunch. Her hunger would wait despite her stomach's objection. Could life return to normal? She should be inside, joining in with the carefree group. Instead, she risked her life to keep Malda alive, her key to solving the case. There was no question the actress knew the killer.

Birdie counted off the possibilities on her fingertips.

First:

Mary Clary had been the target and killed by a plan launched by Malda Boddy using an accomplice. In that situation, her search would target Malda and an unknown partner, both equally guilty in the savage killing.

Second:

Malda Boddy was the actual target, but due to a mistaken identity, likely caused by the red cape, the killer attacked an innocent, Mary Clary.

Third:

The last option frightened her. A crazy, with a long-bladed axe, walked the streets killing people at random.

Tapping her last finger, she drew a blank.

Birdie liked the mistaken identity scenario. However, not forgetting her training as a former Pinkerton Detective, she'd remain cautious and on guard with Malda Boddy. If her theory had been correct, the killer intended to fix last night's mistake. She was sure. If she got in the way, she'd become a victim of his axe.

Why hadn't she disclosed Malda's name and address, the information she illegally obtained, to Owen Roe?

Was she so desperate to solve the murder on her own, she'd risk Malda's life? Use her for bait?

At this moment, Malda should be under police protection, giving Roe and Nagle names of rivals and boyfriends, anyone wanting to harm her. Another possibility, she'd gone into hiding, fearing the police couldn't protect her, or she'd orchestrated the attack, an option Birdie couldn't shake. Malda's performance tonight, running out before the show, gave the appearance she feared for her own life, eliminating other motives. Birdie recognized she may be dealing with a clever and cunning planner or merely a frightened young lady. Birdie couldn't lose either motive from her mind.

A set of open pay phones bolted to the wall of the apartment house gave her an idea. Why hadn't she thought of it earlier? Call the phone number on Owen Roe's business card. He often worked late and especially now, having her as a rival. They would not release the information to the public. She hoped since the three officially "worked" together, they'd disclose to her if Malda Boddy had shown up asking protection.

The number repeatedly rang before a gruff voice answered.

"Midtown North, homicide."

"Detective Nagle, please," Birdie asked, hoping Roe was too busy to listen in.

The line hummed in her ear for several minutes. Finally, a voice she knew came on.

"This is detective Owen Roe. Nagle's not here."

Birdie had no choice.

"It's me, Birdie. I heard you might have a break in the case."

There was a long pause. "As usual, your information's wrong."

"Turn up a witness?"

"You and the mayor will be the first to know."

"Owen! Don't bullshit me." Birdie expected the line to go dead, regretting her words the moment they flew from her mouth. She heard him mumbling, knowing he did when deciding.

"We've got nothing. Honest."

"It's still early," she said.

"Hell, the morgue lost her personal things."

It surprised Birdie to hear the admittance. "Sorry to hear that."

For a second she considered it a ploy. Did he suspect her? He often played confused and lost to gain information—one of his endearing cop tricks. Malda Boddy could be in his office at this moment.

"I'll share if I learn anything." A lie, but she needed to remain on his right side.

"Sure, that would be nice," he said.

"No witnesses at all?" Birdie asked again.

"Honest, we've got less than nothing. Captain's all over us."

Birdie covered the mouthpiece. Was this her chance?

"How 'bout you?" Roe asked.

"I'm waiting on the M.E's report."

"Killer used a long, thin-bladed instrument, something like an axe. He struck once, almost decapitating her."

"Defensive wounds?" she asked.

"None. 'Victim never saw him coming."

"Motive?"

Roe cleared his throat. The sudden cooperation surprised Birdie. Pangs of guilt hit. She deliberated confessing she'd taken the missing property, along with her suspicions.

"We're ready to write it up as a random attack… some nut job. The only thing Nagle and me saw was her purse and cash. Nothing was taken." Roe took a long breath and continued, "Now that evidence is missing."

"I wish I could help," she said, not sure how much of it was true. She wanted to believe him.

"Sure. Gotta go," Roe said.

Before he hung up, she thought he asked, "Are you sharing?"

Despite the deadline, she answered, "I like yellow mustard on both sides too."

Birdie stood in a phone booth two years ago after calling her agent. Thanksgiving approached, and she'd auditioned for a role in an upcoming play, "Guys and Dolls." It also happened to be the day detective Owen Roe entered her life, smearing mustard on her best dress.

Not sure if she'd gotten the small singing and dancing part, she stepped into Katz's for a late lunch. Long, slow lines at the meat counter had her head to the door. About to leave, she heard Roe's husky voice.

"Like pastrami?"

He looked directly at her, or so she thought. She was starved and gave him her best stage smile. "Are you sharing?" she asked, moving to him.

As she did, a tall man stepped from behind her, taking a seat at the same table.

Flustered, she turned and prepared to fight her way through the crowd and away from the eatery. At that moment, a hand touched her shoulder.

"Yellow mustard both sides."

"Is there another way?" she answered.

A hand banged the side of the booth, ending the reverie.

Did Roe bait her, sending a signal, leading her to believe he was desperate? Did he know she'd visited the morgue? Somewhere down deep, she cared for him. The visit to Mort's Jewelry surprised her, the unexpected feelings she suppressed. On the return visit, she'd try on the ring she'd envisioned receiving. Whatever Roe had up his sleeve, she'd forgive him this time. He was the old mustard stain she'd been unable to washout.

Birdie did not doubt Owen Roe. Malda Boddy did not run to the police. Her actions were puzzling. What did Sid Breen hide? Why did Malda Boddy run before her starring opening performance?

What did she wait for? She'd march up to Malda's apartment and confront her, or possibly the stalker. Birdie reached into her purse, patting her revolver and lock picks, regardless—show time arrived. Her first test as a PI.

CHAPTER FIFTEEN

Three months ago, Joe Nagle spotted the wash and fold used by Victor Gregory. Like clockwork every Monday, Victor visited, dropping off a white pillowcase stuffed with dirty laundry. The routine never varied. Two days later, he carried off a wrapped package of bundled clothes along with five dark blue military style shirts heavily pressed and on hangers. Nagle learned his mark was a member of the NYC Transit Police.

He'd found his man.

Working off the books on his own, Joe Nagle could not afford more damage to his career as a detective. The pension inched closer, only eight years off, and he'd be spending his days in a sunny beach side condo in Naples, Florida. He needed to remain discreet, recruiting Victor Gregory to keep tabs on the Russian ship and Lev Reznik.

Removed from the elite organized crimes unit; he had no authority on the Russian investigation. It no longer mattered. The US Attorney General forced his former unit to drop its interest in the Liberty ship.

The Russian Jew laughed in his face as he and his boarding team were escorted from the ship nine months ago. He needed someone with access and a relationship with Reznik, who would be careless now that no one watched.

That night in the middle of a cold February, he and two officers broke into the Russian ship after several nights of surveillance, intending to search the ship for contraband. Human and arms trafficking, drug trafficking, along with smuggling, were suspected. The operation had been secret and illegal, with no substantial evidence, only suspicion. Nagle had been confident he would turn up several illicit business activities Reznik and other Russian immigrants ran.

The year prior, Soviets threatened American capitalists. Many Americans feared an atomic war with bombs dropped on United States soil. Nagle saw a different attack, one from within our borders. The gruff former general and now Russian premier, Nikita Khrushchev, released millions of political prisoners and common criminals. Many found their way to the United States, legally and illegally, and continued to immigrate, making Brooklyn home. Most were honest shopkeepers and hardworking, skilled laborers. Nagle had no problems there. He worried about Reznik and his fast-growing group of followers.

Nagle and his small commando team cut open gates and entered the Liberty ship's bridge. They picked locks and sled-hammered cabinets open searching the ship's documents and sailing records. In the middle of the break-in, Lev Reznik unexpectedly interrupted them. The short, plump Russian Jew appeared from nowhere. Given no choice, Nagle arrested him, handcuffing him to a water pipe. The victory was short lived. In minutes, uniformed agents of the United States Diplomatic Service stormed the ship's bridge, giving Nagle his first encounter with the new Israeli Uzi submachine gun. They pointed six at him as he fell to his knees.

The offense passed beyond breaking and entering. The Russian liner belonged to the USSR and part of their diplomatic territory, which enjoyed protection from search in the United States.

If he wished to continue surveillance inside the Russian ship, he'd need to enlist Victor Gregory without involving New York Police.

Joe Nagle put on his best smile, holding his detective badge near the manager's face.

"You have time to talk?"

"No discounts," he said, inspecting the identification.

"It's a favor."

Despite the cold outside, Nagle felt the heat inside the laundry and wiped beads of sweat from his forehead. The manager stood across the counter in a white armless tee shirt, smoking and dripping with sweat.

"Do I look like a personal secretary?"

Joe Nagle nodded, pulling a ten spot from a money clip. "How 'bout now?"

"I don't know. This about my business with them?" He nodded to the Brooklyn Army Terminal nearby.

"No one's gonna know." Nagle slapped the money on the counter.

"What's the favor?"

"Give this to a customer." Joe Nagle came prepared with a note written days ago and pulled it from his coat pocket.

"Got a name?" The manager waved at floor to ceiling shelves crammed with bundled white packages. "I do lots of business."

"It's private," Nagle said. "Give it to Victor Gregory. I want no one to see him get it."

"Sure, by magic?" The manager said after rummaging through a shoebox of index cards.

"Slip it in his laundry," Nagle said. "Can you do that?"

The manager took the handwritten note from Nagle and slid the ten spot into a back pocket.

Nagle paused, butting out his cigarette on the floor. "Put it in his undershorts."

Outside, Joe Nagle looked back toward the large Liberty ship. Its conning tower and three flashing red beacons raised over the roof lines of abandoned tenements.

He wouldn't make the same mistake. There'd be someone on the inside doing his dirty work. He had no risk. The plan appeared foolproof.

CHAPTER SIXTEEN

Birdie stared at a few dimly lit windows of a mid-rise apartment building set between shabby row houses of Greenwich Village. She'd knock on every door if needed. Malda's life was in danger. Unlike the Upper East and West sides, no uniformed doorman stood guard in the Lower Manhattan building's entrance as she searched for a mailbox or a doorbell with a name.

She entered the small courtyard of the Arbor Manor apartments through a narrow-arched passage next to the pizza joint. To her surprise, she discovered a postage-size plot of ground bounded by surrounding walls of the apartment buildings. Something rustled in the hedge encircling the tiny square of land. She froze, waiting. Did Malda's killer hide here?

After more bush-shaking, which seemed like an eternity, a blond, long-tailed cat pushed its head from thick, bare branches, slinking out, mouthing a squealing mouse. The feline paused, arched its back and sauntered toward tangled, wilted vines of a fall vegetable garden. She nudged open a corner of a chicken wire fence, disappearing behind a compost pile.

At the far end, Birdie spotted a wrought-iron gate, guessing it accessed Malda's apartment building lobby. It swung with a long squeal and opened into a cramped foyer. A dusty, bare fluorescent light flickered above a row of tenant mailboxes. As she hoped—M. BODDY, 401, appeared next to a button on a narrow strip of yellowed paper.

If everything went as planned and Malda cooperated, the case would be closed by daybreak.

A heavy, locked door barred her from the apartment's staircase. Birdie's hand shook, pushing the cracked intercom switch repeatedly. The apartment sat on the top floor, and she'd be unable to hear it buzz if it worked at all. She pushed again, this time keeping her finger pressed, forcing the push button deep into the slot.

No answer.

Birdie slumped against the mailboxes, slamming the tiled wall with her palm. The latch buzzed and clicked. A waistless, middle-aged woman puffing a stogie barged into the lobby lugging an overflowing trash sack. The door stuck on an uneven and warped linoleum floor. Birdie gripped the handle and jumped inside, running up the staircase before the stogie smoker noticed. She would wake Malda and everyone on the floor.

Taking the first set of stairs, two at a time, Birdie slipped. Her hip and leg collapsed, forcing her to take a seat on the concrete landing. A doubt flashed through her mind. She needed to convince herself; again, Malda would not have rushed from the theater, missing her first starring performance, replacing Mary Clary if she'd been part of a plot to kill her. The more she considered the circumstances of the bizarre killing, it became obvious Malda had been the intended victim. She learned of the murder, panicked and ran from fear. It made sense—at least for now.

Birdie remained seated, massaging her trembling hip and leg, questioning how she'd react to a knock on her door at midnight. She reached into her purse; assuring herself the lock picks and pistol were secure.

She climbed, a step at a time, going easy, guiding a hand on the steel rail while the other pressed the painted cinder block wall. It was a concession, shed hated making to the injury that has never fully healed.

At the end of the hall apartment, 401 sat at the corner of the building. A baby bawled. Angry, drunken shouts came from a door she passed. Sharp, pungent scents of pot hung in the long corridor. She gently lifted each foot, walking on the balls of her feet. No light came from under the threshold of 401. Birdie reached the door and pressed her ear to it. A radio played at low volume—not enough to disturb neighbors but to discourage a robber, she guessed.

Several knocks produced no results. The solid wood door stood secure, equipped with twin deadbolts mounted above and below a brass doorknob. Although out of practice, her entry tools felt comfortable in her hands as she leaned over the first lock. Something didn't feel right as she worked the thin wire pick to lift the individual lock pins. As she lined each of them and applied pressure, turning the rake inside the deadbolt, nothing budged. Had she lost her finely honed touch after all she'd been through? After a pause, she realized the pesky bolt had a six-pin tumbler making it more difficult. She stepped back, looked around, and hoped no one stepped into the dim hall.

After a few minutes, Birdie slipped the lock's pins into place, opening the first deadbolt. A minute later, the second clicked and slid open, conceding with slight resistance. She took a last look at the hallway and twisted the knob open, guessing Malda hadn't bothered to lock the handle, and entered the apartment.

A small light burned in the shared kitchen and dining area. No signs of life—Malda or anyone else. Birdie padded into the simple one-room apartment and closed the door. The drapes were closed. She'd do a quick search.

Modest and sparse described the furniture. Two unmatched chairs and love seat occupied the front half of the long, narrow studio apartment. A bookcase, crowded with National Geographic's, separated the living room from the double bed. Centered on several pillows, a doll, and teddy bear rested on a folded pink blanket.

A leather suitcase stuck out from under a metal framed bed near a beat-up highboy dresser. Dresses, blouses and skirts hung from a tall pipe which crossed the room. The news story of Mary Clary's killing laid folded open, propped near the tiny kitchen sink.

Birdie guessed Malda escaped the theater and ran to someone she trusted, not bothering to return home and pack. She'd gone into hiding; afraid the person she spotted at the theater would show up at her door. Most likely Malda would send someone for her clothes and toilet items. There was also a good chance the axe murderer would show or already watched from a nearby apartment or street corner. The apartment was closed off—window blinds pulled below the sills. Birdie ran out of options; she'd stay put, make herself at home and wait for who came to retrieve Malda's personal things or the killer.

She remembered Jark waited in the car. At the side of the window, Birdie peeked out a corner of the heavy drapes and blinds. She spotted his green Dodge parked in a red zone under a dim streetlamp. His boots rested on the car's dash, faithfully waiting.

Starved for food and, she had to admit, a generous dose of male of affection—the lure of Jark and self-indulgence tempted. An invitation to the apartment put him in danger, someone else to protect should the killer show. The thought wouldn't leave her. She couldn't keep him sitting outside the entire night in the cold. He eventually would become worried and most likely barge into the building, calling attention to her plan, scaring off the killer.

An idea came.

After a rummage through Malda's hanging things, Birdie found a yellow rain slicker and matching rubber boots. With them, she'd make a dash; maybe grab takeout after sending Jark home.

She officially became the bait, sitting alone in Malda's apartment, which suddenly felt like a fishbowl.

CHAPTER SEVENTEEN

Victor Gregory stepped from the Liberty ship's ramp, unable to shake the feeling he had company on board. Something went on inside the craft—he'd suspected that all along. Why would Reznik pay him to watch a vacant ship? Why the erratic sailing schedule, leaving port at odd times, disappearing and mysteriously returning, lacking freight—despite month-long voyages?

Sounds and dull, weak voices were sometimes heard, but not understandable. He'd searched the cabins and bridge with no results. What remained unknown were the cargo holds deep in the ship's belly. The giant compartments were off limits, and he intended to keep it that way. Lev Reznik paid well regardless of the freighter's presence in port. If trouble didn't bother him, he wouldn't bother the trouble.

The waterfront's late-night air stung, refreshing and energizing him. Victor glanced back at the large vessel moored next to rust-decayed warehouses. Roofs sagged, near collapse, waiting for another Atlantic storm and their demise. He avoided his usual route, exiting the docks from a different direction. He planned to confront the elusive mystery man relaxing in his car, puffing one cigarette after another. As a Transit cop, Victor enjoyed peace officer authority and power to arrest. His night-stalker broke no laws, parking legally on public streets among a maze of buildings and shadows.

From the beginning, he believed the driver wished to be seen but remain out of reach, playing cat and mouse, dancing away at the last moment.

A subtle taunt?

Why?

Victor crouched, tiptoeing between rows of stacked wooden pallets approaching the smoker's car. In shadow, he stepped around the corner, anticipating coming face to face with the elusive intruder. He'd failed. The Ford vanished, leaving a scattering of cigarette butts and gum wrappers. Nearby, a thin haze of crimson and blue automotive oil floated on the surface of a pool of water.

A cop or anyone trained in surveillance would not be that sloppy... unless intending to. Victor thought of his shadow as Pennzoil Man— without fail, the car left behind a puddle of oil. Poor maintenance showed it was not a government pool car. It had to be the driver's personal vehicle. Whoever they were, they kept a step ahead.

The gutting and remodeling of houseboats moved rapidly. Many waited on a complete remodel, transforming the rundown vessels into bayside cottages resembling the boats they once were. Reznik promised partial completion and move-in within nine months, confirming Victor's suspicion of Reznik's financial connections inside the city's strong trade unions and inspectors. Money and power greased the slow-turning wheels of progress in the five boroughs.

No light burned at his new neighbor's home. She'd consider him rude, not welcoming her. Introductions needed to be made. Their previous encounter, although brief, remained fresh in his memory. His glimpse of her stepping from the shower had been a blatant invitation, not an accident; their eyes had met, hers held a moment, encouraging....

With that picture riveted in his mind, a smile forced its way to his face. He spotted his destination and quickened his pace, rushing to his errand. The chilly night added a crisp tone to the chiming percussion of the basilica bells hourly round. Victor paused, touching his temples, massaging a hammering pulse. A throbbing migraine crept, clawing at his thick neck muscles.

Victor continued walking, almost running, leaving the dock area, passing rows of gated and steel-barred, single story shops. In the distance, the church's tall spires appeared as jagged spikes, piercing a low hung moon. The stoic church gave so many newcomers solace. Why did he feel like an interloper?

Polish, Norwegian and Finnish immigrants once settled Sunset Park, laboring as tailors, grocers, and shoemakers in the modest middle-class community. Today, a new group invaded, spilling in from Brooklyn's Brighton Beach. Russians took over suddenly failed businesses, reminding Victor of the Italian families' rise to power in the city and nearby Jersey. There was no question of the coming ethnic wars and the growth of Lev Reznik's private army of refugees.

His day would soon be over, ending with a hot bath and consulting his meditation bowl, looking to fix his blunder. Malda somehow escaped Chief Red Jacket's iron tomahawk. Was this a sign? Should he allow her a second chance? Could redemption occur?

Harbor Wash and Fold, brightly lit and empty, sat at the far end of the street, centered in a neglected block of row houses. He avoided the laundry, except for nighttime, only he and the night manager. The Transit Police uniform became a magnet for citizens' nagging complaints. He'd wager a week's salary few used the subway. Most lived and worked their pathetic lives at the docks. After the painful loss of the Dodgers, he guessed there was little else to talk about besides late trains and dirty rat-infested stations.

The glass door banged against the plaster wall, driving the handle deeper into it, tripping a wheezy chime. Steamy air and bleach sickened him as he crossed the room to the rear counter, past lines of empty dryers each resembling a giant Cyclops. Shading his eyes against the glare, Victor stumbled and kicked aside laundry carts and chairs.

He banged the desk bell. "Magoon."

The night manager yanked open a curtain and nodded. In a moment he returned with a paper bundle tied with thin string, dropping the package on the counter.

"My shirts?" Victor asked.

Not saying a word, Magoon disappeared, returning with blue uniform shirts hung on white metal hangers.

"Pressed and starched." He slid the ticket along the table.

Victor pulled three wrinkled dollar bills from a shirt pocket, counting them, placing each single note on the cash register one at a time.

Magoon flicked a long ash from his cigar and grabbed the cash. After slamming the drawer, his eyes swept around the laundry and fixed on Victor.

"Three bucks, never more, never less," Magoon said.

Victor leaned over the counter and picked up the package. "Just habit."

"Just habit," Magoon repeated, turning away.

Victor took the shirts. "This everything?"

"That's it."

"Magoon," Victor said. "Can I ask a question?"

"Yeah, shoot."

"Why's your hair always greasy?"

With a hoarse cough, Magoon ran his palm over his scalp. "Habit."

* * * * *

In his houseboat, Victor re-hung the uniform shirts on sturdy wood hangers, spacing them in the closet. Curious and needing a distraction, he peeked from his bedroom porthole. No sign of life from next door. He reminded himself he must return the favor of entertaining his not-so-shy neighbor.

The scene outside struck a chord, his quiet home would be taken from him. Tall stacks of lumber, tools and heavy earth-moving equipment all worked to turn the once calm boat yard into shambles.

After demolition and rebuilding, Seashore Villas would appear, bringing unwelcome neighbors. Reznik's folly would fail—he'd see to it. Relocating to Rockaway Beach didn't suit his taste.

He grabbed a bottle of Ballantine ale from the icebox, taking a long swig. The opened bundle waited. Clean socks, tee shirts and shorts needed placing into compartments within his tall dresser. Once done, he slid the top drawer open and tripped a hidden latch. Inside the secret space, a Crown Royal pouch sat. Inside a diamond and pearl earring along with a silver button he'd removed from the actress he mistakenly killed.

It felt heavy in his hand. Silver lobes of the button-shaped a shamrock's four leaflets. Frayed thread hung from its loop where he'd ripped it from the blood-red cape. He laughed at himself after another long drink of ale. How could he have been mistaken? Malda still lived. The red cape and shamrock buttons were her good luck charms. She'd often reminded him Eve removed a clover from the Garden of Eden to remember paradise. The odd similarity struck him—Malda left him for her career. To his surprise, touching it brought no satisfaction. With his eyes shut, he saw the flashing amber lights of the ambulance carrying away the body he thought to be hers.

A slip of paper fluttered from his clean folded white shorts, landing on the bed.

Victor: Our country needs you. You are in a position to help the United States rid itself of communism and the criminals invading New York. I have watched you and you are on the side of law and order. We both wear a badge as brothers in law enforcement. I will look for you tomorrow at Gig's, your regular time.

Victor turned the sheet over. The note ended, unsigned.

What else did the writer know?

Victor hurried to each room, pulling curtains shut and returned to the bedroom. He dropped to his knees and reached under the sofa bed. The satchel remained safely hidden. He pulled it to him, touching its shape through the heavy leather. The tomahawk was safe, undisturbed.

What did they want? How closely had he been followed?

Grabbing the meditation bowl and bamboo mat, Victor sought guidance from the copper and gold bowl. He sat, crossing his long legs into the lotus position with the bowl cradled in his palm. With a small, wooden mallet pressed against its lip, he circled it slowly along the smooth rim. Gradually, muscles relaxed, yielding soothing warmness. Tension and fear fled mind and body. A deep, calming song radiated from the metal. Gentle rhythm overtook him, guiding mind and spirit to a dreamscape. A realm touching another dimension.

A voice warned, no, no, deep in his mind.

Victor's hand weakened, releasing the mallet. The meditation bowl continued vibrating on its own, growing stronger in his palms. He levitated in a haze, translucent, beyond physical form, void of sensation and emotion, free to explore his new awareness. He passed onto another phase of life, scenic and peaceful. Trees and eroding boulders jutted from sloping hillsides materialized along a path entering a massive stone gateway. A vision of Lazarus and the Lord's Resurrection appeared.

He passed through the portal. The chant in his mind formed a smile, showing the path sacred and led to a safe location to meet the man following him.

The bowl fell, clanging to the mat, mute. Aromas of lilies, roses, and fresh tilled soil lingered inside the cramped houseboat.

Meditation acted like a sedative to frayed nerves, releasing tension better than the occasional visits to the Bowery's brothels. Could he continue? He wasn't sure a get together with his mystery man would occur.

He crumbled the note, burning it in the galley trash can. Tomorrow, the satchel would hang on his shoulder to finish a task in Greenwich Village. Another piece of unfinished work waited in Hell's Kitchen—a date with a red-headed shoe clerk. He wouldn't allow her to disrupt his revenge.

CHAPTER EIGHTEEN

Joe Nagle rose early, leaving his two-story Brooklyn Heights home. The sun hid over the cold Atlantic, hours from peeking between red brick colonial homes crowded together on Willow Street. The coffee timer set. His wife would wake to Maxwell House, perking and aromas filling the house he could no longer afford.

He'd be late and planned to call his partner from the diner, citing a personal problem. For a police officer, it was all he needed to say.

The trap had been prepared. Today, Nagle planned to make first contact, recruiting a new snitch while keeping Roe out of the secretive investigation. The hatchet killer case, along with the mayor, was enough to worry him. It took twenty minutes to drive south to Sunset Park in sparse, pre-dawn traffic. The next hour could reverse his career and perhaps save his marriage. If he wished to remain in his heavily mortgaged Nineteenth-century home, he needed to regain his captain's rank and pay grade within the elite organized crimes unit. His best and only option had full access to the Russian ship moonlighting as a security guard. Victor Gregory fits the bill as a loner obsessed with habit, and according to his personnel record—ambitious. After investing months of surveillance, Nagle saw he had the right man and the ideal bait the transit cop could not resist.

A handful of customers occupied Gig's diner. There were plenty of open seats for him to pick from, giving a good view of his mark when he arrived. Nagle caught a whiff of fresh paint while he tapped a new pack of Camels on the tabletop and ripped away the cellophane wrapper and seal. A painter had patched and touched up a battered wall near the pay phones. Buried among the chips and scars, Nagle recognized a splintered hole made by a large caliber bullet.

He struck a wooden match, inhaling his first cigarette of the day. Soothing nicotine vapors drew deep into impatient lungs, immediately calming him. A mug of black, steaming coffee rested next to his elbow. At a nearby table, a shapely waitress filled sugar bowls, distracting him for a moment. He liked his spot, tucked in a corner, hidden near the phone booths, viewing the entrance. Outside, tolling church bells sounded, and Nagle smiled, looking at his watch, expecting Victor's arrival.

No sign of his recruit. Nagle expected him to be on guard and assumed he took precautions. The few transit cops he knew carried chips on their shoulders the size of a brick, fighting for respect. Nagle viewed them on par with the cities' meter maids, maybe less.

Trust came hard for Nagle. He had to be one-hundred percent sure Victor was not involved with the growing Russian crime groups. If he were, Victor would not be alone; someone would watch. Nagle wouldn't be lured into a new trap by Reznik.

He couldn't afford another snafu with the Russian ship. Foot duty in The Bronx was the only option remaining—if he kept his job at all.

His future snitch appeared and approached. Confident he remained unknown to Victor, Nagle hunched over the table and casually sipped coffee. He looked away as the glass door swung open. Victor entered. No heads turned his way, at least from where Nagle positioned himself. The transit cop took his usual seat at the counter. Nagle held a long look at his future new partner.

With eyes straight ahead, Victor Gregory dropped a folded copy of the New York Post in front of him, sliding it aside as the waitress arrived, placing a mug of coffee in front of him. His brown leather satchel stayed on his shoulder, hanging opposite a holstered Colt .38. He centered his plastic covered patrol cap on the tall stool next to him. If not for the sidearm, Nagle would have mistaken him for a postman.

No hint of eye contact between Victor and anyone in the cafe came. Victor's eyes remained locked on the paper. If a signal passed between the new recruit and an accomplice, Nagle missed it. Months of surveillance work went into putting them together in the same room. He'd have one chance and wouldn't risk a hasty move.

Joe Nagle watched for stray eyes. Anything suspicious and he'd abort. No one in the diner, except himself, appeared interested in the transit cop. The only attention his target received came from a husky waitress refilling coffee.

It was time.

Nagle pulled a coin from his pocket and stepped into the nearby phone booth and slumped into its low wooden seat. He dropped the nickel into the slot, pulling the folded door closed, blocking out the clatter and rattle of dishes. He called the phone number for Gig's listed in the Yellow Pages and hoped someone answered.

After a dozen rings, a rushed cashier picked up a wall phone near the cash register.

Nagle didn't hesitate. "This is police business. There's a Transit officer in your diner. I need to speak to him."

The silver-haired cashier glanced at Victor, set the phone on a glass shelf and walked to the far end of the busy counter.

Victor nodded and creased the newspaper to its original fold. While doing so, he turned and scanned the cafe.

"Pick up the phone," Nagle mumbled to himself. "You want to open and close train doors all your life?"

Victor sipped his coffee and leaned forward, resting both elbows on the counter, staring into the open kitchen.

"Come on. Come on!" Nagle whispered.

Victor turned his back to the counter and picked up the newspaper. This time, he rolled it tight and tapped it against the countertop.

Nagle fought the urge to rush from the booth and approach Victor face to face. Although he had spotted no one, he felt confident someone watched. Did he wait for approval from the same person who tipped Reznik off on his illegal raid of the Liberty ship? The new immigrants, Russian-Jews, were cash rich, organized and patient with well-paid lawyers, unlike the street criminals he dealt with as a demoted third-grade detective.

Victor slid from the stool and pulled loose his leather jacket, exposing his service revolver. He walked toward the door, eyeing the room. Before arriving at the phone, he gripped the satchel's shoulder strap, squeezing it near to his body.

This was the first good look Nagle had of his recruit. Up close he was taller, with a firm athletic build, moving with the fluid grace of a dancer—someone he could not chase down and physically handle. Nagle guessed him younger, although the full black beard hid all but his eyes. Even with his training, Nagle doubted he'd recognize Victor clean shaven.

Victor arrived at the counter and took the phone. Before placing it to his ear, he paused and looked around.

"Come on," Nagle said, palming the mouthpiece. "You've used a phone before."

"Hello," Victor said.

"You got my message?" Joe Nagle asked. The transit cops gentle, soft voice surprised him.

"Who is this?"

"I'm a cop, just like you, Victor."

"You've been watching me."

"I have something you can help with."

"What's that?"

"It'll wait until we're alone."

Nagle watched Victor, hoping not to scare him off. The transit cop acted jumpy, shifting his weight from one leg to the other. From where he sat, Victor appeared to be heavily sweating despite the cold chilly morning.

"Victor, you okay?"

"I'm a subway cop. What do you want from me?"

"For now, just talk," Nagle said. "That's all."

"When?"

"Now. Thirty minutes. You won't be late for your shift."

Nagle watched his recruit shake his head in quick jerks, holding the handset near the chrome hook.

"America needs your help," Nagle said.

There was a pause. Victor held the phone at his side, pressed against his jacket.

Nagle watched him through the booth's wire mesh glass. He got a bad read on the transit cop's reaction. The surprise invasion of his personal life, the note in Victor's laundry, may have pushed too hard.

Victor avoided eye contact with anyone. His only distraction, the heavy leather satchel gripped against his side.

"I'll listen. No promises," he said.

"Green-Wood Cemetery. Know it?"

"Who doesn't?"

"The chapel. Go inside and have a seat."

Victor placed the phone in the cradle with the care of a mother placing a newborn to rest and returned to stool. He retrieved his hat, tossed two quarters next to the coffee mug, and walked out the diner's door. Nagle remained behind, seated in the booth, watching for anyone to follow. In a moment, he slipped from the stuffy box unnoticed. Nagle pulled a dollar bill from his billfold and laid it on the counter, pointing to the shapely waitress. He exited and ran to his car, Nagle planned to be waiting at the cemetery, watching for unwanted company.

Nagle liked the park-like graveyard as a private rendezvous, its expansive grounds open and free of people. A single entrance made it easy to spot those arriving and leaving. Victor's attachment to the satchel raised Joe Nagle's cop curiosity. If the opportunity arose, he'd look inside. What was so important he carried? It wasn't the case so much as how he guarded it, keeping it attached to him.

That was not all that bothered Nagle. He'd seen that face recently—somewhere besides the Liberty ship. He'd think of it. His memory never failed.

CHAPTER NINETEEN

Birdie Kelly woke as she always did following her accident. Cold, damp days like today drove the stiffness deeper into her damaged hips and shoulder. The comfort of the overstuffed chair, along with swallowing her last two Darvon tablets, had cradled her into a deep sleep. The prescription painkiller expired months ago, but not her growing dependence. Disoriented, she stumbled in the dark, unfamiliar room, finding her way to a window. The question crossed her mind as she yawned. Was she alone in Malda's Greenwich Village apartment? She'd failed to reset the deadbolts after breaking in.

Holding her breath, she listened for a telling sound. To her relief, the one-room studio flat stayed quiet. Malda, or her stalker, could have entered while she'd slept. After a search, she was confident she remained alone.

At the window, she yanked the heavy curtains apart, revealing early morning blackness. Specks of drizzle dotted the glass. With a quick glance across the street, she located Jark's green and white Dodge parked near a dim streetlamp. Birdie warned him of the danger and had tried to send him home, at least for the night. Unable to spot any sign of him, her fear rose until she remembered his military training. He was likely slumped in the seat sleeping or relieving himself in an alley. She admired the loyalty of her driver, although unnecessary. She admitted she found herself attracted to him physically. He was ripe and ready for a slightly older woman. The seduction would be mutual. She was a lady.

Birdie grinned and recalled the recent peeping neighbor at the boatyard. After dropping her towel, she smiled into the steamed mirror. His eyes lingered. The thick scar on her shoulder was an aphrodisiac to the men she favored.

She turned on a small kitchen light over the stove and boiled water. Above her, a large grinning Felix the Cat clock stared at her. Its question mark shaped tail swayed back and forth. It showed 5:16. The sun would rise in a half-hour, awaking the city, exposing its raw, uncaring self. Workers rushed, bombarding streets with cabs and crammed buses. Overcrowded subways would rattle beneath sidewalks while the Village's free spirits, poets, and artists slept.

To desert the case and turn over evidence to Roe and Nagle tempted her. To pursue a killer was one thing. Leapfrogging into jeopardy risked her winding up next to Mary Clary, decapitated in the morgue. Her client, Sid Breen, placed faith in her. She would finish the job finding his daughter's killer.

She'd gotten away with breaking and entering twice. Her luck would run out. Like a modern Goldilocks, she'd made herself at home and spent a comfortable night in Malda's home. No point to rush. She had no other lead other than Malda Boddy. The vigil in her apartment was the only alternative, as Birdie became convinced Malda led to Mary Clary's killer. Why would Malda, on her opening performance, in a starring role, replacing Mary Clary, bolt from the theater? The only explanation which made sense—Malda had seen the killer and ran for her life.

Birdie recognized few unforgivable sins and allowed exceptions to few. This morning she granted herself forgiveness as she poured boiling water into a mug of instant Nescafe coffee. Despite an Irish upbringing, she preferred strong coffee over Ireland's beloved traditional tea. Somewhere, her forefathers cringed.

She clutched a steaming cup and turned on more lights; sure her absent host would understand the intrusion.

If Malda took part in the conspiracy and killing, there was a chance evidence remained in the apartment. Beginning near the bed, Birdie pulled open the dresser, running her hands through drawers, finding only a few folded summer slips and scarves. The precisely made bed had a pale-yellow satin comforter with matching pillow covers. She lifted the fabric and found crisp white sheets, which appeared fresh and unused. The cramped bathroom, its sink smaller than a drinking fountain, contained a spare roll of single-ply toilet paper and nothing else.

On her knees, she checked under chairs and the bed. The search continued for a half-hour, finishing in the tiny kitchen. Nothing turned up but dust balls and hairpins. Malda lived with few indulgences. The red cape seemed to be the most luxurious item in her small wardrobe—and now she'd lost it. Birdie wondered how Malda could again wear the garment. Could she forget the bloody murder of her friend wearing the cape?

Absence of family pictures and mementos bothered Birdie. Nothing personal hung on the wallpapered flower print walls but framed movie and theater posters. No pictures of Malda existed, at least not displayed. For a budding actress, there should have been plenty of headshots and publicity photos. Nothing! No magazines, newspapers, or bills proving she'd lived in the apartment. Later, Birdie planned to go door to door, hoping to locate a nosey neighbor, anyone who knew the tenant in 401. Someone had to know her habits and whereabouts. Every building in the city had a prying neighbor. It could be as simple as Malda sub-letting her place, a common occurrence during holidays. Manhattan became a mecca for tourist, while urban families escaped, seeking a Norman Rockwell farmhouse complete with a sleigh ride.

Where did she run to last night? Birdie asked herself, knowing in time of stress, animal instincts take humans to where they feel safe and to someone they trust. She made a mental note to ask Sid Breen to get Malda's personal information from her agent.

The small refrigerator, hidden under the counter, was bare, not a bottle of milk for her bitter coffee. A tall, narrow cabinet contained few dishes, enough for a table setting for two. A near-empty jar of peanut butter sat near another clean mug. Birdie craved a real brewed cup.

Actresses who sang and danced on the stage lived on permanent diets, but the Spartan contents told Birdie Malda ate out often and likely with the killer she hunted. The other possibility, she hadn't thought of until now, Malda had a second home, maybe a boyfriend or sugar-daddy. That would explain the expensive, well-tailored red cloak.

Birdie had become at ease in the small apartment, and hunger pains gripped her stomach. From somewhere she smelled bacon frying.

Could the walls be that thin?

A peek out the blinds revealed the green Dodge parked across the street. Jark could not be found. She hoped he napped in the back seat; however, the early light of morning would have wakened him. Birdie's concern grew. Did someone watch them arrive and attack her unsuspecting driver? The killer may have set a trap, waiting for her to return to the Dodge.

The case grew more complicated, and for the first time, Birdie feared for Jark's safety. Should she call Owen Roe? It may not be too late. She'd have lots of explaining and faced the possibility of jail and losing her PI license. The Pinkertons would not rehire her with a criminal record, and Sid Breen would prevent her from working as an actress.

"Who are you, Malda Boddy?" Birdie asked the empty room.

In the hallway, the floor creaked. Footsteps approached the apartment. Birdie jumped from the kitchen chair, tiptoeing to the door. She engaged the two deadbolt locks and pressed her back next to the wall. The .38 Ruger remained in her purse that rested next to the chair she had slept in. Not wanting to reveal her presence, she stayed put, frozen, pinned against the wall's oversized flowers. Her breathing controlled, no one would know she was inside unless they had a key.

The rapid knock rattled the door. Birdie jerked, bumping the wall. No key entered the doorknob or deadbolts. She pushed an ear against the thick wood, listening.

"Open up, I know you're there." The voice echoed from the hallway.

CHAPTER TWENTY

Detective Joe Nagle waited, parked near Green-Wood's massive Gothic arched and spired entry gates. His tactical position allowed a view of anyone approaching the historic park-like cemetery. On five-hundred rolling acres, and the highest point in Brooklyn, granted visitors spectacular views of New York's bridges and skylines. He enjoyed the serene setting and thought of it as his urban escape. While masses of people rushed to the city's public parks, few knew the secrets hidden in Green-Wood.

A subway stop was a short walk away, outside the cemetery's gates. Nagle expected Victor Gregory's arrival soon. Without him, the plan would not get off the ground. Despite the bleak day, the cemetery attracted visitors and tourists, lured by a morbid enticement to view the recent burial site of the Gambino crime family boss, Albert Anastasia. The killing remained fresh in Nagle's mind.

The bloody assassination occurred in the Mid-Town barbershop of the Park Sheraton Hotel. Last month, October 27, Anastasia sat enjoying a shave and haircut when two gunmen burst through the door, shoved the barber aside and filled the mob boss full of lead.

The cemetery represented a who's who of New York celebrities, respectable and corrupt. Nagle intended, someday, to find the grave of Frank Morgan. The stodgy actor portrayed the great and powerful Wizard of Oz, a misplaced conman behind the curtain, pulling strings, fooling Emerald City citizens with make-believe powers—much like his strategy. He lacked department authorization, and he'd keep his cover behind Victor, using him as a puppet, gaining entrance to Reznik's illegal activity aboard the Russian liberty ship.

As a cop, Nagle relied on instinct and couldn't shake the feeling he missed something. Why was Victor Gregory hinky? Though confident Victor played no part of the Russian Jew's enterprise, Nagle couldn't trust him. The transit cop hid a secret. Whatever the trouble, it kept him jittery.

Victor appeared, stepping to the top of the subway tunnel. After smoothing down his brown leather patrol jacket, he exited into the morning's light fog. Relieved, Nagle slumped in his seat and lit another Lucky Strike.

His mark crossed Fifth Avenue and headed toward the cemetery's only public gate. A satchel hung over his left shoulder, swaying with each step as he marched into the busy street, stopping traffic with a wave of an arm. The transit cop was much bigger and younger than expected, walking with the confidence of a prizefighter entering the ring.

Nagle looked at his watch—twenty minutes had passed since leaving the deli. Victor stopped beneath the mammoth entrance, staring at the larger-than-life carved biblical scenes depicting Lazarus and Christ's Resurrections. After a moment, he continued through the brownstone gates into Green-Wood.

Nagle remained alert for anyone following. He turned away, caught off guard by Victor's sudden change in direction, approaching his car. The transit cop veered again—passing the beat up Ford.

Victor blended with the worn, sculptured marble angels and demons—frozen, eternal sentinels, watching over the cemetery grounds. He walked, with a bounce in his step, along a maze of roads bending past collapsing mausoleums and aged blackened headstones toward the concrete gothic chapel. Its dull gray, sharp pointed spires sat tall, centered among barren oak's winter branches.

Nagle remained in his wife's car, keeping an eye on his recruit. Cold wintery bleakness closed in, shutting out hope for sunshine. It would be eight long years before retirement and boating South Florida's sunny, tropical waters. Fast moving gray clouds sunk over the medieval graveyard, carrying with them a sudden downpour. Rain splattered, hitting the ground with force, muting nearby traffic. Gusting winds carried waves of water blasting against the car, swaying it side to side. Nagle's only view became an opaque blur.

As quickly as the deluge arrived, it departed, leaving behind a dull, flat sky hanging over the cemetery, promising more rain. Joe Nagle stepped from the car. He had lost his mark.

Victor Gregory was not in sight. He'd vanished.

* * * * *

Victor pressed his back against the stone wall, taking cover from the storm. The mausoleum's over-hanging roof had kept him dry. It had been his first visit to the historic Brooklyn site. None of what he viewed surprised him. His meditation had days ago revealed the scenic and peaceful boulders jutting from eroded hillsides and winter trees shaping paths through the cemetery.

Earlier, as he'd entered the massive stone gateway, he viewed stone carvings of Lazarus and the Lord's Resurrection. What message did his musing intend to reveal? A higher power led him, not the person sending the note. Something he didn't understand manipulated his life. He'd searched for it, attending countless masses in the city's cathedrals and churches.

Hid meditative images were not a substitute for his mother's strict Roman Catholic beliefs, but provided occasional clarity and understanding to his subconscious. Did he carry the mortal sins of his mother? An end-stage approached. He knew it to be. Where did it lead? Daily humiliation and whippings by the sisters and priests of good old Saint Joe's instilled a stern view of religion. He'd long ago cast off the church's sacrament of confession—a symbolic man in a box representing a distant, harsh God judging him a sinner, doomed to purgatory.

As Victor passed the gate, he noticed the idling Ford. He'd felt the occupant's watching eyes since stepping onto the grounds. His thoughts on more pressing tasks—the red-headed shoe store clerk saw him in the street. She'd identify him. The police would find her. Time worked against him.

From habit he tapped the side of the leather case, enjoying the touch of his iron tomahawk, Victor stepped from under the mausoleum into the murky day and continued his stroll through the park beneath dripping, leafless trees. He glanced back at the beat up old Ford. White exhaust puffed from its tailpipe.

He'd soon meet his mysterious stalker.

* * * * *

Joe Nagle spotted the tall, uniformed figure splashing through patches of standing water. Athletic and nimble, Victor's pace quickened as he approached the chapel a few hundred yards away.

Nagle's confidence grew with the arrival of the transit cop. He pulled the Ford coupe from the curb and looped around the graveyard's perimeter and found the rear private entrance of the century-old Gothic chapel. Using his cop's authority, he parked in a red zone reserved for service vehicles. Suspicious of a tail, he'd stay in the small sacristy behind the altar to observe Victor arrive. The parking lot remained empty. They'd have the place to themselves. He'd convince the transit cop to assist him; it would be the two, no one else, including his partner, Owen Roe. Once he exposed Reznik as a Russian criminal boss, Nagle was confident he'd regain his captain's rank in the organized crimes unit. As insurance, Nagle held a final carrot, an inducement Victor Gregory could not resist.

The heavy chapel door pushed open. Victor Gregory entered, his walk matched a self-assured poise, his footsteps the only sound in the empty sanctuary. The leather bag hung from one shoulder, opposite his holstered revolver. He removed his cap and walked to a corner, taking a seat in a pew. The dark beard gave him the appearance of someone much older. Nagle guessed late twenties, early thirties. His approach was critical, a cop, even a transit officer, would be skeptical of assisting another law enforcement agency. Police were territorial, guarding their turf against poachers.

Nagle hoped not to appear anxious, stood tall, took a breath, relaxed and pushed open the narrow door hidden behind the altar. As he entered the chapel, he got a heavy dose of freshly applied Johnson paste wax—God's cologne, he thought, as he stepped across the chancel, tip-toeing.

Did he fear disturbing a slumbering God?

Long absent from church, Nagle wondered if he should kneel or bless himself? He chose both and strode across the tiled floor, turned down an aisle which split the chapel, never removing his eyes from the transit cop.

Victor remained motionless and appeared tranquil, bathed in weak shapes of light falling from high-arched windows. The moment of truth arrived. Nagle stepped into a pew fronting Victor, extending his hand.

"Officer Gregory."

Victor tapped his transit shield. "It's Sergeant Gregory." With unexpected quickness, he thrust out his arm.

"Thanks for coming." Nagle shook his hand.

"I didn't catch your name," Victor said.

Joe Nagle flipped open his badge. "I'm a New York City detective— for now, that's all you need to know."

This was no time for pulling rank. Although Nagle outranked the transit cop, he had no authority over Victor Gregory or any New York City beat cop. This was a courtesy between two lawmen.

Nagle motioned to the pews and took a seat, forcing himself to appear casual, intending to drop the use of names and ranks. Nagle turned in the pew and threw an arm over its back, looking at Victor.

Victor's dark eyes fixed on Nagle. A tiresome plop of water drumming a monotonous beat interrupted the stillness.

Joe Nagle forced his face closer, hoping for a response.

"You've been following me," Victor said, using a low voice.

"No. I've been watching the ship you guard."

"Nothing else?"

"Just the boat."

Victor pushed, leaning against the pew, arching his back, keeping his satchel close, clutching it.

"I wanted to speak to you,"

"So you put a note in my laundry?" Victor said.

"I needed to get to you without being noticed," Nagle answered, lowered his head and smiled. "... For our protection."

Victor shifted again, sliding the leather bag to his side. "I took the bait. What's so urgent?"

Nagle heard Victor's calm voice and words. However, he felt the transit cop's intense eyes lash at him. His promising snitch was jumpy. Sweat droplets formed on Victor's forehead despite the coolness.

Victor's preoccupation with the leather bag continued, gripping and re-gripping it. Nagle couldn't help wondering what he guarded. It was more than lunch and the daily reports sergeants in every precinct completed. For now, he'd set aside his curiosity. They were here on a much more significant matter.

He came prepared with an easily believed white lie, one he hoped Victor would not bother to check. He was dealing with a transit cop, and they needed little build up. They understood directness.

"I run an undercover organized crime unit," Nagle said.

Victor remained quiet, fixing his eyes on Nagle's.

"We think the ship you're guarding is involved in international crime."

Joe Nagle hesitated, waiting for a comment. None came. Victor sat there, gripping his leather shoulder bag.

"We suspect Lev Reznik to be engaged in criminal activities with ties to illegal Russians."

Nagle watched the transit cop for a moment. The only sound continued to be the foyer's dripping roof.

"Why tell me?"

"You have access to the ship."

"You want me to spy on Reznik?"

This time, Nagle moved closer. He rose from his pew to sit beside Victor. As he took a seat, the transit cop slid, moving nearer the curved armrest.

"Basically that's it," Nagle said. "Will you help your country?" After the words came out, he felt he'd oversold the patriotic pitch.

"Why not go through channels? Your boss and mine."

Nagle read Victor's file and knew he'd been a drama and dance student. How much of this was an act? The transit cop's face remained unchanged. Was he being played, or was Victor this bland? He'd expected a rush of questions. Most low-level police officers jumped for such an assignment, an opportunity for quick advancement. Instead of offering more explanations, Nagle mimicked Victor's almost sullen demeanor. He had one more lie to tell.

"I'm running this, and there's a leak in our office," he said. "No one knows about it."

Victor shifted in the pew and stood. "Sounds risky."

Nagle took a chance, raised, putting a hand on Victor's shoulder. "There's a place for you in my department when this is over."

For the first time, Nagle sensed reaching the transit cop. Victor's deep-set eyes intent. The rest of his face, hidden by a thick, neatly trimmed beard, prevented a read on the stoic man, although he thought he caught a trace of a smile.

"Do you think so?"

"You're the kind of man we're looking for," Nagle lied.

Victor took a seat. "What do you want me to do?"

"The same thing you always do," Nagle said. "Patrol the ship and tell me what's going on."

"That's it?"

"Reznik, tell you anything was off limits?"

"The cargo holds. There's nothing down there."

Nagle nodded. "Look at the ship's log. They might be locked in a cabinet on the bridge or captain's quarters."

"What am I looking for?"

"I doubt it will list the actual shipments, but tell me what the log claims," Nagle said. "I need to know where the boat goes and for how long."

Nagle wanted to ask more of his recruit but chose not to push, fearing to scare him off. Better to ease him in.

"That's all?" Victor asked.

"The ship have a name?"

"Reznik called it *The Yojo*."

"You're helping already," Nagle said. "Look for registration papers."

Victor unzipped and pulled open his leather jacket, revealing a sweat-stained blue shirt. From his slacks pocket, he removed a folded white handkerchief and dabbed his forehead.

"How do I reach you?" he asked.

Pleased with his recruit, Nagle reeled him in. "I'll be watching the ship. You know where I park. If it's urgent, flash your light twice and meet here."

Victor smiled for the first time.

"I'll be waiting," Nagle said, returning the smile. "If it's not critical, flash once and leave a note in your laundry."

Shaking his head, another smile came from inside the heavy beard. "One if by laundry, two if by chapel."

"Something like that."

Joe Nagle recognized he dealt with someone special. The man he sat next to displayed quick wit and athleticism. He wouldn't underestimate his new snitch.

"Understood." Victor raised to his feet.

"One more thing," Nagle said. "Don't use names."

Nagle came prepared, "Call yourself, Tin Man. I'm Scarecrow, Reznik, The Lion and the ship, Emerald City."

After a few seconds of silence, Victor nodded. "The Tin Man has to go to work in the tunnels."

"One more thing," Nagle said. "Search the ship's holds tonight."

Victor nodded.

Nagle relaxed, thinking the rendezvous yielded results better than planned. As he turned to retreat, the chapel's main door pushed open. A stooped man in a heavy gray overcoat, buttoned top to bottom, shook and closed a black umbrella. Walking with an up and down hobble, he genuflected and slipped into a pew on the center aisle, near where they sat.

Nagle kept his eyes on Victor, but remained aware of the intruder. He didn't know the face but remembered the pronounced limp rushing from the Harbor Wash and Fold laundry.

CHAPTER TWENTY-ONE

Birdie stared at the door.

Another sharp knock rattled the flimsy security chain.

"It's me, your driver, Jark. You there?"

Birdie eased her back from against the wall and retrieved her revolver. With it at her side, she returned to the surprise visitor.

"Prove it," she said.

"Come on, let me in. I spent the night in the car."

With the safety chain in place, Birdie undid the pair of deadbolt locks, inching the door open. Jark's bright blue eyes greeted her through the narrow space.

"Are you crazy?" she whispered, pulling him inside. She glanced down the hallway, thankful no neighbor watched.

"Beats instant coffee." He held a sack of bagels and a shoebox containing a half dozen paper cups of steaming coffee. She nearly collapsed from happiness.

"I told you to go home. What are you doing here?"

"Nothing better to do." Jark arranged small breakfast on a copper-topped bistro table.

"This is breaking and entering, you know."

"The red cape?" Birdie asked. "Is it safe?"

"Locked in the trunk."

"It belongs to the lady that lives here."

"Malda Boddy," Jark said.

"She was supposed to be wearing it."

"Strange, being here."

Birdie nodded, slurping hot coffee, holding a cup in both hands.

Jark ripped opened a wrinkled brown bag, handing her a water bagel covered with cream cheese.

"A schmear would have been fine," she said, catching a thick clump of heavy spread in her fingers.

"What happened?"

"I couldn't help myself." Birdie raised an index finger, took a bite of bagel while scraping remains from the edge of her mouth and nose. After more swallows of coffee, she pointed to an overstuffed chair.

"I played Goldilocks and fell asleep."

Jark walked around the compact apartment, examining the barren room.

"I thought my place was small."

Finished with breakfast, Birdie slumped into the deep chair, eyeing Jark. It had been a long time since she'd enjoyed a man's company.

"You shouldn't be here."

"That so?" Jark opened a narrow refrigerator wedged between the sink and stove.

"Don't bother... the cupboards are bare."

Jark waved a bagel near his face. "No, I've been to the bakers."

"This apartment puzzles me. I'm spinning my wheels."

"You're doing more than the police."

Birdie laughed. "Besides picking the lock, I've stolen and withheld evidence and attacked an usher all in the last twenty-four hours." She stretched both arms overhead, yawning. "I guess I have."

"You plan to search the place again?" Jark asked.

"You bet your life. This apartment belongs to someone who was a target for murder or made it appear like she was."

Jark flashed a grin while he slid a narrow table, covered by pots of ivy and cacti, away from a window, replacing it with a kitchen chair. After grabbing a fresh coffee, he nudged a heavy curtain open a few inches.

"Thanks for the treat, it brought me back to life," Birdie said. "But for now, it's better if you wait in the car."

"I'm not budging."

Birdie stamped her foot. "I mean it."

"That's a bad plan. You need a look-out."

His confident look made the offer difficult to refuse. Birdie returned his smile and began her search.

As an investigator, she'd searched suspect's homes and offices, seeking proof for arrest. Rummaging through Malda's clothing and possessions affected her. Birdie hoped combing through the young girl's belongings would eliminate her as an accomplice and secure a lead to locating her and securing police protection. Instinct and the red cape told her the killer had targeted Malda for the grizzly public beheading. That night, two actresses, and possibly close friends, innocently exchanged winter coats, altering their lives, costing her client's daughter, Mary Clary, her life.

Last night's half-hearted look around yielded nothing. Today, the search would be thorough, pulling contents from drawers, checking clothing pockets, opening purses. She'd examine the stacked shoe boxes, high in the narrow closet. This time, Birdie promised to turn over all leads to Roe and Nagle.

A glimpse of the few dresses, skirts and shoes found in Malda's wardrobe surprised Birdie. The matronly clothes were painfully long out of fashion.

Actresses in the city, desperate for roles, starved, spending meager earnings on expensive wardrobes. Obligatory dinners and cocktail parties demanded a chic, eye-catching look on the off-chance a producer or agent noticed. A contrived, casual meeting with simple hellos and handshakes required less dressy but attention-grabbing attire for a climbing actress.

Over the years, it had been Birdie's mantra. Broadway's successful people dealt with beautiful, successful people. An actress's sexy clothes worked as bait for power brokers. Birdie doubted much had changed.

After dragging a kitchen chair across the room, Birdie reached a hat box tucked deep on a shelf. She slid the round box forward and it tipped. Something from the top slipped forward surprising her, falling, glancing off her arm, hitting the wood floor with a soft ringing tone. A stubby wood club followed, striking her forehead.

The metal bowl rolled and stopped against the wall. The crash brought Jark running from the window. She handed him the dusty box and stepped from the chair, rejecting help.

"What is it?" Jark asked.

"Looks like a copper bowl and wooden stick."

"They sell 'em on the street in Greenwich."

"For what?"

"Who knows with beatniks."

"I plan to find out." Birdie rubbed the tender spot on her head.

Jark tapped the hat box. "What's this?"

"Nothing." She placed her hands on his muscular shoulders, giving a gentle shove. "No questions. Back to the window."

Birdie inched the yellow ribbon, sliding it from the round box, keeping the knot tied—avoiding tail-tale signs of a search. White tissue paper lined the interior and wrapped the contents. A silver-framed photo displayed a smiling girl dressed in a soft blue graduation gown. Birdie guessed it to be Malda. A second photograph showed a cheerful group, garbed in colorful coats and scarves, gathered at the base of an ice-covered waterfall.

A wooden cigar box grabbed her attention. After several gentle shakes, she suspected it held the photographs she'd looked for. Nervous, she fumbled opening the latch, spilling loose Kodak's over the bedspread.

Birdie examined each glossy black-and-white photo before returning them to the container. There were no signs of a boyfriend.

She shuffled through them again, this time eyeing the background—stage scenery and props, recognizing many of the theater locations.

The photographs of Malda and Mary Clary together had been taken during rehearsals and acting performances at off and off, off-Broadway venues she knew too well from her brief career. Malda Boddy's looks were ordinary, far from beautiful; however, Mother Nature blessed the young actress with an hour-glass figure producers and directors favored.

Few mementos remained in the hat box, baby shoes and a withered, smashed wrist corsage. Birdie guessed the blue and white ribbon wrapped Malda's high school diploma and left it as it was.

Stumped, she set the hat box on her lap. Its contents revealed nothing of the mysterious occupant's adult life, nor hint of boyfriends. The apartment offered no evidence of Malda's involvement or clues to Mary Clary's murder. Its sparse furnishing appeared secondhand, thrift store rejects or worse, reclaimed from the curb, except Malda's elegant bed.

The focal point of the single room stood tucked half-way into a nook. Sculpted, twisted brass and smoothly curved steel loops gave an illusion of ocean waves to the grand, tall headboard.

Birdie braced her arm against the elevated bed while easing to her knees and aimed a Boy Scout pocket light under the frame. She pushed away thick cobwebs and dust balls. If no eight-legged creatures were unearthed, all would be fine. She'd endure anything found crawling in people's dark hiding places except creepy, hairy spiders.

Birdie stopped and looked at Jark sitting in the kitchen sipping coffee. "You're supposed to watch the street."

He shot her a crisp salute and turned back to the heavy drapes he held open.

A wave of pleasure gushed through her ego. Jark, at least ten years her junior, took notice of her. She caught him staring.

The trauma of her injury brought occasional anger and depression during her extended recovery, preventing her from connecting with people. However, her women's instincts were returning. Once again, she sought relationships. The previous night's shameless experimentation, while bathing, excited her while providing confidence; she'd begun her comeback as a woman. A slip of her fingers allowed the towel to fall away, ladylike from her toned body. His eyes peeking between the blinds tingled her wet flesh.

Birdie scanned the beam of light back and forth and spotted a pair of fuzzy slippers, a box of tissues and a flattened tube of K-Y jelly.

She replaced the items as she'd found them and climbed to her knees. "This girl got around."

Jark turned to her. "What?"

"I underestimated Malda. I'm taking another look."

"There's a cop down there. He walked out of the drug store."

"What's he doing?"

"Nothing but standing across the street."

"Cops don't do nothing. Watch him," Birdie said as she poked her head under the bed. "Let me know if he does anything."

"He looks like he plays ball for The House of David."

"What?" Birdie asked.

"Their players have beards and long hair."

"Tell me if he comes this way."

Jark pointed a finger-gun at her. "You got it boss-lady."

Her dimming flashlight caught a sparkle at the far side of the bed, beyond reach. She inched, squeezing between the smooth floor and wood slats of the heavy box mattress.

The narrow, cramped space tightened around her, reminding Birdie of the accident, pinning her under a half ton of stage rigging. Hot lights and metal pushed against her, crushing a shoulder and hip.

Shortness of breath and suffocation paralyzed her under the metal framed bed. Her lungs failed, unable to draw a mouthful of air. She'd use her precious last gasp to shout for help.

Sliding on her stomach, pulled by her ankles, Birdie's head bumped against the bed frame. She rolled onto her back the moment she escaped, finding Jark standing over her. His puzzled look told her she owed him an explanation.

Before she spoke, Jark walked to his place at the window, peaking at the street, watching the cop.

Clinched in the palm of her left hand rested a gold cufflink.

"He's not a real cop," Jark said.

Birdie remained on the floor, taking rapid deep breaths, recovering, staring at the dazzling find. It could have been a gold nugget pulled from an Alaskan stream.

"Private security?" she asked, ignoring the panic attack.

"Transit cop, the ones riding subways and buses."

"What's he doing?"

"Holding the wall up, reading a paper."

She inspected the cufflink, gripping it by the stem. Centered on its polished gold face, a solitary diamond. She guessed two carats at least, and real.

Birdie slipped it into her pocket, and returned to her search of the bed.

Another surprise waited, peeking from under the bed. A splinter of glass poked from a wooden picture frame caught her attention. Moments ago, she'd given up finding clues to Malda's life. Now, as if by a miracle, they jumped at her from every direction.

As she turned it over, jagged, shattered glass fell away from the smashed frame. A smiling Malda embraced a uniformed bearded man at least a foot taller than her. Birdie blew off light dust and shook away remaining fragments of glass. She guessed it hadn't fallen, instead thrown in a fit of rage. Metal fasteners which held a cardboard backing twisted away, allowing removal of the portrait. Folding the photograph, she slid it under the waistband of her slacks—no use letting Jark know she continued her wicked ways, removing evidence.

Encouraged by the find, Birdie pressed on, returning to the place women keep secrets—makeup and jewelry drawers. This time, she reached deep into a drawer earlier searched.

How did she miss it?

A silver heart-shaped locket, the size of a half-dollar, rested inside a white folded lady's glove. She guessed Tiffany, being a frequent window shopper of the exclusive jewelry store.

Birdie twisted open the clasp, looked twice at the photograph and snapped it shut—surprised.

Stunned, she almost missed Jark's passing as he headed to the toilet. Once the door closed, she dropped the locket into her pocket.

The bathroom door opened after the flush.

"Where's the cop you were watching?" she asked.

"You weren't listening. He looked inside his leather bag and walked away in a hurry."

"That's all?"

"He may have been followed."

"Cops?"

"Old guy with a jerky limp," Jark answered.

CHAPTER TWENTY-TWO

Victor Gregory checked the war axe and snapped his shoulder bag's lock in place after taking a last glance at the top-floor window. No signs of Malda came from her one-room flat. Each morning, without fail, she had opened the curtains, allowing early sunshine to her cherished plants.

Today, someone new did. Whoever peeked through the blinds looked for her as he did.

Victor had another obligation uptown and tossed the newspaper into the bodega's trash can.

He had much on his mind. The offer to join a New York undercover police operation caught him off guard—advancement to the elite crime unit couldn't be passed up. He knew the Russian freighter from bow to stern as well as anyone, including Lev Reznik. The code name, Tin Man, given him by the unknown cop, had been ironic. He privately enjoyed the bizarre joke.

As he recalled from Frank Baum's original Wizard of Oz, The Tin Man wielded an axe, lopping off heads of animals threatening Dorothy's journey. Scuttlebutt among street cops had it the special unit acted outside standard police procedures, skirting laws to apprehend sophisticated criminals. The lure of power appealed to

Victor; but a personal matter required his attention: Malda and the red-headed shoe clerk stood in the way.

* * * * *

At seven o'clock, Victor Gregory stepped from the crowded morning rush of passengers exiting Columbus Circle station. Street vendors pushed wheeled carts, vying for positions along sidewalks near the subway terminal. Early arrivals sold coffee and rolls to impatient commuters. Late-arriving merchants threw down blankets, claiming space near the street, hoping to gain shopper's attention for their neatly arranged books, purses, gloves, and scarves.

Victor leaned against the side of a busy cart, helping himself to coffee and Danish. Nothing had been said about payment once he pointed at his badge. After a second cup, he walked to the scene of his botched attempt to kill Malda.

From habit, he pressed the leather satchel close to his body, feeling the trustworthy weapon's sturdy, long, curved handle. General Washington's gift of the pipe tomahawk to Seneca Chief Red Jacket symbolized a new country's thanks for the chief's victory against a mighty British Army. When the war hatchet's work ended, it would again rest in a place of honor, a museum exhibit—undetected, never to be used as evidence.

A loose end remained from his mistaken attack. The attractive redhead, working a window display, saw him near the murder scene. An off-duty uniformed transit officer in the vicinity of a savage murder would bring unwanted scrutiny. He couldn't afford more slip-ups. The innocent clerk and Malda could not speak to the police.

He passed close to the church, which gave him refuge last night, calming his jitters and fear. Not recalling its saintly name, Victor raised a gloved hand, making a sign of the cross, as if he were a bishop, anointing it, Saint Promise the Broken, a church like all the rest—all promise, no delivery.

With a backward glance, he laughed at his joke, wondering if the two babushka-covered heads he spotted before continued to pray in the heavily incensed house of worship.

As a child, he'd spent marathon sessions kneeling at a marble altar repeating senseless prayers learned by rote. A black-robed nun administered well-placed lashes to the backs of his legs while conferring reminders of mortal sin's pain and his unworthy mother's excommunication. Victor knew what dirty deeds went on behind closed doors of the powerful parish priest.

The murder scene was no longer cordoned off. The police had removed strands of rope, which had wrapped utility poles and sawhorses. In Hell's Kitchen, vandals and gangs roaming streets could have done the task. Strangely, the white tape remained, profiled a twisted body—the wrong body. Mary Clary, daughter of a big shot producer, sacrificed her life for Malda.

As a precaution, Victor stayed across the street, should the police have the site under surveillance, expecting the killer's return, admiring his grizzly handy work.

Misty haze formed low in the western sky, moving toward him, reaching tops of abandoned docks and warehouses. Fog slinked from the Hudson River carrying clammy dampness. Moisture hung, suspended in heavy, cold air. Victor experienced the same wetness in his palms as last night and ripped off his snug fitting gloves. No blood. Relieved, he pulled them on, feeling tight leather mold to each finger. His fist drove into his palm. He had a job to complete.

Fog draped the landscape, a thick canopy shrouding streets and buildings, seizing the life of the city. Victor guessed The Flying Horse Lounge only fifty feet away from where he stood.

Along a wall of dirty brick storefronts, he spotted the orange and white neon sign of the bar his misidentified target had exited. In his mind, Victor heard the same blaring Chuck Berry tune, "*Roll Over Beethoven*," playing as his victim, wrapped in the red cape, marched toward him last night. Although they brushed against one another, she failed to acknowledge him.

Victor quickened his step as he passed the nightclub and turned the corner. Hell's Kitchen, despite nearness to Broadway, housed ancient tenements, soup kitchens, and sleazy bars; contrasting sharply to the nearby luxurious homes and fine boutiques of Fifth Avenue and the city's well-known Millionaire's Row.

In a few minutes, he located what he searched for.

In the narrow storefront entrance, brightly colored and polished shoes glowed under bright lights.

This was where the redhead entered his life, dooming hers.

A well-lighted display of women's red and green flats, pumps, and loafers sat against a backdrop of cotton ball snow-covered mountains. The presentation held his eye, a work of art. The artist wouldn't enjoy her creation much longer.

Pointy-eared elves leaned against candy canes and smiled from behind the glass. A skinny Santa sat in a sleigh formed by green pumps, pulled by eight brown, five-inch stilettos. The jolly rider held a paper clock—Victor had less than an hour until the store opened.

A groan rose from a dark corner close to the door. Victor stepped back, aiming a flashlight toward the sound. Long, shaggy blond hair rested on a foot mat. Tucked near the entry, a tramp cuddled, his face hidden inside a quilted sleeping bag.

The idea struck Victor the moment he spotted the fetal shape of the foul-smelling vagrant. Inside a pocket, he touched the handle of his knife and backed from the storefront.

Thick fog behind the shoe store provided Victor more cover than needed. He hid behind garbage bins lining graffiti-covered brick walls. A folding security gate stretched across the staff entrance. The small shop likely paid two clerks, maybe three for holidays. He worried a store employee; maybe the same late-working redhead would arrive to chase off the slumbering hobo, or worse, ask a patrolman's aid.

Victor opened his knife and settled in, crouching between trash containers, palming the jagged three-inch blade. Should she have a weapon, his uniform and badge would distract her—by then, he'd close in and finish the task.

The night he killed Malda, an eight million to one chance encounter doomed the shoe clerk. Their eyes met in the window display of holiday high heels and flats she arranged,

Osgood's Shoes would not open its doors today.

From his satchel, Victor removed a flat rain slicker compressed to the size of a folded man's handkerchief. He pulled the thin plastic over his head, tying it snug under his chin. The poncho, not department issue, protected against blood splatter.

His knees ached, crouching in the cold. Forty-five minutes passed and no sign of her. Osgood's opened in fifteen minutes, according to the paper clock in the storefront. He couldn't keep the surveillance much longer. The dense fog wouldn't last all morning, and he'd be spotted from surrounding buildings.

A quick glance at his wristwatch reminded Victor of his carelessness, losing his engraved pocket watch at the murder scene.

His rubber shoes and gloves, which he'd burned, left no foot or fingerprints, nothing traceable. There had been no reason to return. None. If he hadn't, last night's well-planned killing would be untraceable. The pocket watches' engravings were scratched away. Did he miss something the cops might read under heavy magnification?

Footfalls of high heels arrived, moving at a rapid pace. Unseen, they clicked on the alley's brick pavement, approaching the rear door. Sounds from passing cars and street vendors' shouts almost kept Victor from hearing the soft snap of a purse latch. With a hurried glimpse over the trash container, he spotted his prey. Wisps of long red hair clung across her nose and mouth while she eyed the contents of a shoulder bag—distracted and an easy target. Why did women make themselves vulnerable? She was taller than he remembered. He squeezed the knife's smooth, bone handle in his hand. Sweat dripped from his forehead. For an instant, he froze, kneeling on the damp ground. Something constrained him. Did she have a family, children? Had she cared for an elderly parent? His hunting for the killer's weapon might easily explain his presence late last night. While today, he'd returned to question her. What would the redhead think, when days later, the two detectives showed?

He needed certainty.

Victor arrived at her side. She looked up, protesting the intrusion. Her bright blue eyes met his while her red lips pursed together, muted.

The knife blade sliced against her slender throat, a little beneath her chin, half-way between it and her ear, severing the carotid artery. With a quick motion, Victor tilted her head downward, pushing her chin against her coat's velvet collar, reducing blood splatter.

Death—seconds away.

Her purse dropped. Its contents spilled on his polished shoes and over the dirty doormat fronting the back door. He sensed a momentary connection of hunter and prey as she succumbed and crumpled in his arms. He lowered the redhead, inhaling her soft, clean fragrance. Her head dipped forward to one side. So light and graceful, she might have danced beside him on a Broadway stage. Victor squatted over her open handbag, pulling out a black leather billfold. Her dime store diamond watch and rings slid from long, slender fingers

The fog remained, keeping him hidden. At the far end of the alleyway, pedestrians rushed to work, unaware of the killing only steps away.

Victor removed the blood splattered slicker and merged into the fast-paced crowd and slipped away, disappearing into the misty fog, pleased. He sniffed several times, placing the redhead's scent.

Youth Dew.

A touch of Channel would have been more fitting for a lady her age.

Impressed at his cunning, he walked from the alley, his job not finished, and strolled along the sidewalk, returning to the display windows of Osgood's Shoes. The tramp remained asleep, where he'd left him, snuggled with his knees pushed against his chest. No walkers approached, allowing Victor time to finish. Violent killings in Hell's Kitchen were common and rarely investigated. He'd do the patrolling officers a favor, solving the stabbing and robbery for them. Should a passerby bother to stop, they'd see a uniformed cop and assume he aided a poor street beggar.

He pressed the open pocketknife into the vagrant's palm, closing his grimy fingers over the bone handle, and placed it close to an empty pint of Four Roses. Victor wiped the redhead's billfold and jewelry clean and stuffed it into the sleeping bag. Next, Victor rolled up his blood-streaked parka, placing it near the entry door.

The tramp's shoulders jerked and turned, groaning, snuggling against the dirty sleeping bag, pulling into a tighter ball. With a quick sniff, Victor knew the sad-looking man had dumped in his pants.

"Rest in peace, my friend." Victor stood over him, imagining the vagrant's life.

Could he have been a Wall Street tycoon, a husband, and father? The soiled suit jacket appeared cashmere. Victor walked away, knowing there had been an oddness about the bum. They had crossed paths recently. It wouldn't matter. Today would be Daddy Warbucks last night in a drafty storefront. The City would soon feed and clothe the penniless man.

The moment Victor turned the corner a bright beam descended on the sleeping hobo. Seconds later, the light vanished, leaving no sign of the vagrant and his belongings.

CHAPTER TWENTY-THREE

Birdie sat on the edge of the bed, eyeing Malda's tidy, one-room apartment. It had yielded secrets into the private life of the young, struggling actress who remained in danger. Responsibility for her safety belonged to Birdie. Had she not removed Malda Boddy's red cape from the morgue, the police would have also deduced the killer targeted the wrong person and given Malda protection.

She held the open locket and the men's cufflink. The deeper she dug into the grizzly killing, the more connections she discovered between her client, Sid Breen and the intended victim, Malda Boddy. Birdie suspected a great deal more information had been withheld. An experienced PI would not tolerate a less than honest client. The wealthy and influential Sid Breen chose her knowing this.

What else did he keep from her?

The moment she snapped open the locket, it became clear where she'd find Malda Boddy.

"Why in blazes didn't he tell me?" she said to no one.

Jark stopped as he gathered empty coffee containers and napkins.

"Tell you what?"

"We're wasting our time." Birdie slipped from the bed, turned and ran her hands over the satin covers, smoothing wrinkles and creases.

"You're an angel, Jark, but the less you know is better."

"But it's okay if you break into an apartment?"

Birdie looked at her driver, regretting she dragged him into what had quickly grow into a complicated murder. He'd become an accessory to her crimes. "What did the transit police do?" Birdie hurried around the room, straightening what she'd moved.

"He kept glancing up here." Jark pointed to the window he had watched the cop from.

Birdie continued moving, adjusting Malda's few belongings. "Why would he do that?" she asked.

Jark slid the kitchen curtain open an inch, looking down to the corner where the transit cop once stood. "Police protection? Someone tried to kill her?"

"They wouldn't assign a—"

Two quick, sharp bursts came from the kitchen phone stopped Birdie.

Both stared at the ringing intruder. Its echo filled the one-room apartment.

"Let me answer," Birdie whispered, pointing at her chest.

She lifted the handset from the chrome hook as if she were about to be bitten.

Jark moved near her. She held the handset between their ears, covering the mouthpiece. Neither dared breathe.

"Someone's there," Birdie said in a low voice.

Jark nodded, pressing a finger to his lips.

A low buzzing hum came through the line.

After a minute, Birdie began to hang up.

Jark grabbed her hand. "No. Listen. They're in a train station."

Birdie pushed her ear closer to the phone.

"Hear the announcements?"

"I saw you this morning." A muffled voice spoke.

Jark held a finger over his lips.

"Where is Malda?" the voice asked.

A long pause followed.

"What are you doing there?" the caller demanded.

Birdie jumped, dropping the handset, letting it fall, banging the wall.

She grabbed Jark's arm. "Let's get out of here."

She pulled the apartment door, closing it soft, as if their exit would disturb the caller. The two rushed along the faintly lit hallway, dodging a minefield of tricycles, toy trucks, and cars. Birdie held out an arm as they exited the staircase, stopping Jark.

"What did the transit cop look like?" she asked, catching her breath.

"Tall. Couldn't tell much with the beard. My guess—fairly young."

She felt a jolt of memory from earlier. It had not been a coincidence the bearded, uniformed cop passed her leaving Saint Luke's. She ran, believing he pursued her for the removal of Mary Clary's red cape from the hospital's morgue.

"I'm not taking chances," she said, pulling a .38 from inside her leather purse.

The courtyard remained vacant and quiet, no sign of a milkman or a lurking transit cop. Birdie motioned to the arched entrance leading to the street.

"I'll get the car," Jark said.

She grabbed his arm, drawing herself close.

"We stick together." This time, she patted her palm against his muscular chest.

They ran to the gate.

Jark pointed to the green Dodge. "In front of Rexall."

Greenwich Village smelled of baking bread and smoke. Thin, grayish-white lines rose from clustered brick chimneys of row houses, brownstones, and mid-rise apartments, melding into thick early morning haze. Few cars passed in the narrow tree-lined street void of pedestrians. There were plenty of alleys and shadowy places for the transit cop to hide. Birdie guessed last night's revelers remained in hibernation and would be of no help.

"Stay close to the buildings," she said as they walked to Jark's car.

Signs of life came from an all-night bakery and coffee shop. Steamed over windowpanes blurred early morning customers occupying tall stools, sitting at long rows of tables fronting the sidewalk. As they passed, a white-aproned baker slid a metal tray filled with glazed doughnuts into a window display. Birdie hesitated, only to be pulled away by Jark. He'd grasped the seriousness of their situation. After passing a closed dry cleaner and a tattoo parlor, they reached the car. The street remained empty. No one appeared to notice the two.

"Get your keys," Birdie said in a low voice.

Jark tapped his pockets several times, staring at her.

"Don't even!"

A grin flashed across his face. They looked at each other. Her scowl, she hoped, sent a signal disapproving his ill-timed humor. He returned her stare, exhaling puffs of steam while digging out a set of keys attached to a small, black eight-ball chain. He opened the trunk and handed her the blood-red cape.

The case had taken an unexpected twist, forcing her to confront her client with the items found in Malda's home. The silver heart locket changed things, and she needed an explanation from Sid Breen.

This time, Birdie took the front seat, no longer feeling like an escorted celebrity. If she didn't handle the upcoming meeting with kid gloves, she'd find herself unemployed. Without a client, she'd have to rely on the job taken at Reznik's boatyard.

"Where to?" Jark asked.

"Wait, a second. See who comes out the coffee shop."

Nothing happened for several minutes while they sat waiting.

Was she paranoid? There were too many surprises for a case of a misidentified murder. She didn't want more.

"We work pretty good together," Jark said. "Need a partner?"

His pronouncement came suddenly, as if a hungry panther had just turned the corner, baring its fangs.

Birdie continued to stare at the bagel and coffee shop's fogged windows, although convinced no one inside watched. She had nowhere to look, feeling the gaze of her driver's eyes expecting an answer.

He had been a help, rescuing her at the theater as she walked in the rain, not to mention the coffee and yanking her from under the bed. She enjoyed his presence and admitted, to herself, a growing temptation to ravage his firm, tight body.

Jark broke the silence, trying to start the cold engine. After yanking the choke lever in and out several times, the Dodge sputtered and roared, sending a white plume of exhaust from twin, chromed tailpipes.

A short block away, the gate to Malda's apartment building swung open, catching both her and Jark's eyes. Before they said a word, the same blond, long-tailed cat from last night sauntered out, scraping its dull fur against the edge of the building. This time, instead of a mouse, it carried a struggling wren. Birdie winced. Had this been a foretelling? How long could she evade Nagle and Roe before they learned of her interference?

"Where to?" Jark asked.

She knew the destination. No other option existed after finding the locket and cufflink.

"Sid's office."

"It's early for him." Jark put the car in gear.

"Then we'll wait!" Birdie said in a harsher tone than intended, feeling an unexplained distance creep between her and Jark—one which she placed there. She had driven Owen Roe away after he'd entered her life. She'd gone as far as selecting an engagement ring. Was it a defense nurtured decades ago by an abusive father? She learned to stay out of his reach. His anger fueled by alcohol and pent-up rage over the loss of many jobs and squandered inheritance. Although it had been years since his accidental death, he ruled her emotions. She had never pleased him and feared she could never please a man. What chance did she have now? She wanted a normal life, free of the reins he continued to pull from his watery grave.

"Traffic's building," Jark said, breaking Birdie's thoughts.

She considered apologizing for her abruptness, but remained silent. Regardless, she knew it was a good idea to lighten up, relax, and enjoy the ride back to the Theater District. Birdie hoped it would work out and intended to confront her client with her discovery.

She'd almost forgotten about the pocket watch left at Mort's. There'd be time to follow up before seeing Sid Breen. Mort's Gems stayed open at all hours, catering to actor's varied schedules and eccentric lifestyles. Stories circulated that a top star proposed to his co-star after a late dinner and several bottles of champagne. In a stupor, he'd made the short walk from Sardi's to Mort's and purchased a half million dollar diamond ring and waited hours while Mort set the cluster of diamonds. Afterward, the star, disappointed by his lover's rejection, tossed the gleaming band into the East River, sending hundreds of treasure hunters into the polluted water.

The sun had risen. She'd take a chance. Mort on occasion slept in a cot kept in a sub-basement—she'd knock on his door. If anyone could read the scratched-out markings on the pocket watch taken from Mary Clary's belongings and keep quiet, the reclusive jeweler was her man.

"I admit, you've been a lifesaver," Birdie said to Jark, glad to have gotten the words out. She didn't want him to feel unappreciated, nor did she need his help. He was the driver, nothing more, not deserving to be dragged into a murder and obstructing its investigation.

"Pleased to help a lady," he said with a smile, not taking his eyes off the street. Heavy traffic built as they headed north approaching crowded billboards and glaring advertisements of Times Square, the hub of Broadway's theater district. He signaled with each turn and lane change, steering past lines of traffic, maneuvering through New York's streets. Jark drove unafraid among the predator city buses and yellow cabs, not exhibiting the aggressiveness to survive in the cut-throat business of people moving in New York.

A few things about her driver didn't fit for Birdie.

Birdie forced a laugh, turning sideways in the seat and asked. "How did you know Malda's apartment only had instant coffee?"

"Lucky guess." His eyes remained on passing traffic and hordes of workers streaming from busses and subway exits into the caverns of Manhattan's high-rises.

"I'll let that pass," she said. "I want a straight answer to the next question."

"Hit me with it."

"I don't know your full name."

"That's not a question."

"Does it have to be?" She tapped his shoulder.

"Sure you want to know?"

"I'd like to know the name of the man who saved me from the evil bed," Birdie said with a laugh. "Besides, you know mine."

"It's Breen, Tilson Breen. Jark's a nickname from the Marines."

Birdie's eyes closed for a moment, making sure she heard correctly. "I haven't slept much lately. You said Breen. Like Sid Breen, my client?"

"Mary Clary is my sister. She took our mom's maiden name."

"She wanted no favors," Birdie said, nodding her head. "Mary planned to make it on her own. I admire that."

Jark glanced at her. "You're looking at the prodigal son. I hardly knew her. I ran away to Amarillo to be a rodeo cowboy but joined the Marines."

The car came to a stop in the heavy traffic of Broadway and Seventh. He looked at her.

"I can still be your driver."

Birdie became uneasy. This time she knew why. She hiked her white socked foot to the plastic seat cover, resting her chin on her knee, staring into a thin sliver of winter sunlight wedged between buildings. She had a paying client, a car with a gorgeous driver, along with an office to work from. Sid Breen had kept vital information from her, and now her driver kept a secret. What motive did Jark have? What was she to do?

She'd not been honest with Roe and Nagle, not to mention her theft of evidence. She closed her eyes while her brain churned. The almost closed case became more complex. Collecting the sizeable fee would have to wait if she remained employed after her crucial meeting with Sid Breen.

The Dodge jumped forward, thumped through a pothole, turning toward 42nd, and the Theater District. Birdie let herself fall against the door and stared at her driver, trying to decide. His fingers twitched light on the steering wheel, returning her stare with his charming smiles.

"What did you say?" he asked.

The tune was off key, but she recognized, "Give My Regards to Broadway."

Birdie reacted with her all-too-automatic gesture of shrugging. One she needed to stop, not only did it aggravate her healing shoulder but signaled uncertainty. Confidence is what she sold, and well-heeled clients paid for.

"I'm thinking," she answered. "I'll decide after speaking to Sid."

Birdie spotted the Tiffany lamp shop. Below it, at basement level, sat the grimy hovel of Mort's Gems.

"Circle the block, I'm checking on a lead."

Birdie postponed her visit to Sid until she cooled off. Confronting someone powerful like Sid Breen would stop her fledging career as a Broadway PI. A visit with Mort would be therapeutic. She also pondered if she enjoyed the self-reproach, seeing the ring she'd selected. The one Owen Roe should have placed on her finger.

Watching the Dodge pull away into the morning rush hour traffic, she wondered what else she didn't know about Sid Breen and his supposed prodigal son.

CHAPTER TWENTY-FOUR

A pinprick of light came from the rear of the long room. Birdie spotted it through the round stained-glass window as she made her way down the narrow steps. Seeing past the grime of wire-reinforced glass and heavy bars guarding the jeweler's locked door proved a waste of time.

A blurred image moved across the speck of light. Somewhere inside, she guessed, Mort hunched over his cluttered worktable in the company of Jim Beam or Jack Daniel's—preferring not to work alone.

Her watch read a few minutes after seven. Despite the early hour, she could use a stiff drink after her adventurous two days. Birdie attempted to straddle the pooled rainwater blocking the entrance, sinking her penny loafers into stagnant, muddy water. She bent forward, pushing open a tarnished mail slot, shouting to Mort. After several attempts, she raised to look inside the darkened room. The tiny spot of light remained unchanged. New morning light failed to penetrate the gloom of Mort's cave. It wouldn't take a strong argument to convince Birdie he'd transformed into a nocturnal owl-like creature existing alone in his basement grotto. Round oversized glasses and tufts of bushy eyebrows added credence to her theory he belonged to a Tolkien fantasy. Once an avid stage devotee, he attended Broadway opening performances, offering critical reviews and had been cited by *The Village Voice* as a rare, unbiased reporter serving the theater-going public.

She hoped Mort might read the damaged inscription on the pocket watch she'd stolen from Mary Clary's belongings. She sensed the killer carelessly left it behind. As courtroom evidence, it became useless once removed from the police chain of custody. To Birdie, it remained the only solid piece of evidence linking the murderer to Mary Clary. For now, it rested on Mort's skill to uncover the watch's crude scratched-out engraving which she believed hid the murder's name. Until she spoke to Malda Boddy, all she had was speculation.

Did the cold blooded attacker have a grudge against Sid Breen, savagely murdering Mary Clary as revenge? If it were a twisted love triangle, there were many possibilities given Sid's reputation with young actresses. It was too much for her to think about. For now, she wanted one piece of hard evidence.

Sacrificing her new shoes, Birdie stepped deeper into the run-off water and placed her face near the mail slot. As she did, the door swung open. Mort, in a green and white plaid shirt and brown corduroy slacks, stood looking down.

"Something about the mail slot or my worn cords you admire?" he asked, laughing at his joke.

"My downfall. Temptations of the flesh," Birdie said, then slipped. Her foot skated on decaying leaves blocking the stoop's drain, splashing deeper into the collected runoff. Mort's hand shot out, grabbing her arm as her feet sloshed in stagnant rainwater.

"Join me for breakfast?" he asked. "I spend too much time in this cubby hole."

The jeweler reached inside the door and yanked a wool pea coat, floppy hat, and a black umbrella from a wooden peg.

"I came for my pocket watch," Birdie said.

"So you have," Mort said, leaning close.

The smell of whiskey brushed her face. She couldn't help noticing the deep lines etched in his forehead and face, gnarling Mort's handsome features. The creases had not been there a year ago when she'd selected the engagement ring anticipated from Roe.

He pointed the umbrella's nubby handle upward, toward a sidewalk of rushing pedestrians. "I'm starving for a bacon, egg, and cheese on a roll."

Jark's Dodge passed as they climbed from the entrance of Mort's Gems. The sedan's long cluster of tail lights soon faded into the damp haze that settled over the island. She recognized Sid Breen didn't trust her, assigning his son, a former Marine, as her chaperone.

Jark was a pawn in Sid's power game. Did her client have plans to avenge the brutal death of his only daughter? She understood his motives and empathized; however, she would not be part of a lynching. What lay ahead, she wasn't sure, but she wouldn't hold a grudge against the son—the sins of the father and all that.

Mort pushed open the single glass door, holding it, allowing Birdie to pass in front of him into the dimly lit bar. No heads turned from the three bulky overcoats hunched over a mahogany and copper bar. His arm hooked her waist and pointed her toward a booth in a far corner near a quiet Wurlitzer and an out-of-order cigarette machine. After he removed his coat, Mort waved a hand over his head.

"Make it two."

From a narrow serving window behind the bar, a raspy voice sang out, "Bacon, egg, cheddar on a roll with a hole. Double Bloody Mary, no garnish for the boss."

Birdie slid into and scooted along the red leather, half-circle seat, stopping in the center. Although famished, she regretted accepting Mort's offer of breakfast and preferred remaining in the shop, learning his findings. After a deep breath, she realized her long-time friend recognized her anxiety. Sid Breen would not arrive in his office for several hours. What else was there to do?

Mort tossed his coat and umbrella into the next booth and slid beside her.

He placed a black cloth napkin on the table and pressed it flat with the palm of his hand. After positioning it between them, he pulled the pocket watch from his breast pocket. He dangled it and smiled before placing it in front of Birdie.

"I realize you're in a hurry."

"Find anything?"

Mort twisted his face and rested a stubbled chin in his palm.

"Obviously, this timepiece doesn't belong to you?"

"Someone I know."

"Cheap silver plating. Most of it flaked off when I tried to clean it."

Birdie turned the watch face in her hand, examining the scarred case.

"The knife did much damage, leaving me little to work with." Mort leaned to one side, nudging her shoulder. "Later, I may have something that'll cheer you up." He gave her a wink.

"Why wait?" she asked.

Mort sniffed and pulled a folded sheet of lined paper from a pocket.

"Here's a sketch of what I saw."

Before Mort explained, their meal arrived along with a tray of highball tumblers filled with ungarnished Bloody Marys. He offered no toast, taking the glass to eye level and guzzled down half.

"I found this," he said, and took a bite of a drippy egg and cheese bagel. Chewing and talking, he pointed. "It may have been a name. Maybe an 'I' or could be anything. Here, the other name ends in, 'LDA.'" He circled it several times.

Birdie ate quietly, examining the sketch as Mort spun a pen in his fingers, watching her.

"It's Malda," she said.

The name had not been a surprise. Birdie had the red cape, which also belonged to Malda, confirming she'd been the original target.

"It's not much, but here's something interesting." Mort used his pen as a pointer on the watch case.

She smiled, recognizing what he'd uncovered. How did she not see it on her own?

"See 'em?" Mort asked.

"Theater masks intertwined by ribbon," Birdie said. "Like lovers."

"From Greek drama—joy and sorrow."

"Something happened between them," she said.

Mort tapped his note paper. "My guess the two thespians struggled to reach the big stage. Otherwise, we wouldn't be looking at inferior plating."

Remembering the silver locket she'd found searching Malda's apartment, Birdie pulled it from her slacks pocket.

"This isn't plating," Mort said, taking the sweetheart locket in one hand and letting it spin by its chain near his face.

"Any ideas?"

"Tiffany!" He paused, admiring its glitter. "It's a classic design. Notice the white sheen. Platinum will never fade or lose color."

"I'm betting the watch and locket came from different people?" Birdie asked.

Mort laughed. "No question." He studied his Bloody Mary long after answering, chugging the last of it, making his point.

"You're sure?"

Wiping tomato juice from his chin, he nodded. "The watch is five and dime."

Birdie's fingers inched close to the heart-shaped locket and twitched, wanting to grab it before Mort's curiosity took over. No one could see the cheek to cheek picture until she confronted Sid Breen.

Mort pushed away his empty plate and patted a napkin across his lips. He signaled the barman, mimicking tipping a cup to his mouth. In an instant, a carafe of coffee and two cups resting in saucers arrived, delivered by a white-aproned server.

"The police may discover more." Mort leaned close while filling their cups.

Birdie shook her head and sipped coffee.

Mort grinned. "I understand. No cops."

Birdie sought to be alone, sit, relax, and ponder Mort's findings. She expected the meeting with Sid Breen would require her best skill as a diplomat. Clients with deep pockets, especially the powerful, were demanding. Her time as a Pinkerton taught her she could not accuse Sid of withholding vital information. She had less than an hour to work out the problem. Otherwise, when the day ended, she'd be pushed to return to her job as leasing manager for rundown houseboats. Everything she'd rehearsed in her mind came out as an accusation against the one and maybe last client she'd have in the only town she knew.

She took another sip of coffee, chasing it down with the last of her Bloody Mary.

Mort tapped her hand. She thanked him, and both exchanged pecks on the cheek. He understood her desire to be alone.

"Stay long as you like." He waved toward the bar and small kitchen. "They'll take care of you."

She smiled, and he walked away. The coffee did her good. Its soothing heat relaxed her. The offer to remain hiding in the warmth of a homey bar tempted her.

Nothing ever went as planned, nothing. Her driver, Jark, wasn't who she thought. She didn't need more surprises. An axe-wielding madman hunted his victim—a terrified Malda Boddy. Birdie guessed she hid in the city or close by. The pocket watch likely belonged to him, representing a bond he and Malda once shared.

Mort's discovery of the theater masks convinced Birdie she looked for someone with a theater connection, somebody Malda may have recently spurned. A stage actor turned hatchet murderer. Whoever they were, she believed it had not been a coincidence—her brushing past the bearded transit cop as she left Saint Luke's and then outside Malda's home. It all remained a hunch. Malda needed to be located for both information and protection.

As a last resort, she'd make a list of theaters, including off-Broadway and off, off Broadway. In addition, the many acting schools and workshops in the city and Jersey. Running them down would be tedious and time-consuming, with a strong chance it would do nothing but waste her time. So many of the so-called schools came and went, promising students entry into Broadway's inner sanctum.

A shuffle of feet interrupted her planning. Birdie snapped from her thoughts to find Mort standing at the foot of the table. He'd reappeared with a steaming glass of milk.

"This relaxes me." He placed it on the polished wood table and slid the tray near her hand.

"Thanks." Birdie smiled.

Mort leaned over the table. "I have something else."

"Good news?" she asked.

"Depends. Were you planning to look at your ring?"

"If I had time."

She surprised herself with her flippant answer. On many days, thoughts of her ring pulled her up from the dumps, proving someone could love and accept her as she was.

"It's gone," Mort said. "I finally sold it."

Birdie resisted showing a reaction, although Mort knew her feelings about the simple, half carat diamond.

"Some cop took it off my hands."

She lifted her face to Mort.

He grinned. "Detective Owen Roe paid cash."

CHAPTER TWENTY-FIVE

Birdie needed to speak to Sid. She took a breath of wintery air, hoping to relax while she looked for the pale green and white Dodge. Jark, as always, seemed to sense her location. Had it been more? Did he spy on her? He was a marine and son of her client. What else did he keep from her? For now, she'd hold the suspicions private.

Her fingers twisted around the Tiffany silver chain and locket. Why had Sid kept information from her? And, she asked herself, why she felt no elation. She'd pictured swinging on a lamppost when Owen Roe finally popped the question. Would he return her ring to Mort after discovering she'd removed the murder cases' only evidence?

The blast of the car horn came from the narrow alley. There Jark sat, asking the first question as she walked toward the rear door he held open.

"Where have you been?"

"Sid in the office?" she asked, slipping past him, taking the passenger spot while noticing the folded red cape in the back seat.

"No idea." He pulled the car into morning traffic.

With Mort's aid, she'd connected Malda's cape and scarred pocket watch, at least to her satisfaction. Reconstructing the slaying became clear. The killer had stalked Malda Boddy on the dark street and spotted her distinctive red cape worn by Mary Clary. The murder had been possibly an unfortunate case of mistaken identity, nothing more. A man's pocket watch found with the body belonged to the killer, Malda's former boyfriend. Birdie recalled examining the cape and rose to her knees, grabbing the hefty cloak. She had been right. A button was missing. Maybe later she'd ask Mort to examine the coarse thread under his glass. For now, she'd bet her handgun and favorite purse the unique button, a silver, four-leaf shamrock, had been removed as a souvenir by the axe-wielding killer after nearly decapitating her client's daughter. The killer's small memento created direct evidence linking him to Mary Clary, was no longer admissible in court. She'd make sure the unusual button would be found on the killer or hidden in his home.

Finding him became easier this morning. She knew what he looked like, and once she'd spoken to Sid Breen, he'd lead her to Malda and the name of the killer closing the case. A sizeable fee and bonus waited. They'd settle her personal loans and growing hospital debts. Birdie feared becoming optimistic, counting her money too fast.

Jark pulled from the alley's loading zone, swerving into sluggish traffic. Taxi horns blasted, greeting their arrival. Birdie remained patient despite moving at a pace slower than nearby pedestrians. Eventually, their crawl and stop brought them to the intersection they looked for, Forty-Second Street and entry to Broadway, her once upon a time Emerald City.

The old, worn-out line jumped into Birdie's head. How do you get to Broadway? Practice, practice, practice. Each telling never failed to gain a faint laugh. Her fairytale stage career, singing and dancing under the bright lights ended with the collapse of stage rigging. Broadway failed her or she'd failed Broadway. It didn't matter. New York City Theater had plenty of up and coming bright stars waiting their turn. Her challenge waited a few blocks ahead.

Without glittering and flashing marquee lights, the Great White Way did not differ from other cities gritty roadways. Double-parked service and delivery trucks clogged both sides, leaving a single, narrow lane. Jark navigated congestion, using alley openings and occasionally straddling empty sidewalks. With her palms pressed against the dashboard, Birdie sat at the edge of the seat shouting directions and warnings. To her relief, she spotted Sardi's landmark neon signage. Sid's offices occupied nine floors above.

Unable to park curbside, Jark pulled into a red zone, shutting off the motor.

"Let me guess?" Birdie said, exiting. "Dad has friend's downtown."

"Need me to come up?" he asked.

"Find a place to clean up," Birdie said, poking her head into the open passenger door. "Then meet me inside."

"You're on to something."

"Depends." Birdie tapped the roof, walked away and entered the building's lobby. She had no appointment; but something told her Sid Breen expected her.

The elevator jerked and stopped a foot short of the ninth floor. The gray uniformed operator made several lurching passes, missing each time. Before his next try, Birdie, no longer amused, rested a hand on his shoulder.

"This will be fine. Slide open the cage."

"Watch your step," the operator said.

"New on the job?"

"First day."

She hopped down a few inches to the tiled floor as the metal door slammed.

Had the inept operator given her a subtle prompt—a warning to watch her step and mind her manners with her client?

Polished chrome letters affixed to tall, arched wood panels announced Sidney Breen Productions. The compact lobby outside his office overflowed with suited and casually dressed men and women. It mystified Birdie. How hard could it be to finance a stage play? Fire a director, a PI?

Birded distracted herself, hoping to relax, looking over the gathered crowd. Several directors and writers seemed familiar, although she'd forgotten their names. Most, she guessed, looked for work or pitched a script.

As she announced herself to Breen's private secretary, he stepped through the pair of doors, ignoring waiting visitors and waved Birdie inside. She had no doubt Jark called ahead, supporting her suspicion. Jark did much more than drive—he watched her.

While Sid waited, he used the tips of his stubby fingers to remove a speck of lint from his tailored, double-breasted suit. Birdie withheld a laugh, recognizing his enjoyment, flaunting his commanding presence before a waiting audience needing his money ... as she did.

Sid Breen looked his old self—the one directors and actors feared when the powerful theater mogul arrived backstage following a poorly reviewed play.

Today, he wasn't the person grabbing attention.

Not a soul dared object to her interloping; however, Birdie noticed glances aimed at her and a blaring whisper. "His PI. Not bad looking for her age."

Before either took a seat or Birdie being offered one, Sid stood staring out his window, puffing a short stub of a cigar he'd lifted from a star-shaped ashtray.

"How do you like that?" He blew a plume of white smoke toward the ceiling. "I go all night without a report and now... here you are."

Birdie rubbed her aching shoulder, stepping near his desk, measuring her confidence. It wasn't in her to be contrite, especially being close to solving the murder. She'd treat both their anger as a balancing act. Sid paid for the right to complain about being neglected. She'd do her best to control her annoyance with her client—being kept in the dark on his relationship with Malda Boddy.

While Breen's rant continued, Birdie's Irish got the best of her.

"Oh, go spit, Sid."

He turned from the window and took a seat behind his desk.

"What do you want from me?" she asked.

"Find who did this," he said.

"I plan to." As she finished, she pulled out the chain and locket, placing them on the desk. "Explain this!"

"Yeah, I kept that from you." Sid looked at Birdie, then the jewelry. "What difference does it make?"

Birdie resisted the urge to lecture her client. Her ears rang inside her head, holding back pressure, which built since discovering the locket in Malda's home.

Would she look back on this moment as she returned home, unemployed as a PI? She'd find little solace retelling the story of how she'd blasted the great Broadway mogul. Was it worth her future, to relieve pent-up frustrations? If she wanted off the job, the opportunity presented itself. Instead, she inhaled and forced her best stage smile.

"You've been seeing her for a while?" Birdie looked straight into Sid Breen's eyes.

"Few months." Sid lowered his head, staring at the open locket and his smiling cheek to cheek pose with Malda Boddy. "I loved her. You can't imagine."

Birdie agreed, recalling similar feelings for Owen Roe.

"I found this under Malda's bed," Birdie said, using a soft voice. Her anger ebbed seeing the tear in her client's eye. She put the gold and diamond cufflink on his desk near the locket.

Sid Breed opened a desk drawer and removed its mate.

"I made a house call last week. I know how it looks. Our age difference...."

"And you thought it was none of my business," she answered.

Birdie placed the cufflink in Sid's hands. She didn't need to say more, nor did her grieving client need a lecture. Instead, she summed up her investigation.

"It's clear. Revenge is the motive."

Sid pushed both hands forward, stopping her.

"My daughter had no enemies."

"And I believe you, Sid. Here's what I think happened."

Sid nodded after butting out his cigar.

"Two probable motives, both driven by revenge." Birdie raised two fingers and pointed to one. "The killer knew it had been your daughter and stalked her. He retaliated against you for taking his girlfriend."

"I'm to blame...."

Birdie delayed Sid's interruption, tapping a second finger. "Let me go on. He killed Mary who'd borrowed Malda's cape, mistaking her for Malda."

Sid slumped. "I'm the reason she's dead, no matter how you look at it."

"I looked at other angles and kept coming back to these possibilities."

"Whoever this madman is, find him!" Sid rose from his chair. "Put out a reward. Spread money around."

"Let me finish." Birdie stood facing Sid. "I know what he looks like. He's stalking Malda." Birdie wouldn't lapse into feeling pity despite the tragedy. She had a job to do. "And I have questions for Malda."

Sid nodded before she finished.

"When?"

"She's distraught and taking sedatives."

"Librium?"

"We couldn't stop her trembling and shaking. I gave her an extra dose. She'll be awake this evening. Jark knows my Long Island beach house. Around seven."

Sid stood and moved next to Birdie, pulling a side chair close, his knee brushing her thigh.

"Finish the job. Know what I mean?" He squeezed her hand.

Birdie looked her client in the eye. The veiled message sunk in.

"I don't want some judge letting the bastard off."

"I wasn't hired for that," she whispered. Birdie knew retaliation led both parties to similar fates. She'd been told—if planning revenge, dig two graves.

"Is that all?" Sid asked as he stood.

"That's why Jark's with me." Birdie said and rose.

"You've already figured that out.

"You want me to find him for your son, that's all?"

"Just catch the animal. The Marines trained Jark to handle dirty work. He'll take care of the rest."

"I'm his bloodhound?"

"A well paid one," Sid answered.

Birdie didn't need the subtle reminder they had maneuvered her and pondered making the trip to Long Island without Jark.

I want you to find this...your son, that's all. *Jark said the same...The answer...tell back to the Gallery with... I'll take care of the rest.*

Put his foot down?

Well, pull the...Sid intervened.

Milo and Verna's...the car he remembers, then back in any way he... and would be making the trip to Long Island without him.

CHAPTER TWENTY-SIX

City traffic and the bright lights of Manhattan steadily faded as they traveled east. Jark steered his green and white Dodge along Old Montauk Highway, passing West Hampton and scattered villages near Long Island's coastline. Birdie remained quiet, allowing occasional glances to her driver and the faded narrow strip of yellow paint dividing the dark road. The hum of tires on washed out asphalt replaced small talk that once had been casual and easy. Birdie's misgivings mounted. She'd find herself in another battle when the killer was discovered—preventing Jark from carrying out a father's vengeance.

The historic so-called gold coast, east of Manhattan, populated by affluent old money New Yorkers, reluctantly made way to post-war new money and urban sprawl. Aloof mansions dominated its coastlines; however, beach cottages and ranch homes of nouveau riche began to make appearances.

"Gets dark early out here," Birdie said, breaking the silence.

"The stars get brighter once you leave the city." Jark pointed to the broad, coal-black sky. "This is where I plan to live."

"Not if you allow Sid to manipulate your life," she said, not looking at him.

"He's not."

"What do you call making you a hired killer?"

"I killed in the war. This is family business."

"You'll spend the rest of your life in a cage. That what you want?" Birdie turned toward him. "Take a good look at this. It may be your last."

"You got it wrong. Sid asked me to drive."

"What if I give up the case and go to the police?"

"Your word against Sid's. He's got money, and the mayor's on his side."

Birdie stopped. She had gotten the words out, letting Jark know she was aware of Sid's scheme to use him as a pawn in a deadly game of revenge. She'd planned to prevent Jark from becoming an assassin—taking the law into his own hands.

Spent from the previous two days, she slumped deep into the car's seat, forcing herself to rest for the remainder of the drive.

How long would Sid Breen keep her after they'd questioned Malda and learned the transit cop's name? Sid's lack of patience and desire for swift justice would not deter her. She'd been hired to find the killer—not execute him, and that's what she'd do, despite her client's plan. Roe and Nagle would be notified once she discovered his name.

If Jark carried a weapon, she could not spot it in the usual places, under the arm, waist, back, and ankle. Inside his snug blue jeans, near his groin, was unlikely. She guessed he carried off body, perhaps in the Dodge's glove box. She could not be part of a planned slaying. To the legal system, she'd be considered an accomplice before and after the fact. A night school assistant DA could easily convict her to an extended stay at Rikers Island.

Birdie's need of sleep caught up with her. She folded the red cape into a square and pushed it against the window, hoping to doze. Between passing homes, she noticed a low moon shimmered at the edge of the broad, cold Atlantic. Warm tropical water waited under the same moon a half world away—somewhere she could afford. Could she walk away and change her life? Once upon a time, she believed

Detective Owen Roe would be part of it. In a few hours, she'd identify the killer. Soon after Sid's ten-thousand-dollar check cleared, she'd have freedom to live a fairy tale life.

The Dodge slowed, veering from the road, bumping over a collapsed curb, slipping into a narrow driveway between a stand of scrubby Bayberry bushes arched and bent awkwardly by steady ocean breezes. Light sand swirled across the car's high beams as they bounced on the gravel paved drive leading to Sid Breen's beach home.

Birdie's eyes resisted opening, and she forced herself awake, pinching her cheeks and rolling down the window, allowing the cold wind and salty spray to revive her.

Jark pointed toward the choppy, white-capped Atlantic. "They found a German U Boat out there during the war."

Birdie smiled. "A Pinkerton uncovered them."

Nearing the remote home, Jark slipped the car alongside a line of Japanese Black Pines bordering three sides of the property. They continued past a barn and stable, both needing repair, and abruptly stopped, opposite an empty carport attached to a weather-beaten, white and brown shingled two-story house.

"It's not Gatsby's place," Jark said.

"Sid's not here?" Birdie asked.

"Last minute plans for Mary's service at temple."

"That's why the black ribbon?"

Jark patted the lapel of his coat. "Symbol of grief."

For a moment Birdie Kelly squeezed her nails into her palms, asking herself how she nearly forgot Mary Clary's funeral.

"I'll send flowers," she said.

Jark pulled the handbrake tight. "We don't do that. Just place a small stone at the grave."

This time Birdie bowed her head. "I'm Irish, didn't know the customs."

Jark turned the car's lights and engine off. "I hardly knew my sister, but I want to do everything I can to find the killer." He paused with the driver's door partially open. "You think Malda could have had anything to do with this?"

Birdie stopped. She looked her young driver in the eye. She'd let him talk. He may let family secrets slip.

"Why do you ask, Jark?"

"There were jealousies between Malda and my sister."

"That's common between actresses."

"They were the same age. Mary resented Malda and dad's relationship."

Jark quieted, stopped and pushed open the car door, nodding to the pathway. Birdie judged he had more to say. She hoped he'd talk when he was ready. Their meeting with Malda and a stiff drink waited.

"Can't be easy living in the Hamptons," Birdie said, regretting her sarcasm as the words left her lips.

Jark led, tromping through blowing sand and dry crunching leaves. "I like it in winter—fewer tourists."

They walked along a cobblestone trail that crisscrossed the garden. Close to the house, they passed under a pergola, overgrown by leggy wisteria, forcing Jark to twist back barren branches, allowing Birdie to duck through.

"Malda's fragile," Jark said. "Go easy."

Birdie almost missed what he'd said as a crashing wave pounded nearby rocks and beach.

She grabbed Jark's arm, pulling him close. "Her old boyfriend's an axe killer and plans to kill her. All I need is a name."

The home appeared blacked out. A few lights burned near the rear of the house. Tiny lines of light escaped between wood slats and hinges of the house's window shutters. Jark pulled open an aluminum screen door and knocked, shouting Malda's name. After closing the flimsily outer door, he grabbed the stubby rope of a bronze bell nailed to a post on the side porch. No response came after several clangs and knocks.

"Must be a sound sleeper," Birdie said.

"Sid keeps a key under a garden gnome," Jark said, swinging a leg over the metal railing. He nailed a perfect landing in a patch of clumpy, dormant prairie grasses, and crouched to face a short, plump elf in a red pointed hat holding a flute to his lips.

"They bring good luck," Birdie said and slapped the side of her wool slacks, wanting to take back poorly chosen words. She glanced at Jark, who seemed to ignore her.

Jark tipped the stone figure and ran his hand under the flat base, finding nothing except cold, sandy soil. He tramped through an overgrown summer garden, thrashing dead corn stocks and a patch of slumping sunflowers, searching for a gnome hiding an entry key. Birdie watched him march to a distant corner of the house. He walked into a shadow and disappeared.

Birdie waited at the door, should Malda awake to the racket. After a moment, she no longer heard Jark's thrashings and worried. A roar rose from the sand dunes as white-capped waves continued to collapse on the open shore, while long tangled vines of wisteria scraped the house's weathered shingles.

Not sure what to do, she pressed her ear to the door, hoping to hear a sign from inside the isolated home. Could Malda be confused or unconscious from heavy doses of anxiety drugs?

Somewhere on the isolated stretch of land, dogs howled, forcing Birdie to imagine the ghostly black hounds of Conan Doyle's Baskerville Hall prowling remote moors of Western England. Birdie no longer hears Jark's footsteps crunching in the tall, dried, wild grasses surrounding the house.

The baying dogs became silent. Could there be packs of roaming, killing hounds stalking the remote beach? Long Island's remoteness attracted eccentric residents and their exotic pets. She quickly tossed away the thought. Jark could take care of himself.

Were they followed? The killer could know Sid owned a home on the island. After attempting to peek around the frame of a shuttered window, she knocked again—still no answer. Impatient and getting cold, Birdie wrestled with an urge to bang her fists against the heavy cedar door and shout for Malda. At any moment, she would lose her composure and kick the door from its hinges. Instead, she gripped the short rope of the bell and rattled it repeatedly, releasing frustrations. No one appeared. The pair of dogs howled once more, this time raising a fresh chorus of voices, watchdogs from unseen, distant beachside homes.

Birdie stepped away, removing the temptation of launching a full assault with a well-placed foot near the door latch. Picking the security lock would be an easy task, but out of the question. Chances were good a house alarm existed, guaranteeing a visit from local police.

She'd wait for Jark's return if he survived the attack of ghostly dogs. A grizzly picture of the diabolical hounds standing over Jark ripping out his throat invaded her thoughts.

Looking over the sand dunes to the lonely moon-lit Atlantic, she'd made up her mind.

Malda needed help now.

The wind and pounding surf grew, becoming a ceaseless roar and would cover the crash of splintering wood.

The door abruptly swung open. Jark's face, wet and angry, stared at her.

CHAPTER TWENTY-SEVEN

Victor Gregory returned home with a new energy. His big break had arrived in law enforcement and needed celebrating. He should be hospitable and invite his attractive neighbor. They were co-workers employed by Lev Reznik—he as watchmen of the grounds and the Liberty ship, she as the leasing agent for the soon to be remodeled collection of houseboats, fishing boats and tugs Reznik dubbed Seashore Villas.

His unknown neighbor lived nearby, a few boats away and, to his regret, they had not been introduced. The brief peek taken into her bathroom window intrigued him. She played her role as an alluring Bathsheba, enticing her audience of one. Soon there would be others, younger and more attractive, seeking his attention. Before long, he'd be more than an ordinary transit officer running down turnstile jumpers and hunting subway token forgers. After this morning's meeting at the cemetery, he'd soon work in the New York City elite organized crime unit. No badge or official title came with the secret undercover assignment.

Later tonight, he'd begin the mission given him by his new boss, known only as Scarecrow. Victor laughed—he had a code name, Tin Man.

An expensive and stylish wardrobe from Macy's came with the first paycheck. No longer would he wear the shirts and slacks of a common transit cop he'd purchased through cut-rate mail-order houses. His destiny—crisp tailored suits with wing tips identical to Wall Street investors. A West Side high rise with a doorman and overlooking Central Park would be home.

Once again, he felt wetness on his palms. Thick red blood dripped from his fingertips, not a drop splattered the floor. At the kitchen sink, he splashed both hands into warm dishwater. The murky water remained unchanged, yet his palms stayed a deep crimson as they had on earlier occasions. The reddish liquid continued, oozing from pores of his skin, climbing his muscled forearms, reaching his elbows.

Thumping in his chest traveled, vibrating in his forehead and temples. Victor recognized it as the matching resonance of his meditation bowl, which increased since his first killing days ago. Thoughts of a reincarnated life shaped and repeated inside his head, not as a mortal's simple words, but those from principalities beyond man.

Flesh and blood. Death and life.

His meditation bowl no longer needed—did death become his purpose? The copper bowl brought visions of Lazarus and The Resurrection. It had been a message. Would he not exit life?

A fast washing of his face and hands, followed by a splash of Old Spice to his neck and chest, refreshed him.

Malda suffocated him, reminding him of his failure on stage. She sacrificed their happiness for a chance at stardom. The big shot producer meant nothing to her, a stepping stone. She manipulated the necessary evils of Broadway, taking home directors and producers. She had written Victor's part out, no longer needed.

Tomorrow, he'd find her.

* * * * *

Flat on his back, Victor awoke, subdued on the deck of his houseboat, staring at muffled moonlight, shirtless and shivering, his thick black beard damp from drizzle. His hands and arms no longer swathed in blood, he stood. Genuine or illusionary, his reality decomposed, hiding behind disorder, shifting, not recalling how life shifted.

Leaning against the metal railing, he looked for a sign of life from his neighbor's boat tucked among the many derelict houseboats stripped to skeletons in Lev Reznik's deserted Brooklyn boatyard.

A tiny light came from her window, attracting his curiosity, pulling him toward her. Should he inspect it out of a sense of duty? He'd learn more of his absent neighbor. The master key hung on the ring, dangling from his belt hook. A check of his watch stopped him. It neared midnight. He needed to patrol the Liberty ship.

Officer Victor Gregory would carry out his first official job as part of the elite organized crime unit and search the Russian vessel. He knew every inch of the top deck of the old Liberty ship. Tonight, he'd explore the ship's prohibited cargo holds for the first time.

Engrossed with the assignment, he'd almost forgotten the package carried home. The stop at the Greenwich hardware store would come in handy for his journey into the ship's bowels.

Unsure of lighting, he picked up a miner's Night Hawk Lamp, hard hat, extra battery packs and shock resistant flashlights. All available at the transit authority; but he wanted to avoid unnecessary questions.

As a subway cop, he routinely ventured into darkness. Nothing he experienced fazed him—body parts and chewed corpses became routine patrolling the city's eight hundred miles of dark underground passageways.

Once he adjusted his hard hat and its lamp, Victor stepped from the deck of his houseboat. In place of his standard uniform, he sported dungarees and a heavy denim coat. Inside, it concealed a tear gas canister, hand grenades, and a backup pistol. The hand grenade's rough, serrated shell fit nicely in his palm. He wouldn't hesitate to use it in an open space on the ship's deck. He'd taught himself to throw with accuracy and farther the better with small bombs. Anywhere inside the ship's steel hull, the compression would kill both him and his attacker. Victor intended this as a last resort.

He strolled past his neighbor's vacant craft, tapping the heavy pontoons. There'd be plenty of time to explore the secrets of his enigmatic fellow employee.

Victor's plan changed as he climbed the long wood ramp alongside Reznik's tramp steamer. He'd forgo his usual patrol of the deck and bridge. He guided a gloved hand along the ship's plate steel and rivets, he again noticed the pulsation. The hull's slight vibration no longer puzzled him. He'd assumed generators ran in the engine and boiler room, the heart of the ship, far below the water line of the ocean-going vessel, supplying power to freighter's lights and the galley's refrigeration.

From habit, Victor walked to the ship's stern, examining cargo hold doors. Curious, he stopped and glanced port side, this time not expecting his usual visitor.

The familiar old, battered Ford sat in the same spot as it had for the previous three months. A red ember ignited inside. Victor shook his head and watched, admiring the cop for his gritty persistence. Whatever laws Lev Reznik broke, he had a bulldog on his tail. Victor walked away, not acknowledging the visitor. He'd begin at the ships aft.

Fragments of a white stenciled number five on the massive cargo hold waited to wash away in the next heavy rain. Victor located the small manhole in the corner of the enormous canvas, allowing entry into the cargo hold. He undid the brass snaps, uncovering a three foot by three-foot opening and the upper rails of a steel ladder.

After swinging his leg over, Victor stood poised, looking around one last time before his descent. It wasn't the depth or darkness which worried him. Had he been setup? A trap? So much rode on this—his career as a city detective and a new lifestyle they would all envy.

Victor inhaled, lowering into his baptismal font, christening a new life.

A click of switch on his hardhat brought a beam of light to life. Dark spaces were nothing new, instead finding peace in the uncluttered void. He'd imagined it as deep space, emptiness free of distractions, only the sound of his heart beat.

The steel ladder's rungs dropped unseen into the ship's dank and stale bowels. The air warmed and brought a dampness to his forehead. Sweat dripped from his nose. Without a safety cage to break his fall, Victor took every step slowly, gripping each rung hand over hand, not letting go of one before grabbing the next. His legs tired and trembled, reminding him of the brief career on stage.

His hard hat and light tipped forward, nearly falling from his head, as he looked down into the hostile blackness.

Victor had tossed his lucky Brooklyn Dodgers cap against the theater curtain and slumped to the floor, exhausted. Rehearsal lasted most of the day, his legs no longer felt as if they belonged to him. His short thirty-minute dinner break would not be enough. In less than a week the show opened with a new opening dance number. The cast appeared fatigued after four weeks of intensive preparation, and he had been the only one who'd collapsed flat on his back after each run through. Later that evening, he gathered his coat and street shoes and walked out the stage door into a pitch-black alley.

Gripping the ladder with one hand, he wrapped the other arm over a rung, taking time to rest and glance toward his feet, hoping the light would reveal the floor.

Nothing but darkness.

Victor's descent continued unhurried into the black and what felt like a thick, enveloping fluid that drained his will to go on. Darkness surrounded him apart from his hat's spot of light dancing against the side of the ship, inches from his face. As he dropped farther, the tiny bit of light, falling through the small overhead flap, shriveled to a flicker. A floating detachment overtook his gloved hands and feet, seemingly moving of their own accord. A misstep could lead to a fall, leaving him stranded and disabled, and easy prey for ship rats. A radio, if he had one, would be useless, unable to penetrate the hull's thick steel plates.

He passed several empty 'tween decks as he descended until finally his boots landed on the lower hold's heavy wood floor. Although on solid footing, trembling in both legs continued. He arrived at the base of the first cargo hold, searching for unspecified evidence against Lev Reznik. His hand shook, pulling an Eveready flashlight from a coat pocket. Victor swung the bright beam around the empty cavern, revealing the ship's side girders, steel beams, wood planks and nothing else.

Groans and creaks of the massive vessel amplified and echoed, triggering Victor's regression to parochial school catechism and Jonah's travels inside a giant fish.

He avoided thought of a return trip—a long vertical climb, and the prospect of four more holds made the assignment far less attractive. If working for the Organized Crime Unit meant this type of physical work, he'd remain with the transit cops chasing turnstile jumpers.

Curious and needing to recover his strength, Victor walked along the thick cedar planks lining the base of the ship. Thin shafts of light darted from his hat's lamp and flashlight, bouncing off side girders and steel beams. Blackness touched him, tracing a chilled finger from the back of his long legs, along his spine until it lifted and vibrated fine hairs on his neck. Victor convinced himself the touch was real. His normal keen senses failed him and he seemed unstable, encased in a heaviness compressing around him. Victor sat on the ship's floor, hoping to regain balance and orientation, something he'd not experienced roaming New York's subway tunnels.

At first, he hadn't noticed. The sound rose and brought to mind the muffled roar of ocean waves breaking on a sandy shore. He guessed the familiar noise came from behind and clicked off both lights and sat, trying to pinpoint the origin of the constant mechanical rumble. If the vessel's motors and propellers operated, he'd know it— living near shipyards his entire life.

Victor took a deep breath and once again turned on his miner's lamp and flashlight, aiming both behind him. This time he saw it, low to the floor, in the light fanning from his cap's bright lamp—a small square bulkhead door sat open. On hands and knees, he crawled toward it. Next, to the latch, riveted above the door, a brass tag read, "Hold 4." The three-foot square, watertight door led to the adjacent compartment. After poking the flashlight into the void, Victor saw the source of the droning—dozens of running, large air movers and power generators circled the ship's number four hold.

What he spotted next caused him to drop his flashlight and tighten his grip on the tear gas canister. How many more sat anchored to the floor?

CHAPTER TWENTY-EIGHT

Birdie Kelly stepped back and looked at Jark, his handsome face somber. Water dripped from his hair and shirt, leaving a puddle. She hesitated to step into Sid Breen's secluded beach house. Aching in her injured hip and shoulder returned. Maybe the Irish in her exaggerated fear, coercing uncalled for caution. Where had this inbred reflex been the day the stage rigging collapsed? Before she conjured more suspicions and backed further from the doorway, Jark pulled the door inward and waved her inside from the pelting wind. If he'd grabbed her, Birdie questioned how her instincts would have responded.

The door slammed the moment she stepped on the foyer's rough wood floor. Jark wrapped an arm around her, steering them to the rear of the spacious house and a massive antique stone fireplace. Birdie at once noticed the familiar light and sweet smell of rye whiskey.

"I turned on the lights," he said.

"That her?" Birdie asked. "I need to wake her."

"Malda's dead."

"How?" she asked, fighting off regret and frustration, knowing she shared responsibility for the needless death.

Her original discovery of the red cape led to identifying Malda Boddy as the intended victim. Despite it, she'd failed to keep the young actress alive. How would it appear to detectives Nagle and Roe she found the only connection to Mary Clary's killer dead in her client's home?

Once Sid Breen spoke to the local police, she would be exposed and arrested for withholding information on someone with direct knowledge of the murder's identity. She had plenty of opportunities after her discovery. She faced jail, forfeiture of her hard-earned PI license, and a lifetime of meaningless jobs. On top of everything, being at the scene of Malda's death implicated her and Jark as murder suspects.

Birdie's knees trembled, stepping near Malda's body. The young actresses' head tilted back, wedged into the wings of a leather Chesterfield chair. Droplets of water clung to her long, tangled brown hair. Bare feet and legs rested on a matching hassock, posed as if expecting guests. Birdie removed a compact from her purse, holding its mirror inches from Malda's nose and mouth, finding it clear of moisture. With care she pulled away the loose cord wrapping Malda's small waist, letting the only clothing she wore, a man's silk robe, fall away. Birdie leaned over the dead actress, searching for cuts, bruises, and punctures, signs of what killed her.

"She's dead, but from what?" Jark asked.

"Was anyone with her?" Birdie asked, gathering and retying the robe.

"Sid drove to Manhattan early this morning. He left her alone."

"That's what he told you?"

"It's the truth."

"This isn't where you found her."

"In the shower." Jark looked toward a hallway.

"And you put the robe on," Birdie said. "That's how you got wet."

Jark nodded. "She was my future stepmother."

"That would have been nice to know," Birdie replied, standing at the den's mahogany bar, examining a prescription bottle.

"Sid gave her something for anxiety."

"The label says Sidney T. Breen, dated yesterday."

"What is it?" Jark asked.

"Librium. You definitely don't take it with Wild Turkey."

Jark reached for the near-empty decanter of whiskey. Birdie grabbed his hand.

"Don't touch anything."

He nodded and backed away.

"Any idea how many pills there were?" Birdie asked.

Jark shook his head. "Sid gave them to her."

"These and booze are deadly and most likely stopped her breathing and heart."

Birdie leaned against the bar. Her only connection to Mary Clary's killer laid dead in front of her. She had nothing without Malda.

"How long she dead?" Jark asked.

"Half-day I'm guessing. Her body's cold."

"This will be too much for Sid." Jark placed the pills in his pocket.

Birdie stopped him. "The police will find the drug in Malda's system. They'll check pharmacies and know Sid bought 'em. It'll look like he's hiding something."

Jark hesitated.

Birdie touched his arm. "Put 'em back. Let the cops find them."

"Sid's gone through enough. Now, this." He eased his hand out and returned the bottle to the table.

"Thanks," Birdie said. "Tell me why you call your father Sid?"

"Thirsty?" he asked.

"Don't let me stop you."

Jark reached under the bar, pulling a clear glass bottle of Miller beer from a cooler. After a long sip, he answered.

"We weren't a close family. I lived in Amarillo with mom. Mary stayed with Sid after the divorce and took our mother's maiden name, Clary, when she started acting." He rested his elbows on the copper bar top, stared at Birdie and grinned. "We're a messed-up bunch."

Birdie finished listening and completed an inspection of the house, looking for faint signs of a break in. The liquor and pills were found in plain sight—perhaps too easily.

She at first suspected Mary Clary's killer tracked Malda to the out-of-the-way remote tip of Long Island and completed the job he'd begun two nights ago, correcting his mistake. The isolated setting had little risk of anyone witnessing his break-in, making it an ideal location for murder.

The theory fell apart—missing the profile she'd put together for the axe killer. She had him as a risk-taker, savoring the hunt, stalking and executing his target, seeing red blood spatter in the street. A gun or knife were better options, fast and easy to conceal. Instead, he used an axe. The gruesome tool he chose intrigued Birdie. She guessed it held significance. In addition, the victim's red cape lent a macabre flair, which he might have taken pleasure in if he'd killed his intended victim.

His second attempt, likely, wouldn't vary from his first, and this bothered Birdie. The same weapon should have been used, not relying on forcing her to ingest pills. He was confident of escaping, knowing he'd be overlooked. After Mary Clary's murder, he most likely mingled with onlookers at the scene, reveling in his conquest. Did he return for a second look only to lose his pocket watch? His confidence and ego became a weakness. This last thought wedged in Birdie's mind, giving her the next move. One that would put her and the axe murderer together in a public place.

What she saw in Sid Breen's den didn't match. The mixture of drugs and alcohol would be lethal, but, not with the certainty the killer, she knew, preferred. She'd decided the scene in front of her had been an accident, mixed with tragic, classic O. Henry irony. Unknowingly, the killer succeeded in eliminating Malda, not with a blade, but with her own fear. He'd continue his hunt, risking capture, fitting into Birdie's plan as long as she kept Malda's death quiet.

Jark spoke. "Did Malda do this to herself?"

"I'm thinking accident," Birdie said. "Why bother to shower if you're planning to kill yourself?"

Long Island's remote beach-side retreats did more than guard the privacy of its well-heeled residents, it allowed Birdie and Jark to escape The Hamptons unseen, avoiding long, wasted hours of questioning by local police. A delay would cost Birdie the chance of capturing her suspect—only howling dogs and mute lawn gnomes detected their presence. She'd keep her plan from Sid and Jark, who she suspected intended to save the killer from a courtroom and jail cell. It was no longer a secret—Jark would become judge and executioner the moment they found the killer. The task of dissuading the pair vanished with Malda's death.

Birdie glanced around the spacious room, spotting Jark using a white handkerchief, wiping off light switches and door handles.

He looked at her. "You were a Pinkerton. Any pull with local cops?"

She smiled. "Yeah, that and a dime... How 'bout an anonymous call to the sheriff, then we call Sid?"

Jark returned her smile. "We're on the same page."

"Not from here," Birdie said. "We'll find a phone booth."

With the second killing, it became impossible to keep her client isolated from the press or police. Sid Breen's notoriety created headline news. New York City and the Long Island police would rush to make an arrest, grabbing headlines in tomorrow's papers. Sid had been the last to see Malda alive and provided her Librium for severe anxiety. Birdie couldn't imagine an alibi strong enough to keep Sid from being suspected in Malda's murder. What else did her client keep hidden? The Hampton detectives would, without difficulty, track his whereabouts for the last twenty-four hours, discovering the drug purchase and matching it to Malda's time of death. Birdie expected to be next in line for arrest and planned to act before detectives Roe and Nagle connected Malda's murder to their investigation of Mary Clary's killing.

Birdie took a last walk, inspecting the interior of the house, wiping down anything she'd touched. An incoming gale raised an already rough sea, carrying blowing sand across a fast-disappearing beach, promising to cover their footsteps. As they exited, she placed a hand on Jark's shoulder, stopping him. Several coyotes circled his green and white Dodge, confronting them.

He dropped to one knee and pulled a snub-nosed revolver from an ankle holster, taking a shooter's position. Birdie grabbed his arm, shaking her head. To her surprise, Jark relaxed, lowering his .38. Witnessing this left no doubt her driver would always be a Marine and ready to kill.

"I have a hunch the killer doesn't know Malda's dead," Birdie said. "What do I wear to a Jewish funeral?"

CHAPTER TWENTY-NINE

Victor ducked and lifted his leg into the hatch, stepping to the next chamber of the Russian Liberty ship. Swirling, damp air moved through the hold and carried a faint odor he didn't recognize.

The moment he entered, he realized something occupied the immense compartment. Sparkly, flecks of light, resembling stars on a clear night, appeared suspended in space. He rubbed his eyes, blaming his imagination or an unexpected reaction to the lengthy climb into the ship's belly. Victor dropped to a knee and squeezed his tear gas canister, planning to release its immobilizing chemicals at the first hint of a trap.

He snapped off his flashlight and in a moment his eyes adapted, enabling him to see deeper into the darkness. Victor looked at a bizarre scene which could be a hallucination. His meditative trances, at their outset producing needed soothing and relaxing serenity, had implanted forewarning images—vague and abstract, concealing his fate. That, he had been sure of.

Row after row of dimly lit railroad passenger cars occupied the dungeon like chamber.

Could this be what they expected him to find?

Victor tripped stepping over crisscrossing electrical cables and heavy rubber hoses running along the ship's thick wood planks. With an eye on the cars, he clicked on his light and pulled a revolver from his holster.

He side-stepped the perimeter of the ship's hold, inspecting his surprising find. Nothing appeared to move, and he wanted it to stay that way.

"Police!" he shouted. "Anybody here?"

Thankful no one responded, Victor approached the nearest railcar, repeating his warning only to be met by mimicking words of his echo. If anyone hid in the darkness, their movements would be difficult to detect over rumbling fans surrounding the cars.

Victor rose to his toes, taking small steps, closing in on a passenger entrance door. He made sudden stops, listening for errant footfalls or a stumble on the rough plank flooring. The practice worked stalking hobos and tramps in the city's subway tunnels. Inside the Russian ship, he'd learn to work with new rules.

With a flashlight and wearing a cap-light made him easy prey for anyone watching from behind the railcar's panoramic windows. He closed in on the passenger car, watching and listening for errant noises. After reaching the corner of the railcar, he turned his light to scan across the car, spotting bold, thick gold lettering—Union Pacific Railroad.

The search in the deep caverns of Reznik's ship tired him. He unzipped his coat—his uniform shirt saturated in sweat. Taking in lungfuls of stale air, Victor grabbed a vertical handle near his shoulder, letting himself sit on a metal step below the entrance door.

With knowledge of western movies, Victor guessed the coaches to be a holdover from the early nineteen-hundreds, maybe older, judging by the ornate roof line and platform gate.

He thought the railcars destined for a well-to-do collector or one of the city's many museums. What he saw changed his mind. The heavy flanged wheels, axels and couplings had been replaced with steel I beams, anchoring the car to the Russian freighter's floor. Had this been Nikita Khrushchev's idea of mass transit or how he intended to bury us deep at sea? Victor forced a laugh, recalling the erratic Soviet leader's threats.

Why did his hands jitter? Dark, confined spaces relaxed him. He took a last look into the hold's darkness and stepped to the railcar's entry platform. With both hands cupped against the door's window, Victor peeked into the dark car. Would he find travelers waiting to begin a journey? Instead, a speck of a burning light glowed, matching the other cars in the collection, reminding him of summer's fireflies.

The door handle twisted with ease, swinging open. The first blast of air sickened him, forcing Victor to retreat, gagging. As he backed away and recalled the odor of cabbage above deck a few days ago.

He tapped the pockets of his uniform pants. He made it a habit to carry matches to combat the raw odors encountered in the cities abandoned subway shafts.

Again, he approached the open door, holding several burning stick matches at arm's length. The stench lingered, lessened somewhat by the sulfur. Victor dropped the burnt-out matches and walked through the center aisle, swinging his flashlight side to side, bouncing the bright beam along the seats and roof of what he hoped to be a deserted car.

Passenger seats remained upright, in the sitting position, others folded open and reclined, forming small sleeping berths. A few curtains covered windows despite darkness inside the belly of the freighter. The car appeared self-contained, toilets, small kitchen and heaters crowded the luggage areas. A few ragged bedrolls poked into the aisle. He guessed the jumbled lines and hoses running along the ship's floor supplied energy and carried off waste from human cargo.

A stronger hunch told Victor they had been overcrowded with human beings recently. No signs remained of its former occupants. Not a scrap of paper, hats, gloves, nothing besides foul odor. At the far end, near a storage area, he came to a small light. A green Coleman lantern burned and likely a similar oil lamp burned in each of the railcars explaining the star lit hold.

A signal?

Would someone return, knowing he'd entered the ship's holds? Lev Reznik's spies roamed the dock area. It had been no coincidence the limping man barged into the Green-Wood Cemetery chapel, interrupting his meeting.

He couldn't allow the Russian to trap him in the narrow railcar. Maneuverability in the dark open space of the ship's immense hold increased his odds of escape. He had no intent to hang around for Reznik's arrival. The Russian Jew valued loyalty like a religion, punishing transgressors. Victor witnessed several bloody beatings administered by the burly Russian. Afterwards, he'd shoveled the few recognizable remains into the harbor.

He had spent enough time exploring and guessed his discovery would satisfy the cop he knew only as Scarecrow. Everything found pointed to human trafficking, enough for a search warrant. At the open door of the railroad car, he spotted it in the bright beam of his light. A chess piece stood on its green felt base, hiding under a passenger seat, poised for a surprise attack. Victor knelt, grabbing the white knight. A thought struck him. He too had been taken in by a ruse, a pawn in a game played by the cunning New York cop.

Why had it taken him so long to figure it out? However, knowledge is power. It became clear, He knew he'd been coned, and the advantage shifted.

How would he use it?

After pushing the piece into his jacket pocket, he took a last look at the fifty-foot- long passenger car. There were too many to search, and he wasn't in the mood. The ship held secrets he no longer wished to be a part of.

The long climb from the ship's hold took much longer than the descent. His legs ached and cramped needing several stops to regain his strength. Once he reached the deck, he scrambled through the top cargo hatch's small flap, relieved to escape the caverns of the Liberty ship.

Had he viewed darkness as Lord Byron's last man on Earth—witnessing the future, a vision of being cast into bleak blackness, existing in nothingness? All he could do was stagger along the deck, gripping and falling against the gunwale, taking in the night's cold air. Once his trembling legs gained strength, he looked to the dock, to where his supposed contact, Scarecrow, waited, chain smoking in his run-down oil-leaking car.

What else did the cop want? His scrutiny had been unrelenting, as if there was a personal reason. What would be his motive besides an arrest? As a cop himself, he knew there were limits to an investigation, manpower being one. Crime in New York grew faster than the police force could manage. The late surveillance, most likely on his own time, made him think the chain-smoking cop had a personal stake in mind.

Victor flashed his light once, paused, and then again. He immediately received a single flash in return. His contact got the message. They'd meet tomorrow, the same cemetery chapel as before. He had much to tell and more to gain. What the ship carried in the holds would be worth more to him if he played this as a chess game. Victor pulled the sculptured white knight from his pocket, looking at his opening move with Lev Reznik. He'd keep the meeting short. Later, he'd make an appearance, paying his final respects to Mary Clary. Hopefully, Malda Boddy would be at the side of a grieving Sid Breen.

Prior to exiting the ship, Victor had one more piece of business, something he didn't intend to tell the New York detective. The discovery occurred his first month on the new job, spotting the partially open wooden panel. After years of famine, the wheel of fortune spun, and he'd come up a winner.

He climbed a staircase to the captain's quarters. Inside, he pushed aside a metal desk and swung a hinged wood bookcase away from a beat-up wall. The entire time, Victor sensed being watched. Whatever occurred in the ship was well planned and an opportunity for him to take advantage of.

Victor grabbed a handful of new one-hundred dollar bills. The tight compacted, banded currency was hidden and neatly arranged in the hidden closet onboard ship. Color and texture appeared authentic, each bill bearing its own serial number. There were not as many as there had been on his initial find. He'd been cautious, removing small amounts from each brick.

Tomorrow, he had a surprise for the grieving Breen family.

CHAPTER THIRTY

Stepping from Jark's Dodge, Birdie shuddered from the icy chill, dreading her day. The risky scheme seemed less and less possible. Reckless would be how the police described her. She wrapped her bulky coat tight against her, making sure her purse and revolver remained in quick reach.

Brittle leaves swirled, scraping coarse, cracked asphalt at her feet. She pulled a black wool scarf snug over her head and face, shielding against frosty morning breezes crossing Mt. Hebron Cemetery. This time, her impulsive plan may backfire. She looked over expansive green lawns and the towering Star of David near Mary Clary's burial site, Birdie asked herself why she'd put herself in the line of danger pretending to be Malda Boddy. The longshot ploy relied on the killer's arrogance and a second attempt, making good his failure.

Behind her, mounted officers held in check swarming reporters and photographers pushing against a line of rickety wooden barricades, many of which had already collapsed. She'd expected Sid Breen's prominence to draw crowds from the entertainment industry. On the other hand, Mary's large enthusiastic fan base startled her. Throngs of admirers arrived by bus, subway, and on foot, carrying sprays of flowers and burning candles. The scene had been more than imagined, making it simpler for the killer to blend in with the swelling crowd and approach the grief-stricken family. Convinced he'd show to kill Malda from close range, she'd provide the target.

"You ready for this?" Jark asked.

She turned and stepped closer to him, adjusting the twisted knot of his tie.

"You look nice," she said, patting the black, torn cloth pinned against the lapel of his dark tailored suit. "What's this?"

"Jewish custom." He ran his fingers along the tattered fabric. "We once ripped our clothes when grieving, remembering Jacob's grief tearing his robes, believing his favored son died after seeing blood on the coat he'd given him."

"Joseph's cloak of many colors," Birdie said. "From the Bible in...."

She stopped herself, thinking of her discovery—Mary Clary's unfortunate death had resulted from the killer mistaking her for Malda. On that day, she'd borrowed Malda's distinctive hooded red cape. Jealousy again, the motive.

Jark pointed toward the gravesite. "Our family got in last evening. Next to Sid is my mother, Nita. He sent a plane for her. She hates crowds and him."

"How's he doing with Malda's death?"

"Not good. He and his lawyer spoke with the police last night."

"Suspects?"

Jark put his arm around Birdie's waist, guiding her over a crushed rock path leading to the grave. "Cops think the same person killed Mary. Maybe revenge against Sid."

"Get their names?"

"Thought you'd ask." Jark pulled two business cards from his wallet. "Owen Roe and Joe Nagle. They knocked on our door about three this morning.

"Those two are supposed to keep me informed."

"Are they?"

She shook her head. "It hasn't been mutual."

Jark smiled and lifted her chin with his finger. "We better go."

"Don't think me rude," Birdie said. "I'll stay back a minute and look over the crowd ... see if anyone seems suspicious."

"Looking for what?"

"I'll know when I see it."

Jark held a finger to his lips. "Watch what you say about Malda when you meet the family."

He stepped away, hugging arriving family members. Birdie used the distraction to slip away and be alone. Her plan hedged on Mary's killer being drawn to the cemetery, unaware of Malda's accidental death.

Dressed in Malda's clothes, she became prey to a hatchet-wielding madman. Deep inside, she feared another tragedy.

She hated the ritual of groveling over a corpse and annoying greetings of sorrow. Wrap her dead body in a canvas bag and slide it into the Atlantic—no, better to dump it on a burning Viking ship pushed into a desolate cold sea. No point troubling friends with wasted melodrama and gibberish of a divine plan. Spare them spiritual platitudes and threats of eternal damnation, spewed by a cleric pretending to care for a cadaver they had not spoken to in life. Who finds pleasure seeing a box lowered into a hole? Instead, celebrate— cake, beer, song and children playing in the pile of fresh dug dirt.

She watched Sid's family gather. In a moment they worked their way past a growing crowd of onlookers to a row of chairs rimming the unfinished walnut casket resting above a simple grave uncluttered of flowers. Sid walked among friends, accepting hugs of condolence. A slight smile appeared as Jark approached. After shaking hands, Sid pointed to Jark's head.

Jark reached into a pocket for his forgotten Yarmulke.

Supported by a silver-tipped cane, a rabbi stepped near the coffin the same time Birdie returned. She found Sid Breen and eased next to him, about to become a bull's eye. She was taller than Malda Boddy and her face, except her eyes, were concealed by the scarf. Jark had objected to the risky plan, but she'd run out of options. The killer could be in the hoard of spectators making his way to her. So far, nothing appeared out of the ordinary.

An unexpected touch of her arm caused her to jump.

Sid Breen took Birdie's hand, guiding her behind him, allowing her to remain standing. He eased into a wooden folding chair placed on a green grave site carpet.

He fit the image of a movie Moses, and the rabbi hunched over, cut the black ribbon near the coffin and read from the Torah, quieting nearby-by mourners. Cameras clicked while news reporters posed before microphones, rambling solemn commentaries of the service. The rabbi raised his voice, overcoming the babble, demanding quiet with stern eyes. After a pause, he bowed and began again.

The media frenzy stunned Birdie. She couldn't help thinking of what would occur once the story of Malda Boddy's death became known? If the tragedy of Sid Breen's daughter brought the current chaos, she couldn't imagine the press' reaction to the scandal of Sid's young, bathrobed girlfriend dying of an alcohol and drug overdose in his remote beach home.

Birdie's eyes scanned the immediate area, stopping on a heavy-set man exiting a crumbling, aged crypt. Her eyes blurred, and she took another look. Unexpectedly, Alfred Hitchcock stepped from inside.

Had it been a delusion? One of his famous cameo appearances?

How long had it been since she'd rested, much-less slept? What had she missed, scrutinizing fans and the many Broadway and Hollywood personalities? Did a lapse of concentration allow the stalking killer to advance toward her? Birdie's eye's refocused, recognizing the plumpish, slow-moving form as a gravedigger. Jolted awake by the convincing illusion, she carried on her surveillance of the gathered onlookers.

She couldn't make out the faces, but guessed she spotted Roe and Nagle. The pair of Mutt and Jeff detectives staked out a hot dog vendor's cart. Behind them, a gray-haired man in a long coat hobbled up and down past a group of transit cops in dress uniforms.

To her right, she noticed brightly polished fire engines and street sweepers staged near the cemetery's entrance—an obvious campaign plug endorsing the mayor's commitment to a safe, clean city. How would it be viewed if the killer succeeded, beheading a voter, spilling blood less than ten feet from his honor?

Birdie tried to rid her mind of the grizzly image when someone stepped from behind the bulky three-wheeled sweeper. She shook her head, taking another look, not allowing an illusion to fool her a second time.

Although a heavy black beard veiled his face, there could be no mistaking the uniform and smooth, graceful walk. He'd passed her as she escaped Saint Luke's-Roosevelt Hospital wearing the stolen red cape. She couldn't avoid thinking of young Joseph's bloodstained coat and the tragedy and deception brought to his father, Jacob.

He dressed, as he did that day, in the winter uniform of a New York City transit cop. The same cop Jark described watching Malda's apartment.

It couldn't be a coincidence. She'd bet her favorite shoes and purse the scarred and damaged pocket watch belonged to him.

Birdie had her man. With luck, the East Hampton Police and their weekly paper cooperated. Her deception, delaying the news of Malda's death, delivered the killer. She'd accomplished this without breaking or bending laws. A new trend, she hoped.

She lacked hard evidence unless he carried the killing axe in the leather satchel hanging at his side. She'd contaminated the cases few pieces of solid proof. Any jailhouse lawyer would discredit the pocket watch, along with the stolen victim's coat and jewelry. Nothing legally linked the killer to Mary Clary's murder. However, when the time came, the pocket watch would come in handy.

To ask patrolling city police to give chase and arrest a fellow uniformed officer would be met with blank stares. The cop's unwritten code of the blue wall lived in New York. She'd act alone, not disturbing Jark's solemn moment with his father and family.

Birdie struggled to keep the transit cop in view as he walked among the milling crowd. Despite her best effort, he'd somehow vanished between the burial tombs and mounted police. She'd set herself up as an easy target, a sitting duck, for the uniformed officer who'd have open and easy access to her. From instinct, Birdie reached, touching her purse, feeling the compact outline of her pistol, regaining a bit of confidence.

An unexpected dull burst disturbed the service. A bank of white blowing smoke rose over the crowded area occupied by cameras and newsmen. Hordes of press and photographers trampled yellow and black police sawhorses, escaping the billowing cloud. Mounted officers and beat cops swarmed to control the scene.

Birdie recognized the sudden chaos as a cunning diversion, neutralizing heavy police presence, simplifying his access to her and providing an undetected escape. She reminded herself he'd attack close up, using the hatchet as he did on her client's innocent daughter. This guy was not a long-range killer using a rifle and scope, hiding on a rooftop. Her prey enjoyed being close, smelling blood, bringing death with his own hands.

All went as planned. The killer came to her, although now she regretted not involving Roe and Nagle in her crazy idea. Excitement, fueled by adrenalin, ran through her, sensing his nearby presence. He'd attack at first opportunity. She had no doubt.

In minutes, a uniformed officer waved a burnt-out canister the size of a soup can over his head and shouted, "It's a smoke bomb."

The transit cop had disappeared. She looked for what seemed to be a ghost among the hundreds of milling guests and celebrity watchers. For her safety Birdie would no longer allow herself to remain a stationary target, she became the hunter—with any luck catching him off-guard. She kicked off her heels, dropped the heavy coat and scarf to the green carpet, slipping away from the gravesite, forcing herself between tightly packed crowds of mourners. Once free, she circled the gathering, staying behind cameras and photographers, which continued to overrun the burial service. The killer wouldn't suspect being tracked on his path toward the grave. Birdie planned to cut him off well before he reached the coffin.

Instead, she lost her bearings in the shifting horde and found herself at the low end of a slope, unable to locate the fast-moving transit cop.

Birdie rushed up the small knoll to the base of the granite Star of David and hid, watching the gathered crowd break up. The bearded transit cop was nowhere in sight and seemed to vanish among massive tombstones and crypts. The killer had been in her sights, and she'd let him get away. Sid Breen suffered enough pain losing his daughter and Malda. His only chance for closure came from an arrest.

Solemn mourners marched single file past the grave, dropping handfuls of dirt on the lowered coffin. Birdie needed to act fast and took a last look at Sid Breen and Jark. There was no sign of the transit cop. Birdie ran toward the cemetery entrance, guessing he'd given up. This could be her last chance, and she'd not allow the killer to retreat.

Confident of not being seen, she pushed her way through departing masses of people crossing through what had been a police blockade. After stumbling through a sidewalk memorial of flowers and burning candles, she spotted him, at least his back as he ran. He reappeared in the rush of people and traffic exiting the cemetery. Pinkerton training taught her to not only recognize and remember faces, but also body types. She wouldn't lose him, although he surprised her with his light and nimble quickness. Birdie remained determined regardless of the dull ache in her injured hip. It was no time to quit. How could he slip past her? Besides the many rabbis, her suspect had been the only bearded man attending the funeral. Was he wearing a disguise?

She stopped her pursuit and looked among the crowd—he seemed to vanish. Her eyes had not left him. Could he have been an apparition, disappearing into shadowy places reserved for spirits? No, she chased an ordinary man who today got lucky losing her in the mass of people.

Birdie bent forward, resting her hands on her hips, breathing in large gulps of cold air. The pursuit ended. The once dull aches in her shoulder and hip turned into sharp throbs. Her only consolation—her plan worked: she'd drawn the killer out on his belief Malda remained alive. She crossed her fingers innocent bystanders were not injured during the ordeal.

A hand grabbed her shoulder.

Birdie jerked around, reaching inside her handbag, gripping her pistol.

Jark stood near her. "Sid's dead."

CHAPTER THIRTY-ONE

Birdie walked from Jark and the confusion of cameras and police. Her bruised honor and dignity prevented bursting into a rage. She wanted to be alone. The killer escaped once again—most likely watching and gloating. It seemed to be a habit according to the profile she'd formed. He'd penetrated a barrier of tight security, and in broad daylight, murdered Sid Breen. Every news station in the area would lead with the tragic story.

Footsteps came from behind, and she stopped and turned. Her usual cat-quick reflexes failed her. Two hands gripped her, pulling her from the path to a patch of grass near a brownstone mausoleum.

Birdie swung a fist at the attacker, only to have it blocked.

"What the hell happened?" Owen Roe asked, after releasing her arm.

"You were here," Birdie said and pushed away. "You tell me."

"We had the cemetery watched."

"Our guy escaped. I didn't get a good look. You?"

Roe shook his head. "He disappeared in this mob."

"I have a hunch I'm missing something obvious."

"You'll tell me when you find it," Roe reminded.

"That's our deal," she said to his back as he walked toward a group of reporters.

"Yeah, it is." Roe turned to face to her.

Despite the atrocious act which occurred under her nose, Birdie thought of Mort's disclosure—Owen Roe's purchase of their ring.

"Birdie, I'm glad we got it out in the open the last time we talked."

"We're different people now. A lot's happened."

"I'm relieved you see it that way." Roe stepped closer.

"I pushed you too fast. You weren't ready."

"Now's not the time, but I've made decisions affecting both of us."

The crowd of reporters and cameras shoved past the sawhorse barricades, advancing across the cemetery, heading toward the two.

Birdie gave Roe a gentle shove. "Talk to them."

Watching him greet the media, she deliberated. He seemed sincere. Should she confront him about the engagement ring? Owen Roe dragged his feet on everything but his job. It could make things easier, or he may feel pushed, and she didn't wish to make the same mistake again. She'd back off, be patient, and let him decide the timing. He spent six months' pay for that privilege.

What about Jark? Could there be a little something there, or was he an imagined flirtation to take her mind off Roe?

She couldn't be sure, and there was no time to allow her personal life to barge into her job.

The case went back to zero as far as ideas to trap the killer. She needed to clear her mind, trusting something would happen, putting her on a new trail.

Sid Breen's covered body rolled past on a gurney guided by two white-uniformed ambulance attendants. Had he been the target? She'd remain visible, retracing steps, returning to the original murder site of Breen's daughter and Malda Boddy's apartment, and this time she'd speak to neighbors and hopefully get lucky. After today, she knew the axe killer was cunning and able to move about the congested city freely and quickly. She'd keep an eye out for anyone straying too close.

In New York City, that would be difficult.

CHAPTER THIRTY-TWO

Scrubbing with cold water and hotel soap carried in his jacket pocket, Victor Gregory's blood-splattered hands washed clean in the station's toilet. Flushing's Mt. Hebron Cemetery became a memory the moment he stepped on the crowded subway. His intuitions had been correct. He escaped detection, immune, moving at will in spite of the heavy concentration of cops.

Curiosity and revenge lured him to the Jewish burial, expecting Malda at Sid Breen's side. He'd loved her and would continue, despite her deceitful betrayal. The moment he arrived and stepped from the bus, raw instinct told him he had company. The feeling strengthened as he moved toward the crowded gravesite. His senses raised to a cybernetic state, operating freely, drawing in information, adapting rapidly, assessing and predicting events.

After the smoke bomb explosion, his route cleared, and he found his way to Sid Breen, besieged by pushing and shoving television cameras and photographers. He'd expected Malda, instead, encountered a faceless woman, her identity shielded by a black scarf.

Sid Breen deserved punishment. He'd stolen Malda from him. It should have been him bleeding to death on the dirty sidewalk of Hell's Kitchen. Victor took advantage of the chaos, steering a confused and weakened Sid Breen to the safety of a nearby crypt. Breen offered no resistance to the uniformed officer's aid, complying as a helpless child, grasping the first hand extended

Inside the darkened granite crypt, Breen had been helpless to the powerful chief's axe. Once again, it struck the kill zone perfectly. The high and mighty king of Broadway didn't see it coming. Victor grabbed the producer's shoulder, jerking him backward and off balance. The edge of the sharp blade slashed deep, carving his fleshly neck, slicing artery, and windpipe. He pushed the gasping victim farther into the tomb, letting Breen stagger and collapse, scattering hanging shovels and picks.

Dark blood puddled the dirt floor.

Un-noticed, he pulled the crypt's metal door shut, pushing his way past the crowd, exiting the Jewish cemetery.

* * * * *

The newspaper cited an anonymous Long Island police source. They found Malda Boddy dead in Sid Breen's beach home the previous night. The probable cause—alcohol and an overdose of a prescription drug. The news came while Victor ate his sack lunch in the Grand Central Terminal Diner. He almost missed the small headline in *The Post's* city section propped against a donut display. He wanted her to live. The meditation bowl guided him to reconcile and forgive Malda for breaching their bond. Sid Breen lured her and other eager young actresses with his forbidden fruits of fame and stardom.

Victor watched many step from the bus, star struck by the bright lights of The Great White Way. They arrived from small and big towns lugging bargain basement suitcases and resumes boasting starring performances in hometown dinner theaters and school dramas. Talent and good looks, none of it mattered, a common commodity on Broadway.

After reading the story a second time, Victor refolded the paper, tossing it into a booth as he walked into the terminal's boisterous main floor, seeking a vacant pay phone. He planned to call in sick, claiming a touch of flu and retreat home. His life would move on as always. In a few months, Sid Breen would vanish from his mind.

*****

That night, on the deck of his dry-docked houseboat, Victor stared at the brightly lit Liberty ship, recalling the previous night's odd discovery. He guessed the obvious. The well-maintained Pullman cars provided temporary living quarters. But for who? The chess piece and stench stuck in his mind. How many had occupied the railcars and for how long? Tonight, he planned to stay home, hopeful his entertaining neighbor would. A surprise awaited her, a chilled bottle of Mogen David, a late welcoming gift to the boatyard.

Thoughts of their first encounter brought a smile. The curved, crescent-shaped scar on her shoulder and the coy pose and grin she flashed standing over her dropped towel. Raised beads of water covered her entire body. Victor imagined her stepping into his arms.

He'd prepared to make a good impression in return. An open, sharpened ivory-handled razor and barber scissors rested on a fresh, white towel next to the shower. The removing would be uncomfortable and slow. Five years passed since he'd used the antique straight razor. It required a steady hand, especially near the throat.

Victor leaned close to the sink and took one last look into the mirror, saying goodbye. The cutting went slower than expected, but he'd trimmed away most of his heavy beard and stepped into the hot shower, lathering what remained of his stubble and scalp.

The results pleased him. A different person stared back in the steamy bathroom. His fresh appearance brought a rebirth, a transformation. The cocoon shed, stripped away, new life waited to merge with his enlightenment.

Despite the cold night, he wrapped a heavy blanket around his shoulders and sat on the deck of his land-locked boat, watching the brightly lit Lady Liberty pose against the backdrop of Manhattan's southern skyline. He assured himself the high rent upper east and west side snobs envied him.

A pair of shooting stars converged and crossed paths in the distant sky over New York Bay. An omen of destiny to Victor; fate brought he and the mysterious and alluring neighbor together. What remained undecided—how to entertain his guest?

After dozing several hours, Victor Gregory awoke, trembling and stimulated after a tormenting dream of wading through flowing streams of blood and screaming, twisted faces. All things come, and all things go. The lifelike hallucination would be replaced with another. Had it been a sign of his transformation? He had been certain one face belonged to the limping man.

Her houseboat was dark and would stay so. He'd made sure during his nightly patrol.

Tomorrow he planned an early get-together with his contact, Scarecrow, the only name he knew him by. Thinking of the code name brought a laugh, as did his—Tin Man, Oz's axe wielding, monkey killing robot. The New York cop, in the beat-up Ford, stalked him for months and coerced him into spying on his part-time employer, Lev Reznik. What the task rerquired placed him in jeopardy. The Russian had a nasty and brutal nature, enforced by heavy-handed dock workers.

What more would Scarecrow want after he'd searched the Liberty ship? Break into the Russian's home and office? Victor understood the methods and arrogance of city detectives—drag you in slow with promises, then continually ask for more until you're in deep, leaving becomes impossible. In his case, the lure had been a promotion to an elite department and wearing a suit and wing tips. Victor shook off thoughts of backing out, at least for the moment. He'd play along.

Victor ran both hands over his smooth chin and scalp, admiring a new smart look, something he hadn't experienced in years. He'd treated the minor shaving rash with baby oil, splashes of Old Spice, and a soothing application of talcum powder. The irritation would be gone in a few days. The few people he knew wouldn't recognize him.

Relationships at the transit department were all business, nothing else. The department, on his first day, took the only recent clean shaven photograph. In many ways, it was a new beginning, a fresh start. No close friends existed, only shallow associations with other aspiring actors, each loyal only to their livelihoods.

He'd met Malda after finishing his late shift as a transit cop and rushed to his actor's workshop. She had been different; they bonded at once, a covenant of trust between them, leaving no room for anyone. Their fledgling stage careers survived famine for almost two years. Auditions and screen tests, hundreds, yielded nothing but rejection. They'd been dropped by the best and worst agents in the city until a chance meeting on a subway. Malda stumbled and, as luck would have it, Sidney Breen caught her. Within a month, she landed a minor role off-Broadway and eventually the back up to a Broadway star. Soon, Malda lost interest in her friends... and him.

Victor folded his canvas deck chair, ready to retire for the night.

The movement slight, a car pulled to where the locked gate once had been. Now only his dented mailbox remained, marking the lot's entrance. Shadows hid the make and color. Victor jumped to his feet, hiding in shadow, trying to spot the surprise visitor. A door slammed, and the car pulled away. Footfalls crunched past stripped boat hulls and construction rubble toward his elevated home. She appeared under a streetlamp, walking to the houseboat he'd watched. His puzzling neighbor had, at last, arrived, pleasing and surprising him. He reminded himself to stay calm, let things happen, don't appear pushy or forward. The groundwork had been laid. She'd have no choice but to accept. The fuses from her circuit breaker rested in his pocket, leaving her elevated home dark and cold.

Not sure if she'd noticed him, he shouted, "Welcome to the neighborhood."

No response came.

Victor leaned over the railing. "I've been hoping to meet you."

She turned, shading her eyes against the glare of the lot's entry light, and quickened her pace.

"I'm security," Victor said.

"Just moved in," she shouted, walking faster over the beaten and cracked asphalt to her houseboat.

"I know."

She waved and continued.

Victor Gregory wasn't about to let the opportunity pass.

"You've got no power," he said.

She stopped and turned, facing Victor. "What did you say?"

"No electricity. Con Edison's sending a man," Victor yelled over a sudden wind gust.

Pulling strings of hair from her face, her shoulders slumped, walking toward him. "When will that be?" she asked.

"All they said was tonight."

She slapped her hands against the sides of her legs. "That's just great."

"It's the construction," Victor said. "Get used to it."

Victor met her at the bottom of the ramp, guiding her to his houseboat.

"There's plenty of food and drink."

"It's late. I'm imposing."

Victor shut the door and waved an arm around the converted passenger ferry. "She's not the Queen Mary."

As she passed, he stepped back, sizing her up. In the harsh fluorescent light, she appeared older but athletic and fit. The smile she flashed showed off brilliant white teeth. He inhaled, recalling the distinct, musty, floral perfume.

Victor pointed to a couch and chair positioned in front of a radio and phonograph as he slipped into the galley, twisting open a bottle of wine. "Mogen David red?" he asked.

"I shouldn't. It's late," she answered, taking a seat.

"It's already open. One glass," Victor said. "Con Ed will be here and gone before you finish."

They toasted and sipped chilled wine. As they did, Victor noticed her jaw muscles relax, returning her youthful smile from the previous night. In a moment, his guest spoke freely of her job in Reznik's planned boat home community. As she did, the tension in her voice eased. Laugher came easy, and she looked into his eyes as Malda once had. He liked that it reminded him of her. No doubt she'd been an actress or studied to. Her posture and poise well practiced—no hint of a local accent. Seated across from her, while enjoying her vitality and enthusiasm, he'd become alarmed, sensing her corrupted spirit, lack of self-control and disobedient nature. He'd rescue her, allowing her to enter the world he'd discovered. Friendship with a corrupt world brought oppression, dampening her spirit. He'd purify her as he had Malda. He'd been the shepherd Birdie had been entrusted to.

She'd drawn him to her window, enticing him with sins of the flesh. She intended to do him harm, although she had not yet realized her future.

He held the wine bottle near her glass.

She placed a hand near it, shaking her head.

Victor returned to the kitchen, placing the bottle of Mogen David into the icebox. As he did, he caught her reflection in the window. She stood, smoothing the wrinkles in her pleated skirt while looking over the room.

He glanced toward her houseboat. He'd make an excuse to step outside and replace her fuses. She couldn't stay.

"Bathroom?" she asked.

"Where are my manners?" he said.

She nodded and smiled. "Just to freshen up."

"The head is that way."

As she passed, Victor inhaled her scent and resisted touching her long, black hair.

"Evening in Paris?" he asked.

"That an offer?" Birdie said, not bothering to turn.

"I'll be outside. Thought I heard something."

Birdie slid the bolt shut, locking the thin door of the compact bathroom. The haggard image in the mirror startled her. No lipstick, her face a wreck, makeup washed away long ago and her once fresh, clean hair gritty with sand. Not much could be done to salvage her appearance. Scooping cold water to her eyes, she noticed short, black strands of hairs near the hand basin and floor.

Why had she accepted his invitation looking like this? He had an eye-catching smile and attractive face. She couldn't resist his deep blue eyes which examined her the moment she'd arrived. They never left her. It was obvious he'd shaved recently, showing redness near his mouth and upper lip. He attempted to make a good impression, flattering her.

There wasn't much she could do with her makeup and clothes. She'd politely excuse herself and return home, electricity or not—she couldn't remain. The next meeting, she'd have her game face in man-attract mode. Thinking of the men in her life, her new neighbor, Jark and Owen Roe, brought a smile to the face in the cracked mirror. Good things came in threes, and she'd have all three until detective Owen Roe placed a ring on her finger, claiming her.

Outside the thin walls of the houseboat, the creaky door closed and light footsteps crossed the room. After tossing her used tissues into the toilet, Birdie made one last check of her face, adjusted her skirt, pulling it up at the waist, flushed and twisted the door's anchor shaped knob. She nearly missed spotting it. A silver chain sat at the bottom of a wicker basket. Examining it in her palm, she saw the small loop, bent and separated. The missing piece, possibly a fob attached to a belt loop or button hole securing a pocket watch. The idea was too much to imagine, and she returned it to the trash.

Her entrance startled Victor as he stood at the galley's sink, scrubbing his hands under a strong spray of water.

Birded remained behind him. "I heard the door."

Heavy soap covered his hands as he turned to her. "All done. Con Ed. finally showed. You're all fixed up."

She took her coat and purse from a hook and stepped to the door. She saw the unexpected glow of lights in her bedroom and kitchen. Her habit had been to leave a single light on in the kitchen.

Victor remained at the sink, making no move to see her out.

"I'll return the favor," Birdie said, pushing the door open.

"No need, that's what neighbors do."

She stepped to the wood deck and took a last look into the living room, spotting the copper bowl and mallet resting on a floor mat. It hadn't been there earlier.

Birdie paused, hearing the water faucet shut off, hesitating before swinging her coat over her shoulders.

"Thanks again," she said, stepping down the stairs. After a few steps, she stopped, hearing light humming tones come from inside. His sudden change of mood perplexed her.

The photo removed from Malda Boddy's apartment remained tucked in her waistband. She'd wait until she reached home before taking another look at Malda's boyfriend's bearded face. Her only other working clue. What were the odds the two chains matched? With Malda's death, Birdie lost the only person able to identify her former client's killer. With Sid Breen dead, there had been no point in continuing her investigation... except her pride. She'd allowed Sid Breen and Malda to die because of her neglect.

Inside a threadbare pillowcase filled with worn out shoes, she spotted the old gym sneakers tied together at the laces. Birdie held her faithful Keds, not worn since her Pinkerton training. Unless she caught a break, she and the Keds would pound the pavement, making rounds to the city's acting schools and transit patrol commanders, showing the picture taken from Malda's home. If she had to, she'd run down each of the thirteen hundred transit officers patrolling the five borough's buses, terminals, and trains. She expected to meet head-on, the city's well-known cop culture. The strong camaraderie bound officers from divulging information against one another. The Blue Curtain, or Code of Silence, went as far as committing perjury.

In the cold, late night, church bells rang, louder than she had remembered. Alarms sounded in her memory, reminding her of her search of Malda's closet and the falling bowl striking her head. The ornate copper bowl matched her neighbor's. She had been positive and doubted it a coincidence.

What should she do?

A visit to city transit offices presented a risk; she'd expose herself, alerting the suspect, taking away her advantage. Although the odds were a million to one, her neighbor had been the illusive transit cop, the temptation rose in her to have another look at the broken watch chain she'd spotted.

CHAPTER THIRTY-THREE

The next day, Victor Gregory stepped from the subway station near Green-Wood Cemetery. Chilly morning air stung his new clean-shaven face. Rubbing a gloved hand over his chin, he recalled why he'd grown the full, robust beard—masking his identity as a failed actor from himself.

Today he'd bypassed Gig's Diner and his usual breakfast, but not the early edition of the paper. He had a choice of many littering the train.

He leaned against the subway terminal's rusty steel post, skimming past the world news section until he spotted what he looked for. A grainy photo of a white sheet covered the body of Sid Breen. The bold headline read, "DEATH'S CURTAIN CLOSES ON BROADWAY PRODUCER." The crumbled tabloid hit the trashcan as Victor rushed to the cemetery.

Unsure if he'd recognize the cop in daylight, Victor intended to arrive ahead of his contact, known only as Scarecrow. The first get together; he remained hidden in shadow. This time, Victor planned to catch a better look at the man he risked his life for.

Unlike previous days, the sun shined. He hurried to the cemetery's chapel, intending to position himself in a lighted location.

After a short subway ride, Victor entered Green-Wood Cemetery, passing the massive stone and steel-barred entry gates. He stopped, as on his past visit, staring at the larger-than-life, carved biblical scenes portraying Lazarus and Christ's Resurrections. After a moment, he continued through the brownstone openings into Brooklyn's historic graveyard. New York's eternal home for the decaying bodies of both the respectable and not so. A prestigious burial site near someone famous came with a price, or so he'd heard. Even in death, prominent New Yorkers sought status.

The shout came from behind. A heavyset man, garbed in a tan zippered coat with matching slacks, stepped from a guard shack and marched toward him.

"You here to meet a cop?" he asked.

"Who's asking?" Victor said as he turned, staring down at the saggy faced security cop. His too snug uniform and scuffed shoes told Victor the man took no pride in his position and wouldn't make the grade as a transit officer.

"He asked me to direct you." The guard pointed to the gray slate roof of a distant maintenance garage. "He's gonna call. That's all I know."

Victor hesitated, smelling a trap, and looked around the area. His promising sunshiny day turned gloomy. This had been a setup.

The cemetery guard held a palm up. "I forgot to say it's about Emerald City."

Hearing the code word for the Russian Liberty ship brought him to an immediate stop. "That's what he said?"

"That's what the man said. The side door's open. There's a desk in the back. Wait there for a call."

The building sat alone at the end of a crushed rock, one-way alley surrounded by leafless oaks and maples. Victor recalled passing it during his first meeting in the cemetery's chapel. The detective he unofficially worked for took odd precautions, something he'd tolerate until he got what he wanted.

The door slid open, and Victor ducked into the doorway, stepping onto a hard-packed dirt floor, sniffing musty wood and a foul whiff of something he couldn't identify. Weak sunlight forced its way past dusty bar covered windows and a skylight centered on the shallow pitched roof. Two light bulbs hung from a tall roof beam, burned overhead, making him an easy target. Sawhorses and a paint splattered door formed a desk supporting a stack of yellowed Granger catalogs and a black telephone. Lacking a chair, Victor paced between two backhoes parked in the center of the garage, keeping an eye on the door and phone.

Last night's search of the Liberty ships holds revealed hidden railroad passenger cars bolted to the base of the vessel. Although suspicious, the cars gave no proof of a crime. He tapped his jacket pocket, remembering the chess piece, a white knight discovered on the floor of a Pullman car. The pattern of the pieces varying, faint grain lines led Victor to believe it genuine ivory and guessed its owner to be someone of substance.

Impatient, Victor continued to pace. He didn't enjoy waiting. His recent new partner had no respect for his rank as a New York City transit officer. Why did he keep his name secret and insist on meeting in a park full of dead bodies? What did the arrogant cop hide? The detective shield he carried appeared authentic. Whatever the police proposed, he'd never trust him.

After a look at his watch, the phone rang, nearly shaking itself off the stack of grease-smeared maintenance catalogs. Victor let it ring, not wanting to appear eager and perhaps worry his contact. After his discovery inside the ship, Victor recognized his importance to the investigation of Lev Reznik. He had information to sell, and it didn't matter to whom.

The ringing continued, echoing in the wood rafters.

As Victor lifted the clunky handset from the cradle, no voice answered, only the hum of a deadline. Angered, Victor held the phone near his face, tempted to shout into the dead mouthpiece, telling his contact he'd become tired of the charade. Instead, he smiled, lowering the phone, placing it in its dusty resting spot.

Before his hand released the handset, the black phone seemed to jump, rattling his cold fingers. The shrill ring mocked him. Victor lifted the phone, pressing it to his ear.

"Find anything?" asked the voice, not bothering to identify himself.

Victor hesitated a moment. "This Scarecrow?"

"Talk to me, Tin Man," the voice said. "What's Reznik hiding in his big boat?"

"It's not a boat," Victor answered. "It's a ship."

"Whatever the hell it is, did you find anything?"

"Pullman cars. Twenty of 'em," Victor answered.

"The kind on a train?"

"Looks like they were lived in.

"Search 'em?"

"Found nothing. Clean as a whistle."

"What else?"

"The cars are hidden deep. The ship's holds have false floors hiding the sleeper cars. Open the deck cargo doors, and you see nothing."

"All of 'em?"

"In the four main holds, yes."

A faded green pickup idled near the garage, pulling Victor's attention. Two maintenance men hopped from the open bed and pointed shovels toward a pile of dirt and rubble covered by a worn tarp. A moment later, the truck rolled away.

Did the three work for his contact, Scarecrow, keeping tabs on him? Soon, he'd be free of the cloak and dagger. He'd evolved, although not completed, life would not return to what it had been but to the newfound state of being. Malda no longer haunted him, and the dead, red-headed shoe clerk posed no threat to identify him. Her savage killing would be blamed on a drunken street bum. The murder weapon, a small knife, along with the victim's jewelry, would be uncovered among the hobo's few belongings. With the mission finished, Victor looked forward to becoming a member of New York's elite organized crimes unit. He'd escape the drab uniform of a lowly transit cop to custom-tailored suits and appearing on the nightly news. This was all part of his destiny. His contact, a powerful officer within the department, promised to pull strings, transferring and promoting him.

Victor picked up the phone. "I'm back. Go ahead."

"You okay?"

"Grave diggers going to work."

Victor heard background voices, recognizing the lingo of cop talk. He dealt with a real player. He knew it.

His contact remained quiet.

Victor anticipated the job offer and told himself to stay patient—let Scarecrow make the offer he'd used as an enticement.

"I need one more thing done," Scarecrow said.

"What?" Victor said. "I searched the damn ship."

"You did a good job."

"I did what you asked. What else?"

"I haven't forgotten about what we talked about," the voice said.

"Good, I'm ready to start."

"I need something on the Russian lion. Believe me; I want you working with me to stop him. Can you do one more thing?"

Russian lion? Victor asked himself. He recalled it as code for Reznik. He couldn't forget the codes. He'd look incompetent.

"Reznik's office. Know where it is?"

"Been there."

"I want his private ship's manifest, not what customs sees."

"Sounds risky."

"I suspect Reznik's using the ship to smuggle people. I'm sure he's keeping a separate record. That's evidence we'll use to lock him up. That's how you get the job. Can I be clearer?"

Victor fought the urge to slam the phone against the desk. This is what he'd expected from New York cops—always wanting more.

"You there?"

"I'm done. You search his office."

"Listen to me. Don't hang up. Hear what I have to say."

"Thirty seconds."

"Be smart. Don't throw this away. You'll be a real cop, wearing nice suits. How does Detective Gregory sound?"

"That's bullshit, and you know it."

"It's true," don't mess this up like your acting career."

Victor slammed the handset into the cradle. His trembling hand remained on the phone.

What does he know?

The phone rang, vibrating in his hand. He let it ring a short time and picked up.

"I know you're pissed. I'm overlooking that."

"Give me a guarantee."

"Here's what I'll do, one cop to another," the voice said slowly. "I'll promise you Reznik will never learn you sold him out—spying on him, Victor."

"I helped because you're a cop."

"What do you think he and his Russian friends will do to you? They kill cops and snitches in terrible ways."

Victor remained quiet, feeling sweat dampen his tight collar. He needed the guidance of his meditation bowl. The promotion would slip away. There had been no choice, working in the gloomy tunnels alongside rats and vermin drove him mad. His so-called stage career went the same as the many young hopefuls landing in the city, with dreams larger than their talents.

After two years of acting school, hauling garbage and spinning pizza in a window, he landed a part as an unstable black and white-faced, mute circus clown, Snookey. His size and acrobatic ability fit both the role and harlequin costume. The character and show failed, entertaining shrinking audiences for its near week far off-Broadway. Malda entered his life, bringing promise.

"I need an answer."

"I want the job. Give me a few days."

"You're on your own. I can't help if you're caught."

"Didn't think you would."

"Put out the signal when the job's done."

"By the way, the big boat's name is *Yojo*."

The line buzzed in Victor's ear.

Victor Gregory walked from the garage, suspecting someone watched him. It had only been a strong feeling, but he stopped and found no one on the road or cemetery grounds. No one appeared in the area. The same two gravediggers he'd seen earlier worked in the distance leaning on shovels and seemed unaware of his presence. Exiting through the massive rock gates, he took a backward glance, noticing a limping, gray-haired man in a bulky overcoat walking toward a running car. He had spotted that awkward up and down hobble before—more than once.

CHAPTER THIRTY-FOUR

Bothered by a lingering ache in her injured hip and shoulder, Birdie slept little, rolling from bed before the sun climbed above an awakening city skyline. Outside her window, blasts of ship's horns and distant yawning tones of a foghorn bellowed warnings to steamers and ferries crisscrossing New York Harbor.

Standing over her thrift store toaster, she sipped day old coffee, waiting for breakfast. She spotted Victor Gregory exit his houseboat through thin, gauzy fingers of fog that pushed into the low-lying boatyard. Last night, spending time with him, raised questions and cautions—why had he contrived a power loss in her home? Had the energy giant, Consolidated Edison, made an appearance uncharacteristically quiet? Their blue and white service trucks routinely arrived with flashing emergency lights, blocking streets, rivaling a Broadway show opening. Nothing like that occurred—she'd checked with Con Ed. His flimsy ruse had been unnecessary. A simple drink offer would have lured her, welcoming any form of hospitality. Her need for a man's companionship reached an all-time high, exceeding her late teen years. She'd initiated contact and knew Victor hadn't forgotten the dropped towel, inviting steamy adult entertainment on the cold night. How far had she been willing to go for romance?

The fresh shaving rash along his strong jawline caught her attention, but she had discarded it as coincidence. It had been laughable to consider him the killer she hunted. However, after discovering a broken watch chain and coarse, black hair in his bathroom, an inkling of suspicion formed, which she at once rejected. The notion of her neighbor being the murderer she hunted in a city this size—the odds approached ten million to one. With the wave of her hand, she brushed away the absurd thought. How could she think that of her new neighbor?

With Sid Breen in the morgue, she had no client writing checks. The retainer would run out in a week, and she would be on her own. Birdie convinced herself to stick with the job. It had been her stubbornness to insist on keeping evidence to herself. There would be two fewer people dead. Her last legitimate option remained, return to the basics of old-fashioned detective work, surveillance and pounding the pavement.

The long, slow process of watching three shifts of transit cops come and go from New York's four command centers and district offices would take weeks or months. Observing thousands of officers check in and out would not go unnoticed, raising suspicion, risking exposing her probe against one of their own, criminal or not. Without a doubt, the cop's blue wall of silence would drop and stonewall her. With none of her ill-gotten evidence allowable in court, she preferred to stay anonymous, not calling attention to her investigation—more small side steps around the laws of evidence were yet to come.

In addition, she'd search for an actor who may have known Malda Boddy, and she'd begin with acting schools.

Before launching long, time-consuming plans, she'd play a hunch she could not get out of her mind. She had to admit; it had been the reason for her fitful night, and she'd keep Jark out of her crazy scheme. She'd keep it too herself, as it promised, too big a risk for Jark and after all, she worked on her own time. After Sid's death, she wouldn't accept being responsible for Jark's actions and his safety.

After a close study of the photograph removed from Malda's apartment, she couldn't deny Malda's boyfriend's deep-set eyes resembled her neighbor's. Disguises hid prominent features, but eyes were difficult to conceal. They were the gateway to a person's soul and revealed much.

She'd not had a good look at the bearded transit cop during earlier encounters. She first saw him as she hurried from Saint Luke's, then from Malda's fourth story apartment to a darkened street and, most recently, from a much longer distance at Mary Clary's funeral service. His facial features, ones she'd been trained to observe, cheekbone and jaw had been hidden by distance and neatly trimmed beard. The hair found on his vanity proved nothing. It may have come from a recent shave or a do-it-yourself haircut. However, her suspicion represented her only clue.

Three people were dead. She owed it to her deceased client. With nothing else to go on, it was time to take a shot in the dark. A quick search of his home would eliminate him as a suspect.

After taking another look at Victor's vacant houseboat, she convinced herself it would also be for her peace of mind.

Her neighbor, an axe murderer.... The thought sounded crazy and absurd. She'd never mention this to anyone or say it out loud. Construction workers arrived in an hour. She could, with ease, enter and exit unnoticed.

She'd force herself to think of the transit cop as a suspect in her search for evidence connecting him to Malda Boddy or Mary Clary—photos, letters, anything he'd kept. The killer had taken pains to remove a silver shamrock button and a pearl and diamond earring from the body he believed to be Malda. Something to admire, personal items taken as gruesome souvenirs, reminders of his conquest, hard-won trophies to be kept close.

Victor's copper bowl—she suspected it an exact match of the one found in Malda's apartment, which tumbled from a shelf, bruising her forehead. The idea came out of the blue. She had no solid reason, only instinct. Any evidence turned up would be worthless, obtained during her committing a crime, and the items she'd removed from the morgue would be argued in court as planted on the accused. Birdie required untainted proof connecting the killer to Mary Clary. Thinking for a moment, Birdie ran to her bedroom and retrieved the scarred pocket watch. Its existence was unknown except by the killer. Until now, it had been useless, but Birdie had an idea how the watch would be used.

Fog crept inland as a rolling vapor, rising from the bay, shrouding the nearby Russian ship and the immense Brooklyn Army Terminal, hovering inches above a coat of early morning frost. Loose gravel crunched, grinding under Birdie's Keds, leaving a trail of noise to Victor's elevated home. If anyone had been inside, she did her best to alert them before breaking and entering.

Her neighbor didn't strike her as the trusting type. She'd be careful, taking her time, watching for tells left behind to spot intruders. Walking up the ramp to the deck, she stopped, listening for anyone inside or lurking outside.

Luck had been on her side. The boatyard remained vacant, and her neighbor appeared gone. She'd be alone. She hoped.

Birdie glanced under the old steel-hulled ferry, using the light of her flashlight. Visibility in the dense fog only reached as far as the rough cedar supporting braces near where she crouched. The wide beam of light found a corroded pick and shovel lying in the dirt near a padlocked metal chest. A paperclip could pop open the cheap lock in less than a minute. Curiosity nagged her to examine the suspicious package, but time was short. For now, her focus would be inside the boat. The box would be low priority and examined later. She hunted for the victim's belongings, knowing they'd be kept safe and convenient, within easy access, allowing frequent inspection.

The crime committed to conduct her longshot search, productive or not, gave Birdie a boost. She needed something, any action to restart her stalled investigation. Fifteen minutes to snoop through

Victor Gregory's home gave her plenty of time to examination thoroughly the four small rooms and a toilet. If she failed to discover anything, she'd begin the tedious canvassing of acting schools and city's transit command offices.

Birdie checked under the welcome mat—no key. Not deterred, she kneeled on a jute rug, prepared to test her rusty skills. Cold dampness and gritty dirt soaked into her only clean wool slacks. After examining the flimsy aluminum and glass door and although her skills remained out of practice, the simple lockset posed no challenge. She kept the pick set in her coat pocket and instead removed a hairpin from beneath her hat.

Before poking it into the lock, she rested a free hand on the door handle. It turned. The door swung open. She jerked back, gripping her handgun, prepared to shoot through the leather purse, expecting to find her neighbor standing over her.

No one appeared in the open doorway.

After a twist of the handle several times, she realized the door was unlocked—another trick to lure her inside? She hesitated to enter and stood at the door, aiming her revolver around the room. Did he hide after circling back, hoping she'd enter? The pungent odor of incense from the past evening had vanished. Her wine glass remained as she'd left it on the end table. Dishes sat in a rubber-coated drying rack. She'd comb the boat's compact space thoroughly after making sure she was alone. Birdie entered each room with her revolver at eye level; eyes wide open, staring down the barrel, keeping her back to the wall. Satisfied the houseboat empty, she lowered her pistol, letting out a breath, trying to relax, knowing she couldn't. With the boat secure, she returned the gun to her oversized purse, resting it in its compartment, ready to be drawn and fired.

The room remained as it had been last night, all but the ornate, etched copper bowl. Something about it made it special to Victor. Birdie convinced herself its twin dropped from Malda's closet during her search the previous day. Everything else in the compact galley and living area seemed untouched from last night. What particular significance did the bowls have to Victor and Malda? Birdie guessed Malda didn't share Victor's interest. Last night she sensed something wrong the moment she stepped into the houseboat as she did this moment. A voice told her to leave.

She started to the door and stopped. This remained her case. There would be no walking out, although Sid Breen no longer employed her. She'd finish, despite uncertainty of her PI career which after yesterday's botched trap in the cemetery appeared doomed.

A glance at her watch told her she had little time. Jark proved reliable and punctual despite New York's congested traffic. His timing and presence were uncanny. Was it coincidence he'd been at the last two murders?

Bedrooms kept secrets, and she'd begin her search in Victor Gregory's. She'd toss it. If the transit cop had hidden anything, she'd find it in his neat and tidy space. A straight front highboy, bed, and ladder-back chair furnished the room. Blue uniform shirts and slacks hung, perfectly spaced, in an open closet near the only bathroom. Finished with her scan of the efficient and well-ordered room, she went to work, beginning with the obvious, and pulled open the side-by-side top drawers and ran a hand over and between socks and handkerchiefs. Each piece of folded clothing rested in its own paper lined space, separated by drawer dividers. Before sliding the drawer shut, Birdie turned her palm upward, feeling the wood top for anything attached. She did the same for each drawer and found zilch. A box spring and mattress rested on black painted cinder blocks. Nothing laid under or between neatly folded and creased sheets.

Birdie couldn't help admiring Victor's need for tidiness. She recognized it as obsession and a feeling of total control.

Time ran short. Jark would soon arrive, and she saw no point letting him know she suspected the transit cop. Birdie looked back at the tall chest of drawers, wondering if she'd ever known a man to use white lace doilies. Pausing, she this time, noticed the loose crown molding outlining the top center panel. Running her fingertips over the carved wood, a small section of trim pulled free and twisted, making a faint, dull click inside. The entire center panel flipped open, revealing a concealed pigeonhole. A crisp tan envelope stood on its long edge.

Birdie gripped it at a corner and slid it forward from its hiding spot. After removing it, she looked outside—no sign of anyone. She undid the cord and opened it. Benjamin Franklin stared up at her from a two-inch stack of rubber-banded bills. She riffled the tight bundle several times, finding only hundreds and guessed fifty thousand in cold cash. She hadn't seen that much money in one place, much less held it. A quarter inch worth would solve her financial worries, wiping her slate clean. She'd escape Brooklyn to a higher quality life, where she belonged, near the bright lights of the city. The cash felt good in her hands as she slipped it into a pocket.

What had she done? She could not let herself slip that far, becoming a thief. Wherever the cash came from—she had been positive it was dirty. No one kept that amount of money on hand unless stolen or counterfeit. After hesitating a moment, the money went back, and the panel closed.

Looking at the highboy dresser, she asked what other secrets it held. She had read craftsmen once built hidden surprise doors into such old pieces. A few minutes remained before Jark arrived. She slid the chest's long, top drawer open, and this time removed it, discovering a false back. A partition, made of the same wood as the drawer, hid an added three inches of space.

Something lay in a corner. Birdie removed a thin wire hanger from Victor's closet, using the hook to retrieve a small velvet Crown Royal bag. Time ran short. Curiosity led her this far. Did she believe her neighbor committed the crime she investigated? She intended to eliminate him as a suspect in case things got friendly between them.

She pulled open the gold drawstring, spilling its contents to the bed covers.

Her mind flashed back to Saint Luke's basement morgue and standing over box twenty-one containing Mary Clary's belongings. She couldn't forget looking at the crumbled, bloodstained navy-blue dress belonging to the innocent victim. She regretted rushing to escape before Roe and Nagle arrived, taking the red cape and paper sack holding Mary's jewelry. Several people, she came to care for, would be alive if she'd allowed the detectives access to the items.

Her knees weakened and forced her to sit on the edge of the bed. The evidence she needed lay in front of her. Stuffing the bag and contents into her purse and running entered her mind, just as she had run from Saint Luke's Morgue.

She jumped from the bed as a car horn sounded.

CHAPTER THIRTY-FIVE

Cold blustery sea air greeted Victor Gregory the moment the B train's doors slid open. The station's elevated platform provided panoramic views of neighborhood low-rise apartments and modest homes wedged tight together in the seaside community. Once favored shops and eating spots, he remembered stood vacant, a stern reminder of how his life changed.

He faced a tough assignment, one he'd placed on himself, allowing the New York detective leverage—threatening to expose him to Reznik and certain death.

Mayhem entered his once orderly world.

Peaceful times with Malda in nearby Coney Island seemed a decade ago. He'd loved and hated her during their two years together. Her zest for life and risk appeared limitless, flirting with every passer-by, allowing no moment unlived. He lost her to Sid Breen's promise of fame.

Persecuted Soviet Jews escaped Odessa and Ukraine following World War Two, gradually transforming the ocean-side community of Brighton Beach. Lev Reznik played an unwelcome role, profiting legally and illegally from the influx he created.

Time had come for Reznik to take on a partner.

His recent railcar discovery provided a valuable negotiation chip, and he planned to make a business proposal to the Russian boss. His previous find of counterfeited American money inside the ship had become his nest egg but small potatoes compared to what the future held. Skimming a little cash would go unnoticed and there was no point killing that golden goose. The card Victor intended to play promised both power and wealth if he survived.

The offer could not be passed up—a cop with inside information assured Reznik, a steady flow of Russians entering New York, bypassing immigration.

Anxious, Victor jogged across Brighton Beach Avenue and spotted the red awnings fronting Reznik Real Estate. A wholesale jewelry business operated behind locked doors of a third floor, one he could not enter. Unlike previous visits, he arrived unexpected and bypassed the entrance after recognizing Reznik's bodyguard hovering near the front door. Curiosity tempted him to have a look at the Russian's private office.

An Uzi 9-millimeter submachine gun hung, not well hidden, under the guard's black leather overcoat he wore draped over his shoulders like a cape. The other watchman most likely waited inside, chatting, sipping tea with young, attractive ladies Reznik described as office staff.

Victor slipped into a vacant rear alley, hoping to remain unseen. A dim light burned behind tall stained-glass windows guarding the Russian's third-floor private suite.

Flat, heavy steel bars crossed the rear alley door. Above it a white stenciled notice warned trespassers of being shot. Victor chose a direct approach, avoiding the Russian guards and a full body pat down. Climbing atop a dumpster, he jumped and yanked down an exposed overhead iron ladder and clambered up two flights of metal stairs. After reaching the third-floor platform, Victor stood to the side, knocking on the steel door.

A revelation popped into his mind. Thoughts, uncontrolled, manifested—played a scene of bullets shredding the closed door he faced, tearing and ripping his flesh. Victor, surprisingly, suffered no pain, balanced in a void between life and death as he sprawled on the metal grating. With a firm grip on the rusted fire escape railing, he rose to his feet as Lazarus returned to life unscathed. Looking again at the heavy door—it remained undamaged, as did he. Lifelike visualizations came without warning, becoming stronger with each occurrence as a foretelling.

His chest thumping, he knocked a second time; certain what he carried in his pocket would grab Reznik's attention.

The click of a remote electronic buzz released a lock. The door opened a crack. Victor gave it a nudge with his shoe and stepped back, allowing it to swing inward. Reznik stood spread legged in the hallway, smoothing back his hair with the palms of his hands.

"Most people use the street entrance," Reznik said, holding the door open.

"A cop's watching your ship," Victor said.

"What about him?"

"You knew?"

"He's why I hired you." Reznik nodded him inside.

Victor Gregory side-stepped two plump blond cats and squeezed past an open file cabinet. He entered the Russian's office, bumping into a kidney-shaped table displacing chess pieces positioned on a black and white leather board.

Reznik took a seat, crossing his legs behind a mahogany roll-top desk.

"You waste no time with chitchat, unlike most Americans."

"Time is valuable to an important man like you. I came on business."

"I am a humble man. Look around. I'm not the Bolshevik many think, only a common worker, part of the masses."

The office door pushed open and a porcelain tea serving appeared. Victor stiffened and recognized the other husky Russian as he placed a tray on a table. An Uzi hung inside his oversized sport jacket as he arranged dishes of sliced lemons, sugar cubes and cookies. Victor eased his hand from his lap and reached to his holster, touching his six-shot side arm, but felt no reassurance against the new Israeli weapon. Outmanned and outgunned, he'd rely on his ability to convince the smug Russian he offered an opportunity to manipulate the New York police force and protect his illegal dealings.

Victor guessed a private signal passed between Reznik and the bald guard, causing him to stop and immediately exit, positioning himself in the hall, blocking the fire escape.

"Black tea?" Reznik asked.

"I came to discuss business," Victor answered.

Reznik waved both hands in the air toward his guest. "Tea first. It takes the edge off. Then we talk."

The Russian held a glass under the kettle's spout. "May I?"

"If you insist."

Reznik flashed a smile. "I do, my friend." He poured from the tall, slender pot with a steady hand, filling two gilded glass tea holders with steaming dark tea.

"Russian traditions are not easily broken." He raised his glass taking a noisy sip. "What you have to say will wait.... Yes?"

Victor followed, slurping a few sips, and returned the glass to the tray. Doing business with Russians, Victor knew them to be difficult to read and deal with. However, in this case, the mob boss appeared open for discussion.

Following a second sip and a bite of sugar cookie, Reznik wiped his hands and lips with a white napkin and leaned back.

"Mongolians are to blame," he said. "They bring tea to Russia, making us slaves to their dried leaves."

"You play?" Victor asked, looking at the chess board.

Reznik laughed. "I am Russian. It is our heritage."

"You're missing a knight," Victor said.

"A casualty of war. The set is rare ivory and cannot be replaced."

"Unfortunate." Victor nodded and slid forward in his chair. "Let's talk about your big boat."

"Ship." Reznik's smile vanished. "Spit it out, as you Americans put it."

"It's being watched because the cops suspect something illegal is going on."

"It belongs to the Russian Consulate, and according to the Vienna Convention, immune from United States laws."

"A cop approached me to search it."

"Detective Joe Nagle does not know when to quit. I threw him off a year ago."

"Tall guy, flat top, heavy smoker?"

Reznik pushed a stubby, manicured finger at his guest. "Like a New Jersey smokestack."

"Said he's with the mayor's organized crime unit."

The Russian leaned back in his chair. "That so?"

"Told me if I keep an eye on you and the ship, I get a job in his unit."

"What else?"

"He's got nothin'. Just fishin'," Victor said. "Wants me to do his dirty work."

"Are you?" Reznik asked as he stood at a louvered window staring down at the back alley.

"I had an idea..."

Reznik slapped his palm against the wall. "He won't give up, this cop. I am telling you this. Nagle got booted out of his job. He is playing you for a sucker."

"He's dangerous and I have an idea..." Victor began.

"I don't give a damn about your ideas," Reznik said, turning to his visitor. "Stay away from him. The man is trash and should be hauled to sea with the city's garbage. I'm an honest businessman. Look around. Ask neighbors. He won't find anything."

Victor Gregory stood to leave. "We have nothing left to discuss."

"... and there is nothing to find," Reznik said, holding the door open.

Victor stopped, savoring what he was about to do, and reached into his jacket pocket, placing the white knight in the vacant square flanking the rook and bishop.

No longer smiling, Lev Reznik stretched his arm across the door opening, easing it closed. "You enjoy chess after all."

"On occasion," Victor said, sliding the white knight to an attack position, centered on the leather board.

"You played yourself into a risky position, comrade."

"I came to offer my services."

"You have my attention." Reznik bent over the table and removed the white knight, examining it. "The set is complete... intriguing. May I ask...?"

"I know what you're hiding." Victor pointed to the piece Reznik held. "I found it in a train car. Nagle may find that interesting."

"Russia starves while the government is in chaos. I give them a home in this great country."

"For a price."

"They pay to escape oppression."

"I can help."

"In exchange for what?"

"It's what we can do for one another." Victor leaned close to the Russian's face, taking the knight from him, returning it to the board.

"Tell me what that is, comrade."

"I keep you informed to what Nagle is doing and you pay me."

"*Nyet*," Reznik shouted, grabbing the opposing black knight, slapping it to the middle of the board. "The cop means nothing."

"For three months, every night, that cop sat on the dock watching your boat. He's not giving up. Pay me now. He'll go away. I'm smarter than him. I got a plan. *Capish*?"

Reznik laughed. "Napoleon failed because he became blinded by his brilliance. He marched into Moscow and lost an army because of an early snow... one he never considered... beginning his fall."

"He lost credibility," Victor added. "Something no one fully regains."

"You have two minutes. Talk."

Heavy footsteps moved in the hallway, stopping near the closed door. Victor guessed the guard responded to a quiet alarm.

Victor looked down on the polished black and white chess pieces. "He's looking for a weakness and then he'll attack. Nagle's not giving up, he's out there. Eventually he'll find something."

Reznik nodded. "... and you propose?"

"Discredit him. Feed him worthless information. Keep him off balance with enough truth so he'll believe it. In time, he'll lose credibility."

"You will be a mole, yes? How do I trust you?"

"I'm sitting here, aren't I?"

"You remain breathing because I trust you... but very little."

"We both benefit," Victor said. "Leave it to me... comrade."

Victor heard confidence in his words, masking his uncertainty with false poise. His eyes glimpsed the familiar over-coated man hobbling, hurrying from the alley. The bright winter sky faded to an icy blue-green resembling a frozen pond. Victor recalled the French general's defeat and hoped the coming storm brought rain, not a defeating snow.

"I will double what I pay you, but I decide how to handle Nagle," Reznik said. He propped his hand on the table and tipped over the white king, letting it tumble to the wood floor.

Victor ignored Reznik's extended hand.

"I'm taking a big chance," Victor said.

"Take my offer and you walk out of here."

"I'll need a small favor when this is done," Victor said.

"As will I." Reznik flashed his brown stained teeth. "When our game is ended—eliminate him. As the cop dies, inform him the Russian devil welcomes him to Waterloo."

Victor exited the building through the front doorway, escorted by the leather coated bodyguard. The Russian ignored the requested favor, which no longer mattered. They both shared a death wish for Nagle, and Victor had drawn the honor. Could he trust Reznik? Victor looked over his shoulder. How long would he remain breathing?

CHAPTER THIRTY-SIX

Jark's Dodge pulled into the boatyard, skidding to a stop as a guilt-ridden Birdie stepped from the wood ramp, leaving Victor's home. With her new illicit scheme, she didn't know if facing Jark would be a good idea on several levels—personal and professional. The case appeared near an end, yet she felt annoyed. His family suffered, and he deserved to know what she was up to. With Victor Gregory behind bars, it would not bring back Jark's sister or father, but she hoped it would be the beginning of healing.

"We got him," she said through the car's open window.

Jark stepped from the car. "Who?"

"The damn killer," Birdie said in a low voice. "We'll talk inside." She nodded toward her houseboat.

They stood at the coffee table she used as a desk. Birdie held the purple bag by its gold string, dropping it next to her Remington typewriter that sat on a wooden beer case.

"The evidence is in there," she said.

Jark remained quiet, unbuttoning his wool pea coat. He stood over the small sack, shaking his head. "You mean it?"

"Positive. Without a doubt." With one hand, Birdie shook the velvet bag open, letting the silver button along with a pearl and diamond earring slide out.

Jark lifted the well sculpted shamrock button, holding it at arm's length. "I'll be. It matches the ones from Malda's cape."

"That button was missing from the cape when I removed it from the morgue."

"A souvenir?"

Birdie nodded.

Jark picked up the single earring. "Sid gave it to my sister on her birthday."

"I figure the killer took it from Mary after attacking her." Birdie took the earring from him. "The studs still in the backing. He ripped it from her ear."

"What's the plan?" Jark asked. "Call the cops?"

"I had the impression you and Sid wanted to take care of him yourself."

"Sid did. I went along."

"Now?"

"Things changed."

"Damn right they did. I got the killer dead to rights, and now there's no client and no pay." Birdie caught herself and stopped. "Sorry, that came from left field. Your father and sister are dead. I don't know where that came from."

Jark placed a hand on her shoulder. "You've been under a lot of stress."

"Money or no money, I'm finishing this," she said.

"You'll get what's owed you and more," he said. "I'm running the business. At least I will once the court settles the estate."

"That could take time."

Jark stepped close to her. "Sid hid a lot of cash. We'll be fine."

Birdie felt Jark's breath against her cheek as he hugged her. She resisted the sudden urge to kiss him, but continued to hold him against her, enjoying the firm feel of his chest and arms.

"Then it's business as usual," Birdie said, reluctantly leaving Jark's warm arms. The innocent embrace was nothing more than what occurred between friends. To her, she wanted something beyond that but forced herself to pull away and return the items to the velvet bag. She dangled the pouch between them.

"What's next?" Jark asked.

"There's a problem," Birdie answered. "The police will eventually know I removed the coat from the morgue and your sister's matching earring was in the same evidence box. Any public defender will spot them on her personal belongings list and argue I tainted the evidence. They'll also claim I planted one earring."

"We'll put the cape back," Jark said.

Birdie shook her head. "By now, the box is secure in the police evidence room. We'll never get near it."

"It still proves we got our guy, but not in a court. You can't give up."

Birdie pulled the scratched-up pocket watch from her purse. "I have this."

Outside her boathouse, construction crews arrived, and sounds of power saws and hammers soon overtook the quiet they'd enjoyed.

"What are you planning?"

"I have more than a strong hunch it belongs to our killer."

"Who is it?"

"That's the strange part. It's the transit cop next door."

Jark stopped; his normal stony, calm manner vanished. "This is crazy."

"This bag came from the boat next to me."

She'd dreaded this moment, uncertain of Jark's reaction. Would he come unhinged, a view of him she had yet to see? To counter his expected response, she stepped close to him, placing both hands on his chest.

"Please let me handle this?" Birdie said. "I know what I'm doing."

She felt tension in his muscled body. His heart beat vigorously under her palms. He inhaled and exhaled several times, then relaxed.

"And?" Jark asked, peeking from a slit in the Venetian blinds. "What's your plan?"

"You're better off not knowing since I work for you."

"You're not safe here. You know that?" Jark said.

Birdie held up her thumb and forefinger inches apart. "I'm this close. I need to stay and finish the job."

"He may know who you are."

"He went from warm and friendly to cold and distant last night."

"You were with him?"

"... A few minutes. Tell you later."

"Want me to go?"

Birdie smiled and nodded. "I need some time."

She watched the green and white Dodge bump through ruts and holes as Jark drove off. Birdie owned up; he'd tempted her with his rugged good looks. She couldn't deny having a few years on the former Marine. Enticing him for an overnighter.... Birdie regained her thoughts, knowing exhaustion set in, letting her mind wander. She had feelings, at least the physical kind, but doubted Jark would reciprocate. She only hoped he trusted her to complete the job... alone. He'd lost a sister and father and faced the unpleasant task of dealing with Sid's estate. Besides, she didn't want Jark involved in what she planned.

Birdie spent the morning completing a detailed report, omitting indiscretions of her investigation. She'd also prepare a summary of the past three days as a quick reference for any estate judge or lawyer reviewing her sizeable bill and expenses. The case neared its end, but nothing was over until she completed the paperwork. She'd prepare another report for herself, leaving nothing out, admitting to her wrongdoings. That one would stay private, locked in a bank security box.

After downing a pot of strong, bitter coffee and several stale Danish, Birdie put the finishing touches to each typed document and signed her name below the title, Licensed Private Investigator. She didn't know how long she'd hold on to her right to work legally in the state of New York. They may be her last official PI reports, but she left nothing out from her personal summary. She solved the case, not necessarily by the rules and laws of New York and certainly not ethically; however, in the end, the killer would pay for the horrible crime.

At eleven-thirty, on the dot, Birdie spotted the arrival of a red and black Metro step van. The large truck rumbled into the job site, blasting a two-tone horn version of La Cucaracha, and stopped, halting construction as labors dropped their tools and headed to the food truck.

In moments, both driver and passenger doors slid open. A heavyset man twisted a latch, lifting one side of the International Harvester van, revealing a display of wrapped sandwiches and steaming stainless steel soup kettles. At the other end, a grinning, dark-haired woman in snug bib overalls snapped a small folding table into place, setting up shop. Despite the day's chill, she sported a tank top displaying a generous cleavage while taking money and making change from a chrome coin dispenser hanging from a nicely rounded hip.

The brunette's tank top and flirting smile kept workers near the food truck and provided Birdie with the distraction she needed to enter Victor Gregory's home and return undetected.

Birdie grabbed the scarred pocket watch along with the purple pouch from the table, looked at the lunch truck and dashed from her houseboat. She hoped the full-figured, classical Rubens model would hold the men's attention another ten minutes.

She used a worn path, hiding behind tall stacks of lumber and cinder blocks. A return to Victor's home had been a risk. She'd managed earlier, but a second time stretched her luck, which had run rotten.

Victor Gregory's work hours were unknown. Most transit cops worked varied days and hours. He could arrive home, trapping her, justifiably pull his service revolver, shooting her, all within his rights.

His door remained closed and unlocked, same as she left it hours ago. After taking a last look at the food truck—a half-dozen men lingered in line, inspecting the brunette's curved hips, twisting and swaying as she eagerly took their money.

Before returning the items, Birdie peeked into the cramped bathroom. The wicker trash can was empty. The silver, broken chain gone from the previous day.

She'd didn't intend to tell Jark about the vast amount of cash found in the highboy dresser. Had it been intentional? Was she becoming a thief? Were the earlier thefts of evidence a result of panic? She had no time to think about it. Everything done had been for her client, Sid Breen. However, she'd failed to protect him, attempting to lure the killer to her. The tragic and poorly thought out scheme cost Breen his life while attending his daughter's funeral. Her actions were irresponsible. Could she refrain from habitual knee-jerk responses under stress of the job?

What she planned to do in Victor Gregory's home was unlawful. His civil rights remained until New York City proved him guilty in court, not by her judgment. As Owen Roe had reminded her frequently, justice often needed a little push.

She would return the earrings and shamrock button along with a new addition—the pocket watch Victor carelessly left behind at Mary Clary's murder. As an act of a Good Samaritan, she'd give it back to its owner.

Time ran short. Birdie looked to the food truck, spotting the rushing driver slamming shut its side panels. In the future, she'd play it straight, following the laws of New York State and the ethical behavior required of a licensed private investigator.

The hidden cash had been hers for the taking, and another opportunity waited to tempt her determination. Her neighbor couldn't go to the police, as a criminal. He forfeited the law's protection. Birdie ran her hand over the chest's carved wood. The small section of trim pulled free and twisted with a faint, dull click, opening the hidden panel. The tan envelope of money, hidden in the narrow pigeonhole, promised to solve her mounting financial problems. The forbidden fruit also guaranteed remorse and sleepless nights. Birdie closed the concealed door, leaving the envelope untouched.

She opened the same chest's long top drawer and removed it. After pulling the velvet Crown Royal pouch from her purse, she added the pocket watch, cleaned of prints, dropping it next to the silver button and diamond pearl earring. She retied the cords and slid the bag to the rear of the secret partition where she'd first discovered it. Planting the watch, she was sure, belonged to her neighbor, had several possibilities. She'd alert Roe and Nagle and allow them to find the killer's hidden stash or frighten Victor into a mistake once he learned the engraved watch left at the murder scene returned home.

Birdie had not found the savage weapon, and guessed it long ago disposed. Without that vital evidence, she'd have to rely on the strength of her plan.

Birdie felt certain she and the police could force Victor Gregory into a blunder, exposing himself as the killer. It was all she had. To her, it became a poker game, and she pushed her small pile of chips to the center of the table.

The future of her PI license and remaining a free woman depended on her next move with Roe and Nagle.

CHAPTER THIRTY-SEVEN

Victor Gregory left Reznik's real estate office, rushing past the Uzi-carrying guard and what he guessed were waiting Russian home buyers. Had these families occupied the railcars hidden deep in the Liberty ships' holds? At the sidewalk, he glanced over his shoulder.

No one came after him.

The second guard vanished, no longer stationed at Reznik's front door. Victor guessed Reznik summoned the burly sentry for a rebuke over the uninvited intrusion. If Lev Reznik intended retribution, the two hefty Russians would have already hauled his weighted-down body far out to the cold Atlantic. Victor knew Reznik stored dead enemies among the hungry coastal sharks.

Pleased with himself, he'd accomplished what he set out to do. Nagle no longer had a hold on him. There had not been a job for him in the city's organized crime unit. The cop's threat to expose Victor to Reznik had been defused and reversed. Victor persuaded the Russian to manipulate Nagle into a trap and kill the troublesome cop—a task he looked forward to.

Patches of sunlight broke through coastal haze as he walked along the busy Surf Avenue. The promised peaceful relaxation from the salty mist of ocean air and cries of gulls drew Victor close to the water's pounding surf. Open sky, free of towering high-rise buildings and honking cabs, gave seashore visitors and resident's freedom from New York's hurried life. The simple Brooklyn beach community's fate laid in the hands of Reznik. Coney Island and Brighton Beach's beautiful ocean views would soon belong to displaced Soviet Jews. Already, Reznik Real Estate signs marked many impoverished areas.

Victor's personal transformation expanded, growing his cybernetic senses—unrelenting choruses of voices and visions battled within his head, perceiving outcomes of events yet to come. At the onset, he relied on the harmonic vibrations of the Tibetan meditation bowl to place him in a relaxing trance, providing intimate peace. Its soothing tones offered divine guidance, and, in time, his orderly life succumbed to its hypnotic incantations—controlling him.

He'd hoped Malda would join in his discovery of enlightenment. Instead, she'd ridiculed his daily practice as witchcraft and pandering to demons. Her Midwest church upbringing constrained her, preventing shared enrichment.

While he struggled, failing auditions, she'd grown her fledgling career, landing minor Broadway roles. In time, only obvious pity held their waning relationship together. He foresaw it, appraising Malda long before she'd announced romantic interest in a much older Sid Breen. He gripped the leather satchel slung over his shoulder, feeling the shape of the Seneca chief's war axe. Could he part with the weapon which gave him strength and confidence as Abraham's test of faith—parting with his only son?

Meditation created his genesis of new understanding. In the beginning, his mind formless and empty in a darkness, viewed a light separating him from blackness. Spiritual and divine, they were not; his ability to raise the dead, as Lazarus had risen, failed.

There would be more transcending as intellectual vision matured. A higher power bestowed him gifts to feel and see thoughts long before they'd formed—why were Reznik's not revealed? Did the Russian block him?

Rotten fish and decayed seaweed broke Victor's reverie. His planned calming stroll took him off course, far from Reznik's office.

Coney Island's seashore and faded wood boardwalk stretched past rows of hibernating plywood covered concessions and idle thrill rides. Large, flamboyant, colorful signs marked home to absent vendors laying claim to world famous cotton candy and foot long frankfurters.

Victor's mouth watered, practically tasting the first juicy bite of a Boardwalk Coney schmeared in bittersweet brown mustard. A moment later, he realized it had not been his overcharged imagination. He smelled cooking stew and didn't recall the last time he'd eaten.

Nearby, a haunted house, bumper cars, and a carousel offered to frighten and amuse for a mere quarter of a dollar. Offering queasy stomachs and whiplash to daring riders, a looming wood-framed coaster and a three-hundred-foot parachute jump reached to touch the sky over the lifeless seaside complex.

Besides a few vagrants, he had the giant amusement park to himself—no boisterous children ran in and out with helium balloons tied to their wrists. Here would be a quiet place to ponder. The quicker he eliminated Nagle, the sooner he would ascend to a new promised life. The money found on Reznik's Liberty Ship provided more than enough cash to live far from Reznik and memories of New York and Malda. The bundles of hundred-dollar bills he'd taken were his rainy day fund.

He planned to take a great deal more of the Russian's stash.

Reznik failed to miss the few stacks of bills he'd removed over the past six months. He'd suspected the cash counterfeit, although the paper had the feel and looked the genuine article. He needed years to spread it around with small purchases to evade calling attention to the large bills. Another option, one he hoped to avoid—sell the forged C-notes to street bookies in Queens and The Bronx for a dime on the dollar.

He'd considered purchasing Long Island beach property, unloading it for a nice profit in a year or two, receiving squeaky clean money on the exchange. He suspected Reznik's real estate and jewelry businesses served similar purposes. The Russian took it a step more, importing illegal Russian immigrants, methodically building a base of loyal followers, providing homes and jobs. Victor guessed Reznik completed the deal, supplying necessary legal documents for citizenship.

Victor wouldn't allow Reznik to manipulate his life. Once they're dealing with Nagle complete and the cop buried at sea, he'd separate from the wily Russian.

Reznik's swift agreement to a proposed partnership sent up a red flag. He'd expected resistance and threats. Gossip of the Russian's past varied from being a defrocked priest to have been the only man to have escaped the brutal Soviet prison, Black Dolphin. Neither rumor mattered. The cagy Russian would not be trusted.

The day which began with promising sunshine faded, turning the sublime sky into gray, threatening gloom. Locals he spotted strolling the boardwalk, and sandy beach vanished, no doubt detecting the day's quick about-face. Large raindrops struck the wood deck with a dull snap. The pleasant beauty of the morning disappeared, replaced by the menacing face of a chilling, wet winter storm. While he searched for shelter near the idle Tilt-A-Whirl, Victor's eye caught slight movement near the boarded-over carousel.

A cloudy reflection flashed across the glass of its ticket booth. The limping man appeared. His coat swayed on his thin frame as he hurried past canvas-covered attractions. Since leaving the guarded fortress of his Russian boss, Victor's senses remained on high alert, ready for anyone. He'd crossed and re-crossed streets several times, walking at a rapid and then slow pace, stopping often, never looking over his shoulder, instead, gazed into drab storefront windows, hoping to catch a glimpse of a tail.

The limping man wrapped his tan raincoat snug against his torso as rain strengthened and ducked into a darkened door of the shuttered carousel. Victor shook off the possibility of a coincidence. Several times in the past few days, he'd spotted the distinct up and down limp. If his stalker worked for Lev Reznik, the Russian already knew of his association with Nagle. Victor suspected the assassin on his trail concealed a weapon inside his long, bulky coat.

There had been plenty of opportunities for a clean kill if his pursuer silenced his weapon. Victor guessed the man knew he'd been spotted and abandoned the tail or it had been Reznik sending a message. Dead, he'd be no use to the Russian in his revenge against Nagle and New York cops. Victor bet his life on it. Reznik could, at any time, send an army of stooges to finish him.

Victor's curiosity bested him, and he couldn't resist learning more about the cripple shadowing him. Was he careless, or did he wish to be seen? Tailing the mystery man—turning the tables, would answer questions. Under the right circumstances, and with the cash Victor had access to; he could turn the limping man into an ally.

The sudden downpour cleared the boardwalk of the few walkers and pigeons, leaving Victor alone to begin his surveillance. In a dry spot near the bumper cars and funny mirrors, he made himself comfortable on a folding chair under an orange-roofed ticket booth. From that position, he remained confident of not being spotted and hoped the carousel lacked a second unseen exit, allowing his mark's escape. In case Reznik had a change of heart and sent one of his Uzi carrying guards, Victor gripped his handgun hidden inside his wet leather jacket.

The hunter becomes the prey.

Rain, carried by heavy wind squalls, continued to pound the midway, threating to flatten gaming booths and food stands. Water gathered in deep puddles, forming streams, washing cigarette butts and gum wrappers flowing past Victor's feet. The surge gained speed, whirling and spinning above a storm drain's iron grating until swallowed and flushed to sea.

Victor's mind wandered back to happier times. Brilliant, shiny horses whirled past as a calliope pumped a hypnotizing melody. A giant Teddy bear rested in his lap. Malda laughed with childish joy, gripping the gold and red stallion's straining neck and flowing yellow mane. Her eyes danced as she spun past, raising and lowering on the leaping horse. Wind blew her hair as she wildly tossed kisses to passer-byes. He'd grabbed life's prized brass ring. Shared love and ambition appeared endless, chasing dreams of stage careers. The carousel slowed. Her raising and lowering limp body sagged over a midnight black stallion. Crimson blood dripped from a thick gash across her slender neck.

A pair of worn and scuffed brown boots splashed into Victor's view.

"Hold on! Put the gun down... please." The intruder stood a foot away.

He spoke in a soft, smooth voice, contradicting his ragged appearance.

Victor lowered his .38 revolver to his lap, staring at the over-coated man. How had he been so careless? For a moment, his eyes left the carousels' door. Could he be an illusion? The figure appeared dry despite heavy blowing rain. The midway had been clear between him and the entry door to the carousel. The crippled man standing near him stood no chance to advance without being spotted.

The visitor pointed to a dry spot under the narrow roof. "Mind if I come in?" He pushed past, not waiting permission.

"What do you want?"

"Relax comrade. I am a poor Gypsy owning no gun."

"You're following me."

"If I meant to harm you, you would already be in the ground."

Victor tasted the sting of salt water on his lips as a gust carried mists of breaking surf further onto the boardwalk. He'd been in no mood for threats by the gimpy, white-haired tramp.

"The weather is dreadful. We can sit inside and talk... yes?"

Victor shook his head. He allowed himself to be caught off-guard by a crippled, wobbly old man.

"You're hungry... no?" The aged man pulled the belt of his long coat tight around his waist.

"You work for Reznik?" Victor sprung the question, hoping to catch the Gypsy off guard.

"Have lunch. Come, you will like."

Victor shrugged and stood, running his right hand over the handle of his holstered revolver. "Someplace dry."

Another squall brought more salty spray, striking Victor walking several paces behind his host as they headed to the boarded-over carrousel.

The carney limped ahead, hobbling up and down, reaching the weathered door and holding it open.

"This chump twister is home," were the last words Victor heard before the crippled, old man slipped inside ahead of him.

The dark entrance could hide an ambush or offer a warm meal a place to shake out his soaked clothes. Victor couldn't recall the last time he'd eaten. His senses failed him. He allowed the lame carney to get close. Could he trust his judgement?

Ducking under the door, Victor entered the dim round room crowded with glassy-eyed, stationary, painted and varnished ponies and stallions floating on a circular stage. Musty air and a dirt floor failed to hold back faint aromas of cooking. The limping man walked ahead toward a cloudy light in the rear of the giant carousel barn.

"Most call me Otter. This way."

The old man swung his peg leg, with a dull thump, to the carousel's elevated wood deck and vanished behind a wall of mirrors circling the hub of the amusement ride. Victor hesitated and stopped, pulling his revolver, expecting Otter led him into a trap.

"Fish and chicken soup—good and hot." The shout echoed from deep in the boarded-over carousel.

Victor proceeded, gripping his handgun in front of him, listening for telltale signs of anyone approaching in the near blackness. In four years, he had not drawn his service revolver. Within the last hour, he'd drawn it twice. The unmistakable smell of cooking cabbage and dill strengthened. He refused to move closer, retreating. Why did he allow the cripple to lead him here? Years of patrolling New York's subway tunnels enhanced his night vision. If anyone appeared, he'd shoot, claiming self-defense.

Heavy rain rattled the corrugated tin roof. Cold dripping water bounced off his leather uniform jacket. His mind played tricks. A spotlight snapped on, lighting a small room and table.

"Russian Gypsies make soup from anything."

Victor played along. Lowering his pistol, he pressed it behind his leg and walked toward the light.

"You will not need your gun." Otter turned his back to Victor.

Victor approached the shaggy-haired Gypsy standing over a potbelly stove, stirring a steaming, dented copper pot. A pegboard wall, crowded with greasy tools, separated the kitchen from a cot and a row of clothes hanging on hooks of nails. A half-empty pint of Four Roses whiskey sat on a shelf.

"We alone?" Victor asked. "... and why should I trust you?"

"There are two of us, and I have not taken the lives of innocent people. Can you say the same?"

Victor hesitated and slipped his firearm into his service belt, curious to learn what his dining companion knew.

Otter pointed to a card table set with two tarnished spoons and an open bottle of ketchup. "Sit."

Victor pulled a stool close and swung his leg over. "Otter... that's your name?"

The Gypsy twirled his arm toward a new varnished midnight black stallion suspended from the roof's trusses. "That is my creation." He lifted his trousers, displaying an intricately carved peg leg. "Otter, like the animal. I give shape and life to wood, unlike those who destroy."

Victor's eyes never blinked nor left the dark stallion—from it, blood dripped, hanging suspended, floating overhead.

Heavy drops of rain splattered on the floor near the table, snapping Victor's image.

Otter pushed a dented, galvanized bucket over an uneven wood floor, catching the steady droplets. The old man's dry overcoat swung open enough for Victor to spot a leather strap falling from his host's shoulder. It carried a weapon or a money pouch or supported his wooden leg. Gypsie's habits defied what eccentric New Yorkers termed strange. He'd allowed the down cast tramp to lure him into the shutdown carrousel, into a trap. Had he lost his edge?

Before Victor looked for a way out, white bowls filled with steaming fish and chicken soup arrived, and a plate of crusty brown bread followed, sliding on the table's oilcloth.

Victor grabbed a thick slice while keeping his eyes on Otter. Did the man he ate with exist or was he a part of the strangeness taking over his life?

"Dip in bowl... is how gypsies eat."

He followed the old man, immersing broken bread into thick broth, eating it from dripping fingers.

Otter swallowed, wiping the back of his hand across his mouth as he did.

"Americans waste so much, throwing good bread in the garbage."

Victor pushed his bowl to the side. "Why follow me?"

"You work for Reznik."

"I watch his ship, that's all."

"He trusts no one."

"We have an understanding."

"To him, words mean nothing." Otter dropped his bread into the bowl. "He uses blood and iron to get his way."

"You don't know me."

The old man pulled wet strands of hair from his face, staring across the table into Victor's eyes. "I know much about you."

"I'm a transit cop. Lots of people think they know me."

"As the dead shoe clerk in Hell's Kitchen?"

"You're barking up the wrong tree."

Otter leaned, rocking his stool sideward reaching into a drawer of a workbench removing a small, bone handle knife.

"You left this."

CHAPTER THIRTY-EIGHT

The four-story building looked more like a refuge for indigents than the home of New York's Mid-Town Precinct. Birdie's cab ride gave her time to organize what she hoped to be a convincing "coming clean" explanation. Her fate rested with Owen Roe and Joe Nagle. The planted evidence, setting-up Victor Gregory, was all she had and would be placed in the hands of the two cops. Hopefully, finding the killer of Mary Clary and Sid Breen would gain her absolution for the sins of withholding and removing evidence.

Two additional white lies would get the ball rolling toward his capture and her hefty fee.

A pocket watch found with Mary Clary's personal items in the morgue was in position. Although the scarred inscription unreadable, she believed it belonged to the killer and intended it as a back-up to trap Victor Gregory, planting it with the transit cop's killing mementos. She hoped its mysterious arrival in his secret stash would disrupt his calm demeanor, forcing panic and maybe an error.

The prospect of a marriage proposal from Owen Roe loomed in her mind since her visit to Mort's Jewelry. Mort let it slip, Owen Roe had bought the engagement ring they'd chosen a year ago at the peak of their love affair. Once the case closed, Roe would no longer view her as a rival and pop the question—she knew it. She'd make the stubborn, hard-nosed cop sweat. A small amount of payback, playing hard to get and letting him squirm, would put the arrogant cop in his place. She was about to present him with a gift-wrapped capture of a vicious murderer, which had the mayor and his cronies breathing down the backs of the eighteenth precinct.

After dropping her change and cab receipt into her purse, she stepped under scaffolding stretching the length of the gray stone fortress. She had taken the trouble and called ahead, hoping the desk sergeant passed her message upstairs to Roe and Nagle.

The moment she entered the lobby, a thin, blue-shirted officer stood and looked away from a group of uniformed cops clustered near his desk and waved her to the staircase. He appeared familiar. She wanted to call him by name, hoping to ease her anxiety; however, it had been a long time since her last visit. She'd go upstairs, as if expected, hoping the signal indicated her right to pass.

Birdie rested her hand on the cannonball sized newel. Were her schemes about to explode in her face? Why did she come to them? She should dictate terms, beginning with a less intimidating environment, at least one not so bland and tasteless. The public library or a Greenwich coffee shop would have been a better choice. Their initial meeting, to review the murder case, had been a simple picnic in a cozy park in Manhattan, relaxed, away from the antiseptic halls and rooms of the station house.

For her to show up, hat in hand, at police central gave the appearance of wrongdoing. She'd admit to minor interference and slightly stepping out of bounds in her role as a PI. Because of her client's friendship with the mayor, there had been an implied right for her to take liberties in solving the murder. She was on her own. With Sid Breen dead, there'd be no one to intercede with city hall. Her best and only leverage—she'd found the axe-wielding killer.

A wave of panic passed through her, forcing her to sit on the grimy black and white tiled stairs. Were the two detectives waiting to interrogate her under a hot spotlight, like an old James Cagney cop movie? She faced the possibility of arrest and could spend the night in the basement lockup. The uniformed officers surrounding the sergeant's desk no longer stared and returned to their discussion. She felt trapped. Could it be an act to lure her upstairs? Birdie propped her elbows on her knees and contemplated her decision—she wanted to leave.

"Would you like to come up?" a voice asked.

Birdie turned to find Joe Nagle standing above her.

"I forgot how cheery this place is." Birdie eased her throbbing hips from the cold stairs.

"Long time, no see," Nagle said, sticking a cigarette into a corner of his lips.

"Been busy."

"Guess it's tough losing your only client."

She recognized the cop's indifference written on his smug face. Over the past year, he'd become more like Roe. Ignoring his brashness, she'd force herself to stay composed, reminding herself of the big favor she needed from the two.

"You got my message."

"I'm all ears," Nagle said, striking a match.

"It'll wait 'till we're upstairs."

Nagle turned and waved an arm for her to follow.

The climb to the fourth floor had been painful, and her hip throbbed with each step, as if the stage rigging, once again, lay on top of her, crushing her. Catching her breath, Birdie forced herself to block out the numbing pain. She stopped and looked for Owen Roe through a haze of cigarette and cigar smoke in the cramped detective room. Nagle disappeared briefly, returning, dragging a heavy wooden chair.

"We've turned up nothing on the dead actress and Breen. That's why you're here?" the cop asked, sliding the chair between his and Roe's vacant desk.

"I know who the killer is."

Nagle stopped rearranging stacked file folders on his desk.

"Can I speak to you and Roe?" Birdie asked.

"He's not in. You can talk to me."

She felt a pang of disappointment, hoping to see Roe's face as she handed them the solved case. She'd bet the last dollar in her wallet he'd kept the recently purchased engagement ring locked in his desk.

"I'll wait." As her words left her mouth, she noticed Nagle take a hard swallow.

"It might be awhile."

Birdie looked around the squad room, wanting to spend little time in the dismal surroundings. Should she return when Roe was present?

"You think you know something, or you wouldn't be here," Nagle said.

"He's a city transit officer named Victor Gregory." She blurted, relieved to get the words out.

"Evidence?" Nagle asked.

"We're neighbors. I saw him with an axe matching the sketch in the coroner's report." Birdie lied and waited to tell her next. She knew it was typical for detectives and uniformed cops to plant evidence and use strong-arm tactics to gain information and confessions. This would be no different. A small fabrication to take a cold-blooded killer off the street would not cause her to lose sleep. All she'd seen pointed to the transit cop. His lean athletic figure running from the graveyard matched the description of the cop she'd passed leaving the morgue.

"You got a good look?"

"I did," she said, nodding her head. "He took it into his house, a boat near me in Sunset Park."

"You're sure?"

"I wasn't until I chased him at the cemetery."

"You took your time to tell us."

Birdie nodded and forced herself to lock eyes with the detective. Like most cops, he studied faces looking for signs of lying.

Joe Nagle remained quiet, staring at her.

She knew his ploy. He'd remain silent and wait her out, allowing her nervousness to betray her. Liars tended to continue talking, rationalizing the story they've told. It was a common interrogation trick she'd used herself.

Nagle smiled. "What did you see?"

"He wiped the blade with a rag and took it inside. I watched him last night."

"It had to be late. You're sure?"

"There's a light over his houseboat. I saw it."

"I'll get a warrant for a search." Nagle stood and put a hand on Birdie's shoulder.

She smiled, pleased with the warrant. Once Roe and Nagle rummaged through Victor Gregory's home, they'd discover the victim's belongings, more than enough for an arrest.

"What should I do?" she asked.

"We'll take it from here."

Birdie leaned forward, touching Nagle's arm. "I can help."

"Let us handle this." Nagle butted out the remains of his cigarette and waved a palm in the air.

Again, she found herself on the outside, relegated to the bench, put in her place and dismissed from the game just as she had been from the Broadway stage. She heard the detective's words through a haze. Spoken as if she were a disciplined child.

"And I'd stay somewhere else for the next few days. For your safety."

Birdie shifted in the chair knowing she faced hours of grueling questions, beginning with her theft of the victim's cape. From habit, she grabbed her purse, feeling the bulk of her .38 bump against her thigh. She could take care of herself. How dare he think her defenseless, or worse, incapable. She'd survived the collapse of stage lights and rigging, crushing her under a mass of steel and glass, not to forget seven years as a Pinkerton detective. Instead of the relief she'd expected, she felt anger, brushed off the case, not asked to take part in the search and arrest instead, told to go into hiding. She handed Roe and Nagle a solved murder, delivered on a silver platter, and she's excluded from the grand finale and the mayor's eventual acclaim in every newspaper and television news show in the city.

She spent the next ninety minutes detailing her involvement in the case, admitting to evidence removal and withholding information from the two detectives. Birdie hid her surprise as Nagle didn't flinch or react with a stern lecture, followed by her arrest for the admitted infractions. Instead, he made notes and occasionally interrupted. Finished, she watched Nagle close his notebook and smile.

"We could charge you with a number of crimes."

"I handed you a killer."

"That's why we'll keep this between us."

Birdie silently let out a deep breath and nodded.

"One condition," he said.

"Name it?"

"Drop the case and stay out of it."

"Just like that?"

"Stay out, and we'll keep you out of jail, and... don't come here anymore. The less you're seen, the better."

Before protesting, Birdie stopped. She had gotten a break for a small price. Sid Breen's estate, soon to be controlled by Jark, and he'd issue her a generous check. She gained the satisfaction, knowing she'd taken a killer off the street. How many more would he have killed while wearing a transit officer's uniform? Jark, on the other hand, what did he have? His father and sister were dead because of her refusal to involve the police. Her pride had superseded reasoning, and Jark's family paid.

Told to stay out of the arrest and allow Roe and Nagle to grab her notoriety was painful but deserved, but she had no intention of running and hiding. Her revolver would remain within arm's reach, tucked under her pillow. There could be no way Victor Gregory connected her to his arrest. She doubted they needed her testimony. Most likely, the detectives would list her as an anonymous source, shielding her from taking part in the capture of the axe killer.

Waving down a taxi proved difficult near the precinct house. Apparently, none of New York's hacks thought it profitable to cruise past the rundown police station. After venturing a short block east, toward the city's pricey hotels and high-rise offices, she stepped into the busy street, waving and shouting at the first yellow cab she spotted.

As she pulled the rear door open, she glanced across the street, noticing the empty parking enforcement cart parked in an alley near several upscale hotels. At that moment, a uniformed New York City meter-maid stepped from The Ridgemont's brass revolving door and adjusted her small bowler hat and side bag.

Birdie froze, not believing who followed the buxom redhead to the sidewalk.

CHAPTER THIRTY-NINE

The early morning downpour, which had swept in from the chilly Atlantic, mellowed to a salty drizzle as Victor Gregory slammed the rickety door of the carousel house. Walking from the shut-down amusement park, it struck him odd the carney's clothes remained dry despite the heavy rain. More astonishing—how had the slow, elderly man approached unseen?

The encounter with Otter left him with an uncomfortable chill in his bones, sensing the miserable cripple belonged somewhere in another unearthly realm. Victor accepted heaven and hell sharing space on earth, existing equally in multiple planes and dimensions. He'd seen it and acknowledged it as he did the invisible light and radio waves bombarding the planet daily.

Where did the carney belong—heaven or hell?

Victor glanced over his shoulder, wondering how much the Russian gypsy knew. Did Otter work for Reznik like so many in Brighton Beach? How long had the ragged vagrant followed him? Vagrants overtook the city, making their homes in alleys, subway terminals, and storefronts, becoming part of the daily landscape, rivaling the cities' growing rat population.

The image of the Hell's Kitchen shoe store and drunken tramp, curled in a filthy, ragged sleeping bag, jumped into Victor's thoughts.

It had been Otter, huddling in the shop's recessed entrance and days later, rescuing him from the storm and offering lunch. What kind of messenger did this?

The late-working redhead saw his face at the murder scene and needed silenced. After slashing her throat, he slipped the knife into the beggar's palm, closing his grimy fingers over its carved bone handle. He'd stuffed the dead clerk's billfold and costume jewelry next to the foul-smelling tramp. Even though he bent close, Victor didn't notice the vagrant's face buried inside the sleeping bag.

Otter's return of the knife puzzled him along with the connection to Reznik's Liberty ship? Had it been a subtle way to let him know nothing happened on the docks without the Russian boss's knowledge?

Victor took a last glance around the subway terminal, relieved not to see the limping carney, and boarded the northbound train leaving Coney Island and Brighton Beach. He'd detour home, instead of his job in Manhattan's Penn Station, to make sure the shamrock button and diamond pearl earring remained hidden. The Russian gypsy spooked him. Had he entered his home finding the prized souvenirs?

Keeping remembrances of his first kill had been an error. The historic pipe tomahawk had become magical to Victor, bestowing on him the bravery of the great Seneca leader. It, too, would return to the Metropolitan Museum's archives, rejoining the chief's belongings.

With the leather satchel tight against his chest, his fingers ran over the axe's form, caressing the weapon's handle and blade. Before the revered weapon rested, he intended to honor it, swinging the war hatchet in ultimate victory.

One last act he looked forward to completing.

The twenty-one-minute train ride and short walk delivered him home in time to spot a dark-hooded figure leaving his houseboat. Victor broke into a sprint, chasing through the boatyard. The high-stepping sprinter hurdled stacks of board lumber and pools of water until reaching the maze of warehouses surrounding the nearby Brooklyn Army Terminal's massive complex and millions of square feet of storage.

After losing sight of the intruder, Victor slowed to catch his breath, hoping to spot the runner in the acres of parked employee's cars. Whoever he'd chased, moved with grace, appearing to glide over the loading yards rubble. On the hike home, splashing through the rain-saturated ground, he grabbed the moist brown envelope sticking from his mailbox. Why did he react, chasing the messenger? Reznik sent a paid lackey to deliver the packet. The old carney came to mind.

Once he'd rung out the cuffs of his uniform pants, Victor stepped into the houseboat's galley and immediately recognized the scent. The familiar scent could not have survived the burning incense used during his meditation after Birdie unexplainably fled the previous evening. Her generous use of perfume, Evening in Paris, made a recent unwelcome and unannounced appearance in his home, confirming the negative aura he'd detected. The distinct, musty, floral aroma might as well have been a blood trail leading to his neighbor's home.

Could she be watching, peeking from her window as he'd done several nights ago as she showered? Would she tail him? He'd guessed her a loner, detached from society as he since losing Malda.

The company of others no longer mattered. Spirits, although unknown, guided his new life. Sacred signs and wonders came in dreams and thought. He'd evolved into a power, foretelling happenings, growing superior to biblical prophets, attaining a higher order of being, demanding worship. Death no longer stalked him.

He had ascended.

Had Birdie returned to his home, hoping to reacquaint herself, rectifying the earlier night's disappointment, resuming what she'd begun inside her steamy shower with the drop of a towel?

The rain-dotted envelope laid on the coffee table. Victor slid the edge of a letter opener under the sealed flap.

The awful spelling and grammar on the typewritten note left no doubt it came from the hands of Reznik. His instructions, to prevent monitoring of his phone conversations, were simple—use a pay phone, calling ten numbers listed in the message. One of the given would find Reznik.

Before slipping on dry slacks, he thought again of his neighbor's unwelcome break-in. How secure was his stash of money, earrings and shamrock button? He'd dispose of it all and the old gypsy. He couldn't afford a live witness to the killing of the shoe clerk. A tragic accident would claim Otter. They would find him crushed in the open gearing of the spinning carousel.

Everything appeared normal after opening the antique dresser cabinet and its hidden slot. Victor undid the braided cord of the Crown Royal bag, shaking it over his bed. The diamond earring and silver button slid out, dropping to the blanket, laying side by side.

He'd worried needlessly.

Something caught stuck in the sack's small closure. He gave it a shake. Could it be an illusion? A pocket watch tumbled to the blanket. The scrapes and scars he'd inflicted on the time peace, after Malda's desertion, left no doubt it had been the one he'd carelessly left at the scene of his first killing. Can it be an ironic twist? Fate meddling in his well-organized life. Why had the Coney Island cripple returned the knife used to kill the shoe clerk? Topping off things, his missing Bulova shows up, mocking him, ticking in rhythmic, perfect time. Something it failed at before.

Trickery or delusion—but no coincidence. Not unnoticed, there had been an attempt to tail him leaving the funeral service. Could Otter or the pushy detective Nagle be behind this?

Victor laid back on his bed. He must stay calm. Several deep breaths brought relaxation, oxygen stimulated his brain, rousing his senses.

It didn't take long for clarity to arrive.

Birdie's soft fragrance, which greeted him moments ago, hung in the room. She'd betrayed him, like Judas. His neighbor entered and searched his home, violating his well-guarded privacy—otherwise, how did the missing pocket watch return? She'd misled him, as Nagle had, taking advantage of his desire for friendship and to work as a New York detective.

The pocket watch was left deliberately, trapping him, a set-up to be found by police.

He smiled, her feeble ploy would instead snare the hunter. His turn came to return the favor personally. Birdie had been no different from the innocent shoe clerk. He'd repay her in kind and wait in his neighbor's home. Her welcome to the neighborhood would put the finishing touches on his mission.

CHAPTER FORTY

After reaching her cab, disbelief gripped Birdie as she stood in the street dodging and side-stepping midmorning traffic. She refused to believe she watched Owen Roe trail Hollis Gail from the hotel. The flirty meter maid had been the reason for her and Roe's recent breakup. Whatever went on between them in the past became ancient history. Birdie had been willing to swallow her pride, forget and forgive the arrogant detective she unexplainably loved.

She understood cop thinking. Public bravado concealed his shy tenderness reserved for her and close friends. The toughness she accepted. The rough edges attracted her. A New York City homicide investigator was not expected to be an altar boy.

The meter maid turned back to Roe, modeling her hand, admiring the recent sparkle on her ring finger. Despite distance and traffic, it had been obvious Roe had new plans for the engagement ring Birdie once cherished.

She gripped the yellow cab's door handle and ducked inside, shamed, hoping to escape unnoticed. How could she allow herself to believe Roe's feelings for her returned? She'd held the door open for him to re-enter. Was she that desperate? She'd lied to herself, believing Roe changed. The run of bad luck in her career and personal life officially hit bottom with a solid clunk.

Roe and his giant ego rapidly advanced from uniformed street cop to detective, and thanks to her; he'd close the current high-profile case and receive a bump in rank, further feeding his exaggerated importance. Her dream to marry and a home with a grass yard in Jersey shattered as painfully as the overhead stage rigging had collapsed, crushing her years ago.

She'd rehearsed the moment. The two, bundled, cuddled under a soft, warm blanket, enjoying a Christmas carriage ride in snow-covered Central Park—he casually held her hand and slipped the ring on her finger, asking....

"Where to?" the cabby shouted over blaring horns.

Birdie shook off the shattered fairy tale. Slamming the cab's door only to see the two embrace had been a body blow. She'd recover, having taken worse, always bouncing back.

"Brooklyn, Sunset Park." She turned in her seat, taking a last look at Owen Roe and Hollis Gail.

Birdie slumped, falling back into the Checker Cab's cold vinyl seat. She'd allowed herself to believe Roe shared similar feelings. She had jumped to conclusions after a visit to Mort's Gems and Jewels, learning her former boyfriend purchased the ring they chose.

There would be no tears or self-pity. She owed her client a case report, an itemized list of expenses and, of course, the final bill. The fee and promised bonus would restart her life, escaping Reznik's boatyard. Returning to the civilization of Manhattan's Upper West Side would be her consolation.

Although she'd handed the solved murder case to Roe and Nagle, she deserved the satisfaction of watching Victor Gregory hauled away in cuffs and being shoved into a patrol car. It had been more to do about vindictiveness than with police procedure—something she'd brought on herself.

Nagle had most likely obtained a search warrant, briefing Roe the minute he stepped into the office. She anticipated the two cops inviting all television, radio and newspaper reporters in the five boroughs. She'd watch, unseen, not hiding, as Nagle suggested. Of course, the arrest would happen early tomorrow, in plenty of time for the morning news. Owen Roe and Joe Nagle would enjoy accolades from the mayor—shining heroes, basking in the city's giant limelight while she served penance.

Her cab bumped onto the rutted road, pulling into the boat yard, inching past staggered rows of lumber wrapped by gray canvas. Birdie unlatched her purse, gripping her handgun for a moment before releasing her hold. Better safe than sorry, although she believed Victor Gregory had no reason to suspect she'd entered his home, planting the watch alongside his victim's belongings.

Tomorrow, an early morning knock would end his murder spree. Nagle knew of the dresser's hidden compartments; but she hoped the search turned up the murder axe, cinching the case, placing a noose around the transit cop's neck, rendering other evidence less important, mitigating her tampering.

* * * * *

Birdie sulked in her darkened room, unable to find pleasure, sipping whiskey and nibbling a stale sandwich alone, celebrating. Was it a sign of age or her injuries rebelling against New York's damp nights? She'd pretended there'd be no self-pity over the rejection. Sleep came between sobs.

Her sound nap ended with an abrupt faint rattle of the entry door. Half asleep, she pushed open the sliding partition and peeked into the next room, expecting the light on over the stove. She'd left that morning facing possible arrest after confessing theft of evidence and may have forgotten it. On tiptoes in the dark, she stumbled over the purse she'd thrown earlier. Somewhere, her new shoes laid, the ones worn to impress Owen Roe. The Italian, high heels became land mines waiting to topple her.

It was over, and emotions ran bittersweet. She finished her first murder case as a PI and uncovered the killer living under her nose. On the other hand, she'd not see Jark again.

In darkness, Birdie reached for a lamp. A slight gasp broke the silence. From behind, a gloved hand slapped over her face, covering her nose and mouth, yanking her off balance.

She attempted to twist away from an arm, wrapping her waist with the firmness of an iron vice. The taller attacker had the advantage and strengthened his grip, pulling her tight into his chest. If he intended to kill her, she'd already be dead. The situation needed calming. If robbery or rape were planned, she had little time. Carelessness led her to walk into a dark room, leaving her purse and handgun on the floor. Left with only instinct, she must stay alert for an opportunity to escape.

"Feel it?" her assailant asked. Warm breath touched her ear at the same instant the sharp point of the blade pressed at her side.

She nodded. His rough skin brushed her neck.

The hands gripping her face and waistline loosened, allowing her to draw in needed air. If the knife had punctured her, adrenaline kept back the pain and terror. Birdie resisted reaching to inspect for blood. She wouldn't risk a move—death most likely followed.

"Think you're smart?" the voice asked, keeping the knife pressed to her ribs.

"Take what you want."

"I plan to. You think you're clever?"

Birdie felt his chest and arms relax, giving an opportunity. She lifted her leg and slammed her bare heel into the top arch of the attacker's foot while spinning to face him. His face remained a blur in the darkness as he swung the knife, grazing her shoulder. Birdie drove her lower palm toward his nose—missing, but making solid contact with his chin, sending him falling back into the kitchen table.

She dove to her purse, hoping to reach her handgun. The kitchen door and roof escape hatch were the only ways out. If he fled, she'd not stand in the robber's way. Birdie wished to survive. The dark figure came at her. This time he kicked, catching her arm, dislodging her grip on the .38. To her surprise and relief, he turned and ran.

The thin metal door and latch gave way to his shoulder and body weight, crashing open. Birdie changed her mind, her anger flared. She had a shot at the running man if she acted fast and found her revolver. With elbows braced on the boat's deck rail, she rushed her aim and fired. In the dim light of a distant streetlamp, the runner stumbled but continued. Unsure of a hit, Birdie raised up and staggered barefoot, looking for a blood trail in the parking lot.

Few footprints appeared on hard-packed ground. She looked toward Victor Gregory's home. She couldn't identify her attacker, but was sure it had been him. The yard remained deserted. Sunset Park inhabitants were accustomed to late-night gunshots. Birdie did an about face and noticed her ruined blood-soaked blouse. She wouldn't know the damage until she returned home ending the nightmare. It took all of her strength to force her cold feet and trembling body home. Tomorrow would be a new day after a homemade patching of her injured arm.

* * * * *

Few diners glanced from their plates and newspapers when Victor limped into Gig's. He rubbed his jaw several times, feeling the ache from Birdie's punch. Satisfaction arrived after he patted the satchel hanging from his shoulder. The bullet meant for him ripped through the leather and had been stopped by the axe's blade. Not only did he misjudge his neighbor, but he's underestimated the power of the Seneca Chief's weapon. Next to it, inside the bag, laid a mushroom-shaped slug.

Although nothing in the crowded eatery seemed out of order, he could draw the axe in an instant—like a gunslinger clearing leather. The thought brought back his shaken confidence. Regulars squatted in their usual places and the few unfamiliar faces appeared harmless, gripping knives and forks feeding their faces. Bypassing the counter and tables, Victor walked to the empty phone booth, confident, ready to carry out his plan.

A round fluorescent light flickered overhead and lit as he dropped onto the low wooden bench. He caught no eyes following him but suspected the strange old carney close by—showing up despite Victor's precautions.

Victor laid Reznik's note flat on the booth's ledge and looked over the list of ten typewritten phone numbers, recognizing the Brooklyn exchanges, Henry, Mayflower and Chelsea and Cathedral belonging to Manhattan. One of them would find Reznik, according to the message, and he had thirty minutes.

The drop of the nickel into the slot came with a louder than usual clang. Did someone watch? He'd cornered himself with only one way out. The limping man, Otter, could not be far off. Had Reznik set a trap? Would men armed with Tommy-guns crash through the dinner doors and riddle his body with a barrage of bullets?

On the sixth call, a Manhattan exchange answered.

Reznik spoke. "Tell Nagle five million dollars of undetectable American counterfeit money is on board the Liberty ship."

"That's it?"

"It is being moved by truck tomorrow night at ten. You overheard me. That is how you know."

"He'll be suspicious."

Reznik laughed. "Do you fish?"

"No."

"Our man, Nagel, is a prison bitch. Show him the money you stole from my ship. He will bite."

Victor remained silent, watching the diner's entrance. What did Reznik know, and how did the gypsy fit?

"Give Nagle my money to inspect," Reznik said. "It will be bait, comrade."

"Ten tomorrow night, it...." Victor had been cut off.

The phone buzzed in his ear. Sweat rolled from his chin, dripping to the wedge-shaped ledge he propped an elbow on. Did the unwelcome gypsy carney stare at him from the street? The face, blocked by the flashing neon window sign, could belong to anyone. Victor ran from the restaurant to the dark street, looking for the limping man.

The road remained deserted.

If anyone watched, they hid behind closed windows of the darkened apartments lining each side of the narrow street. Victor knew firsthand that his body would not be the first or last to lay bleeding to death in the dock area of a rough and tumble Brooklyn.

Returning to the boatyard, Victor spotted a half dozen tanker trucks loading fuel oil into the hulking Liberty ship. Unlike past weeks, today its decks blazed with lights and longshoremen lowering crates into the same holds where he discovered the empty rail passenger cars.

Victor was confident the cargo ship headed to a Russian port and another load of escaping refugees. He had no doubt Reznik planned a double cross. The cagy Russian agreed too readily to cut Victor in on his smuggling scheme. Whatever happened tonight at the docks and on board ship involved a trap for both he and Nagle—that he was confident of.

Victor had plans of his own. Like the white knight he'd discovered in the bowels of the ship—he'd strike, seemingly from nowhere.

CHAPTER FORTY-ONE

Early the following day, Victor pushed past commuters, and a trio of violinist's struggling to play over the clamor and rumble of the 59th Street terminal's departing and arriving trains.

His badge and uniform spoke authority to thousands of faceless New Yorkers filling the dungeon-like caverns of the city's mass transit system. Dreary faces shuffled on and off subway cars, wrapped up in their daily serving of grim news supplied by papers whose purpose was to sell vacuum cleaners and laundry soap.

Four wooden phone booths lined a back wall near the terminal's stairs. After a quick glance, Victor relaxed, relieved to find them vacant. In fifteen minutes, detective Nagle would call. The first door folded open, reeking of urine. It had been the one Nagle selected. Victor examined the round, worn seat and dropped into it. From the enclosed space, he felt secure, isolated from the masses packing the Brooklyn terminal. His bullet hole damaged satchel hung at his side, reminding him he'd become immune to harm. Besides the war axe, he carried the bait, a bundled stack of hundred-dollar bills—counterfeit, but flawless, according to Lev Reznik. He could take the money and run with a full day's head start on the Russian. There were plenty of places to turn the forged currency into the genuine thing. He could be in Canada this evening.

After checking his watch, he had time for one call and dropped a nickel into the slot, dialing Malda's apartment, curious if anyone answered. Did the police stake out her place, hoping to catch her killer? Instinct told him it had been Birdie looking down at him from the window on that morning. After three rings, he hung up, slamming the grimy handset to the hook.

The expected call from Nagle would come in minutes. They would set the trap to do away with the pesky, rogue detective. The cop carried a grudge against Reznik, and he'd bend and break the law in his vendetta for revenge. This morning's phone conversation acted as a setup to assassinate Nagle. Victor confessed to himself he looked forward to swinging the historic axe, bringing down the self-important conman who manipulated him with promises of advancement into New York's elite organized crime unit.

Jittery and with time on his hands, Victor leaned back in the booth, watching the fast-moving crowd. Someone may have followed him. The Coney Island gypsy more than likely watched. He kicked the booth's door open slightly, darkening the overhead light. Victor knew Reznik saw himself above the law and would kill anyone threating to disrupt his profitable illegal activities.

A sharp rapping came inches from Victor Gregory's ear.

"I need the phone," someone shouted.

"Use the other ones," Victor said.

"There're full."

Victor pushed the door open, allowing the intruder to see the badge pinned to his leather jacket.

"Shaved the beard... huh?"

"Got tired of it," Victor said pushing the door.

"I should cuff you now," Detective Joe Nagle said.

"Take it easy."

"Your neighbor's a private eye. She told me everything."

"Don't know what you're talking about."

"She found what you took from the Clary girl in your home."

"Who told you this?"

"Your neighbor showed up at the precinct... said you killed the actress and Sid Breen, and I should search your home."

"That's why you're here?" Victor asked, stepping from the phone booth. "... to arrest me?"

"There a reason I shouldn't?"

"You won't find anything at my place, and yeah, I got a million of 'em," Victor answered. "Want the Russian or me? He's the big cheese."

"I'm think'n."

"Arrest me; you lose Reznik and his illegal business fronts."

"What you got?" Nagle asked.

"Here?"

"I don't have time." Nagle stepped close, shoving Victor into the booth.

Victor Gregory held his open palm in front of his chest. "I'm reaching in my bag." As he did, his hand touched the Indian war axe. For an instant, he considered the pleasure of a public execution performed before hundreds of unknowing commuters, just as John Wilkes Booth had unleashed tragedy on America.

Instead, he gripped a wrapped bundle of hundred-dollar bills, handing them to Nagle.

"Reznik's moving counterfeit money off the freighter tonight."

"Yeah."

"He bought millions from the Germans." Victor Gregory smiled for the first time and tapped the axe inside his leather case. "Nazi's ran out of planes before they could dump them over Europe. Jewish prisoners engraved the plates, thinking they'd save their families. Believe me; they're perfect and undetectable."

"Why move 'em?"

"Reznik's got a buyer."

Joe Nagle held the wrapped bills. "You got these... how?"

"Job perk. He'll never know."

Nagle stuffed the bundles into his overcoat. "If he does...."

"You worry too much." Victor pushed his way past the cop, leaving the phone booth. "Ten tonight, a truck marked, Romanian Folk Dancers, will park at the dock. Reznik will be there."

"You're sure?"

"I heard him on the phone."

"Stay clear of the freighter," Nagle said. "I'll show after I have someone look at the money. If it looks good, I'll be there."

"The other thing?" Victor asked, gripping the detective's arm.

"What thing?"

"The job with organized crime?"

"For now, it's our secret," Nagle answered, turned and walked away.

Victor took a seat in the booth, scrutinizing the cop climb the stairs. He had played along as if the dangled carrot of a detective shield had been real. The cop was dirty, as he thought. Nagle took the bait, planning to steal the forged money, hiding behind his gold and blue badge.

* * * * *

Nagle knew the transit cop watched. The excitement would wait until he left the train station. For more than a year he'd been patient, anticipating, knowing the Russian hid money onboard ship, safe from a search, protected by the Geneva Convention. Reznik could not claim diplomatic immunity once the counterfeit cash reached the docks. They were on American soil.

CHAPTER FORTY-TWO

Birdie rose early to blasts of ship's horns, bells, and crying seagulls, her routine wake-up calls. She'd dressed in baggy overalls and a long flannel shirt while keeping an eye on Victor's houseboat. Touching her wound, it ached. Gauze bandages and liberal amounts of iodine helped. She wished she could say the same for her blouse and only winter jacket.

The kitchen suffered mild damage and needed a new toaster and night light from Sears and Roebuck. The intruder had taken nothing but bruised her self-confidence. Birdie found it hard to admit, her sharp judgment failed her the past several days. Perhaps she should have taken Joe Nagle's warning and moved. Did she foolishly believe Victor Gregory remained unaware of what she'd done inside his home? If it had been the transit cop, she'd beaten him. She'd stay put—at least one more day.

Roe and Nagle, accompanied with a bevy of police cruisers and news trucks, would arrive any moment armed with a search warrant. The earring and silver shamrock button Victor Gregory removed from Mary Clary's body, along with the planted pocket watch, would be uncovered. With luck, they would find the murder weapon, rendering the evidence she tampered with less relevant.

The pain and irritation of not personally putting on the cuffs and shoving the ruthless killer into the squad car would fade in time. She'd given up that satisfaction, hopeful of favorable treatment from the arresting detectives—overlooking her criminal transgressions during the murder case they unofficially shared.

Gratification came knowing she'd soon bank a sizeable, hard-earned fee. Debts, accumulated during her lengthy hospitalization, would be her first order of business. A down payment on a Manhattan condo with a roof patio followed. She'd recline on an overstuffed lounge, staring at an endless universe, pondering the derailing of her once well-planned life. After that, a suitable office for her investigative services—possibly subleasing a suite in Sid Breen's former office. Birdie liked the sound of that each time it crossed her mind.

Despite news coverage, the word on the street would spread: it had been her cracking the Breen killing. Mercifully, life on the Brooklyn waterfront ended. The smell of decaying fish and tugs pushing the city's rubbish to sea already faded in her mind. She'd return to the glamor of the Theater District, where she belonged. No longer part of the trendy Broadway crowd, but near bright lights and excitement. Once again, walking the Great White Way, absorbing the energy and excitement.

After the third cup of coffee, Birdie wrapped a blanket over her shoulders, venturing outside, watching for the dragnet about to drop. Early morning sunshine deceived her; frigid air numbed her face. She'd enjoy the calm before the impending storm of police and flashing lights overtook the quiet boatyard. Remaining silent and out of sight had not been her strong suit; but there was no point aggravating Owen Roe and Joe Nagle.

Tires crunched on the frozen dirt and gravel road. Birdie stepped inside, watching from a curtained window. Battered trucks and construction vans sped past, stopping at a new framed houseboat at the rear of the yard.

No sign of police.

Disappointed, she slumped into a deep chair. Soon, they'd arrive, and it would be over. There had been nothing for her to do. She'd given Nagle the facts, plenty for a judge to grant a search warrant.

Beeps of a car horn sounded, bringing Birdie to her feet. The green Dodge rolled to a stop at her front door.

She'd fallen asleep not knowing Jark arrived without warning. Now that he was her client, she couldn't grumble about his timing. If he'd known anything about the pending arrest, she hadn't told him. She had intended to call him after the transit cop sat in jail, fearing Jark would take his own justice. He grieved the senseless loss of a sister and father because of a spur of the moment random act—Malda Boddy and Mary Clary swapped coats, causing the killer to misidentify his victim. The former combat Marine had plenty of skills to take revenge. There were times Birdie wondered if she would prevent him.

Before Jark knocked, she opened the door, waving him in.

"Coffee?"

"Need help?" Jark asked.

"There's been a break."

Birdie poured two cups from the electric percolator she kept filled. She swung a chair from behind her make-shift desk.

"I kept something from you," she confessed, seating herself close to him at the kitchen table.

"I had a feeling."

"The cops are on the way here to make an arrest."

She noticed Jark remained calmer than expected. His life changed because of the man she lived next to. If she'd been alert, Sid Breen would be alive sitting in his office running his Broadway empire.

"I will not do anything stupid... not anymore," he said.

"I know," she said, holding his hand, noticing his reddened, puffy eyes.

"What next?"

"We wait," Birdie said, peeking out the living room window.

"For what?"

"Their search will turn up hard proof for an arrest."

"You did it." Jark jumped to his feet, walking to her.

She nodded her head.

"How long did you know?"

"Not long. You were a big help."

"Is there enough evidence?" Jark asked. "The weapon?"

"He had the silver button from the cape your sister borrowed, along with her earring."

"The axe?"

"No."

"You searched his place?"

"That's all you need to know. I shouldn't have said something."

"You went to the police?"

"Joe Nagle. I told him everything. He and my ex-boyfriend will handle the arrest."

"I want to see the bastard."

Birdie looked at the kitchen clock. "They should have been here hours ago. I'm starting to worry."

"Probably paperwork." Jark glanced outside. "I came by to let you know Sid's service is tomorrow."

"Same place?" she asked.

Jark nodded. "Won't be easy."

"I can't imagine."

"Having you there helps."

"We'll have this guy behind bars by then."

Birdie allowed her emotions to escape and rushed to him, wrapping her arms around his neck, pressing close, whispering in his ear. "I'm sorry this happened." She pushed tight against him. Jark returned her embrace and kissed her.

Her pent-up passion exploded, gripping his hips, pulling Jark closer until they collapsed as one to her sofa.

She craved him and would not hold back.

CHAPTER FORTY-THREE

The subway doors slid shut behind Victor Gregory, leaving him in the near-empty terminal. Two winos drinking from paper bags huddled in a corner at the back of closed token booths. One of them, possibly Otter. He didn't care, walking past the hobos as an ordinary civilian, no longer a uniformed transit officer.

For the first time, Victor felt vulnerable, his privacy breached, and his home most likely staked out by police. The tall, eye-catching neighbor betrayed him, breaking his trust, entering his domain, discovering secrets. New York City had become dangerous, a modern-day Gomorrah; but, he'd never relocate. To him, the magical city would always be the capital of the world.

Victor trudged to the sidewalk, taking a deep breath of late-night damp air. The leather bag stayed at his side, guarding the Indian pipe axe and the mushroomed slug delivered by his neighbor.

A glance at his watch reminded him an hour remained to position himself. Lev Reznik had lookouts in place, waiting in the shadows of the docks. Across the street, late customers exited Gig's diner, escorted by a plump waitress. She hung a closed sign on a suction cup, giving it a push, swinging it in the window.

Fluorescent lights clicked off, one by one, leaving few to illuminate the long, white Formica counter. No longer would he enjoy his spot at the bar, comforted by steaming hot coffee. Exhausted, he craved the dull life of others. Thoughts of his failed existence bombarded his mind, crowding out reasoning, and triggered a vicious response.

What depth would he reach? Could he recover? Was death his escape? In the cold street, an image of Otter, limping toward him, took angelic form, emerged from a discharge of steam rising from a sidewalk grating, hovering over him. Abruptly, the vision vanished.

A foretelling?

Nagle made a fool of him, luring him with a promotion to a non-existent job. The crooked New York cop would pay with his life. There would be no blue-uniformed honor guard or casket drawn by a team of white horses. Nagle deserved a burial at sea with the city's garbage.

Russians were moving into Brooklyn, gaining power, and Reznik wanted a clean slate, with no intention of keeping Victor as a partner in the illegal operations. He'd be used to kill the cop, and when no longer needed, discarded. Most likely they would make it appear he and Nagle shot it out, killing one another.

Winter's darkness came early. Black overcast clouds shrouded New York Bay, cheating dusk of its brief appearance, bringing heavy gusts and fast falling temperatures. Victor turned up his jacket collar and held his bare hands above a steel drum's snapping flames. He wanted nothing more of the long day—only to return home to meditate. He couldn't; Birdie changed that. Tonight would amend everything. The scars of his life would be healed.

Victor looked at the time; he'd arrived early, hoping to spot Nagle and signs of an ambush. As far as he could tell, no cars approached and the rooftops clear of lookouts. The ruse relied on convincing Nagle Reznik planned to move the counterfeit cash, something the dishonest cop may have sought from the start. Nagle was in for a surprise. Once the raid took place, no forged hundred-dollar bills would be discovered, only wardrobe trunks filled with costumes belonging to a Romanian dance company.

A pair of tugboats pushing a steamship from the Brooklyn Army Terminal distracted him. New York Harbor remained quiet, lit by the lights of Manhattan, glittering on its choppy water. There had been nothing for him to do but wait for Nagle and Reznik's promised moving van. Any time, Victor hoped to spot Reznik's longshoremen transferring heavy chests of costumes from the Russian Liberty Ship to the waiting truck. The scam would draw Nagle from hiding.

Nagle preferred to work alone, that he had been sure of, not trusting another cop for what he planned—the theft of flawless, counterfeit one-hundred-dollar bills.

The rumble of the truck's engine came from between warehouses. Wet brakes squealed, stopping near the Harbor Ship Supply eighteen-wheeled trailer. Men in heavy wool coats came and went, pushing two-wheeled dollies, stocking the Russian freighters meat lockers and storerooms. The surprise diversion gave Victor an opportunity to get close to the ship and keep an eye on Reznik while watching for his target.

Victor pulled off his oversized topcoat, tossing it in the blazing fire. Under it, a slim-fitting pea coat. Pulling on a watch cap, he walked toward the boarding ramp unnoticed, joining other longshoremen.

Reznik and his two bodyguards waited in the truck cab—possibly more hid in the rear, under the white canopy-covered bed. The recently arrived truck, belonging to the Romanian Dance Company, would receive a decoy chest, luring Nagle to Reznik's bait and abrupt demise. All the forged currency, according to plan, would remain secured, locked inside the Liberty ship,

A sudden flair of a match lighting a cigarette caught Victor's attention. Nagle's beat-up Ford coupe sat outside a battered storage building less than twenty yards from Reznik. The cop arrived alone. Victor knew Nagle operated as a lone wolf. He knew the type.

Victor had the upper hand, knowing the positions of his enemies and controlled the situation. Like a chess match, he'd strike rapidly, overpowering his opponent.

A rhythmic squeak of a two-wheeled dolly bumped down the ship's long ramp, grabbed his attention. The metal wheels landed with a thump on the quay's wood platform as a single workman struggled to support the bulky, wooden steamer trunk.

At last, the bait entered the theater, beginning the end of the tragedy, drawing the combatants to center stage.

The red ember flew from the car door, and Nagle emerged. He'd be well armed under the long overcoat. Victor Gregory waited, knowing the cop would pass near where he hid. Nagle's quest for shallow, worldly rewards would be punished as God had disciplined wayward children of Israel for worshiping a golden calf. The cop's last judgment would arrive like a bolt from the blue, pleasing the Seneca war chief.

Fear in his victim's eyes, feeling their final breath against his skin, brought intimacy. Unlike the aloofness of a distant sniper, he watched from close by as the specter of death entered his prey. He'd created a bond—honed steel merged with a fine carved wood handle mated him to his quarry as an umbilical cord, not of life, but death.

Victor gripped the war axe at his side, waiting.

One final deep breath, hold, exhale.

Footsteps approached at a quick pace. Nagle's shadow appeared at the edge of the dirty brick building. Victor lifted the axe, raising it from near his knee, holding it overhead, taking aim. With full force, he swung downward. Nagle walked full stride into the sharp blade as it rammed into his forehead. For an instant, he remained erect, frozen in mid-step, before collapsing on the wet, grimy road.

His earthly labor complete—he'd join his father soon. Birdie no longer mattered, unworthy of his divine attention and bond.

The kill had been executed without a glitch. The great Chief would have been honored. It came time to seek eternal sanctuary, leaving behind the axe embedded inside Nagle's skull. His work concluded. Reznik's men would leave no trace of Nagle. He'd escape, blending with dock workers. Only he knew the secrets the Russian mob boss hid in the belly of the Liberty ship.

Victor took several deep breaths, calming his racing heart. Each killing brought new power and strength.

His time had come.

The bells of the basilica rang, guiding him a few short blocks to the church. Our Lady of Perpetual Help waited with open, forgiving arms. His final destination—his transformation, the promised reward awaited. He'd reached the ultimate judgment of his earthly existence.

The massive cathedral's doors remained open for sinners and saints. Victor entered, walking the central aisle, hearing distant echoes of his heavy-soled shoes rebound off the vaulted ceiling. Surrounded by vacant pews and twinkling votive candles, Victor fell to his knees beneath the life-sized crucifix.

"Take me. My work is done."

He knelt with outstretched arms. "Take me. Take me," he shouted towards the figure of Christ hanging crucified above the marble altar.

Candles, flanking the majestic church walls, flickered and died, leaving the cross lighted by a single, muted scarlet spotlight.

A voice broke the silence.

"Victor Gregory, you have disappointed me."

CHAPTER FORTY-FOUR

The familiar voice came from divergent directions, surrounding Victor. His legs useless, frozen, kneeling on the cold tile floor. The sensation came without warning. Had he drawn it from his imagination or a remnant of his meditation? In the past, he'd experienced gratifying pleasure during deep trances.

Victor slid a revolver from the small of his back, waiting to aim at the first sign of life. Immobilized and locked to the floor but not defenseless, he'd send a bullet without warning into his attacker.

From the half-darkness of a recessed chapel, footsteps approached. Victor Gregory raised the gun barrel, aiming into the gloom.

Otter stepped forward facing Victor, entering the wide nave, showing no signs of a hobbled leg.

"Who are you?" Victor asked, cocking his handgun.

The surprise visitor waved his pale hands near the aimed gun. "I visit those who have reached the end of their squandered human lives."

Victor lowered his aim. "That so?"

"We first met at a church like this. You tripped over me." Otter smiled. "Do you recall the night you intended to kill your girlfriend? A mistake happened. You killed an innocent Mary Clary."

"What do you want?"

"From you, nothing."

"Tell Reznik or whoever you work for, I'm done with all this."

"That choice is no longer yours." Otter stepped close, placing a hand firmly on Victor's head. "I will take you now."

Victor continued kneeling, powerless to rise or pull the trigger, watching Otter stand over him. His appearance, despite ragged, dirty clothes, belonged to another world. He had become someone else yet remained the same man he'd sat with inside the carousel and who'd tracked him for days, knowing details of his actions and movements. Unable to understand, Victor knew something spiritual transpired, altering Otter.

The hand on his forehead turned hot. Victor tried to knock it away. It stayed in place with a greater force, searing his scalp.

"Leave me alone," he shouted to the figure looming large over him.

"I am the Archangel Azrael, ministering to the damned."

"Don't see no wings," Victor said, shading his eyes from the sudden circle of light glaring over him.

"I do not have a celestial form. You are through, Victor."

"I've seen my destiny. I'll be raised like Lazarus."

"No. He died first. You will not," Azrael answered. "You will remain undead but not living, existing as a dream-shadow, never part of heaven or hell, unworthy of them."

"This is a church. Give me holy water. I'll confess...."

Otter extended both arms, touching Victor's shoulders.

In the next instant—in a fiery flash Victor evaporated. No ashes. No residue. Instead, a gauzy, dark shadow emerged from the floor where Victor Gregory once knelt, shaping his silhouette near the heavy wooden cross.

High in the belfry, bells tolled as the cathedral doors swung open. Otter hobbled down the stairs, buttoning his raggedy overcoat, returning home, limping up and down through new fallen snow.

CHAPTER FORTY-FIVE

Birdie and Jark awoke in the dead of night to the sudden burst of light. In a blink of an eye, it blazed like a muted ball of lightning, vanishing as quickly as it came, leaving behind a chorus of ringing church bells.

"What was that?" Birdie said, sitting up.

"Somebody's headlights," Jark answered, reaching an arm around her.

She rolled from bed. "No, we're too high. Something's wrong."

"Whatever it was, didn't make a sound," Jark said.

At her window, Birdie looked toward Victor Gregory's home.

"It's gone!" she said.

"What is?"

She pushed open the heavy curtain. "My neighbor's place."

The elevated steel and wood houseboat ceased to exist. A single street lamp lit the vacant spot. No sign remained of the massive corroded hull and upper deck. The rusted stairs she'd climbed to break and enter her neighbor's home vanished. Nothing remained.

Could it be last evening's wine permitting her vivid imagination to take control?

A thick Atlantic fog had rolled into the low wharf area the previous night. Would it have concealed a tidal surge which floated the houseboat from its base and carried it to sea? Perhaps her neighbor's home sat abandoned on a sand dune in Long Island.

Birdie turned back to watch Jark step into the shower. She'd lived a fantasy with him the past several hours. Time to face reality. Reznik most likely moved the boat while they frolicked in her bed. This was New York City. Big things happened overnight. It bore Broadway stars in an instant, and high-rise skyscrapers seemed to pop up overnight. It was a magical city if you had courage to believe. Jark had been hers, at least for the night. Something in Birdie sensed what happened to Victor Gregory's home wouldn't have a rational explanation. The two, despite ravaging one another, would have noticed or at least heard trucks and workmen moving the large houseboat. She'd more likely believe a sudden tidal wave had been responsible.

She pulled Jark's navy pea coat over a thin gown and grabbed her red and white Eveready flashlight and gun. Stepping to the deck of her boat, her house slippers sunk into powdery snow, chilling her feet and ankles. Birdie felt the sting of frigid air dash up her spine.

Curiosity drove her, and aided by a sliver of a waning moon, she made new tracks, crossing the boatyard's dreary landscape. The fairy tale illusion would not lull her into carelessness. She dealt with a dangerous killer, one she knew. With her destination a few steps away, Birdie squeezed her handgun, resting in the pocket of Jark's wool jacket. She thought of him and his gentleness. Moments ago he had wrapped her, safe and warm, in his arms. What possessed her to leave for the cold snow? The murder case belonged to Roe and Nagle. Couldn't she get that through her thick Irish head?

Seeing the empty site of Victor Gregory's home up close made it easier to accept, although Pinkerton training taught her not to believe everything she saw too quickly and take nothing for granted.

What did she expect to find?

It was gone, vanished as if Harry Blackstone waved his magical shroud, whisking it away without a trace. The space was vacant. No signs of the houseboat or heavy-duty joists which held it upright. Was her neighbor behind the misdirection or whatever went on? He'd deceived her before, and her client, Sid Breen, lost his life. She wouldn't take any chances and began a search.

She dragged her near frozen foot side to side, as a broom, brushing away powdery snow, searching for remains of the houseboat. Five hours ago it sat secure, welded to steel beams anchored to concrete piers. Could anyone possibly move the massive vessel in the short time, leaving no trail?

It seemed unlikely; Birdie kept it as a possibility. Reznik had friends in the powerful teamster's organization, and with enough money, anything could be done or bought in New York City or Jersey.

With frostbite attacking her soaking-wet feet, she kicked away snow non-stop, uncovering nothing. Oddly, the bare ground remained smooth and level, undisturbed by utility and sewer lines. Why bother to remove them along with the beams supporting the hulking houseboat? If they'd been torch cut, protruding nubs of steel would remain, poking from the frozen ground.

Could this fruitless search be something her mind conjured as a dream? Was she, at this moment, snuggled in her warm bed, arms wrapped around Jark? If so, she wanted to awaken, relishing in the pleasure of putting a smile on his handsome face, rewarding him.

Or..., God forbid, a delusion carried over from her addiction to painkillers?

It had been none of those. The reality—she foolishly worked herself to a frenzy in Reznik's boatyard, barefoot, house slippers lost, nearly frozen, wearing Jark's coat. None of what she looked at or did made sense, yet there she remained, playing the part of a despairing, miserable character in a Victor Hugo drama.

Roe and Nagle may have something to do with the unexplained disappearance. Perhaps witness protection?

Snow continued to fall, and Birdie's numb toes and soles felt like lifeless wood clubs at the ends of her ankles. She'd lost her case, every piece of evidence vanished. She'd call the two detectives and, with them, thoroughly comb the property. A reasonable explanation would be discovered. She knew it.

About to end her misery, Birdie took a last swipe, sweeping her foot over a small rise in the snow. A small white crusted clump jarred free and rolled. Her frozen house slippers turned up. She had no other place to search.

Nothing really disappears into thin air.

CHAPTER FORTY-SIX

Detective Owen Roe came face to face with Birdie as soon as he stepped from his car the next morning.

"What do you mean you want an explanation?" he asked, stepping around her.

"Don't play dumb." Birdie persisted, placing herself in his path. "What happened to Victor Gregory's house?"

"Don't know him. Guess he moved. This boatyard is nothing but a trailer park without wheels. Happens all the time. People pack up and move in the middle of the night. He has a right to."

"You had a warrant to search his house. He killed Mary Clary and Sid Breen... maybe more."

Roe gripped her shoulders. "Stop right there. We had what?"

Birdie paused. Her anger nearly took over. She'd never forgive him for giving Hollis her engagement ring. This one time, she needed to keep cool. Something was wrong. She looked Roe in the eyes. He had faults, lying to her was not among them.

"Two days ago, I dropped by your office to discuss Mary Clary's murder," Birdie said. She pointed to the open space where Victor Gregory's home once sat. "The killer lived there."

"You didn't talk to me."

"You were out." Birdie resisted bringing up seeing him leave a hotel with the busty meter maid. After a prolonged deep breath, she continued. "Nagle took my statement. The guy living there is a transit cop named Victor Gregory. I saw the things he removed from the Clary girl after killing her."

"You talked to my partner, Nagle? This is news to me."

"He didn't tell you?"

"You're sure it was Nagle?"

"He took notes and said he'd fill you in. Said he'd get a search warrant and for me to stay out."

"This evidence, what is it?" Roe asked.

"Her earring and the silver button he cut from her cape were in his house."

"In the houseboat, that isn't there anymore?"

"It was when Jark and I went to bed."

"You weren't alone?"

Birdie shook her head. "No." Then waved toward her home.

Jark stepped from her kitchen door and walked down the ramp.

"We both saw a bright light flash early this morning, and the boat wasn't there."

"We guessed someone moved it," Jark said. "Trouble is, it snowed and whoever hauled it off, their tracks got covered."

Roe looked at Birdie and Jark. A tiny smile appeared on his face. "Why don't we look?"

After a few steps, Roe stopped. "Birdie, get me a broom."

She needed him and held back words she wanted to say to the arrogant, self-important cop. Seeing this side of Roe again eased the pain he'd caused her.

Birdie returned with a worn-down kitchen broom. Roe stood spread-legged, hands stuffed in his overcoat.

"This where you say the killer lived?"

"Here, closer to the utility pole." Birdie used the broom's red handle as a pointer.

"Show me," Roe rotated a finger around the area they stood. "Sweep me an outline of where exactly this boat sat."

It would do no good to toss the broom into his smug face, encouraging Owen Roe to remind her of how her well-known Irish temper kept her in trouble. Birdie gritted her teeth and swept a clean path outlining Victor Gregory's boat home. The light snow stopped at sunrise, leaving several inches covering hard packed gravel and dirt. With the wood handle, Birdie marked a crooked X in the center of the large rectangle she had drawn.

"I sat there in his living room a few nights ago," she said, tapping the broom on the spot. "You're acting like you don't believe me." Birdie again bit her lip, stopping herself from calling the cop a moron.

She had more to say, but the look on Jark's face warned her off. He remained her client, despite their recently evolved relationship.

Roe walked the length of the outlined location, pausing from time to time to kneel in the thin covering of snow, holding his bare hand on the raw ground. "I'm not saying I don't believe something once sat here, but there's no evidence that shows me that."

Birdie marched through the snow, wielding her corn broom like a medieval lance, stopping when the blunt, snow and mud-crusted handle rested against Roe's chest.

"You think the both of us are making this up?"

Roe reached out and slid the handle to the side. As he did, Birdie stepped back, flailing her arms, tossing the broom.

"Well, do you?" she shouted.

"There has to be an explanation," Roe said. "As far as I know, the damn Russians and their Sputnik vaporized it. The entire world has gone crazy since that thing went up there."

"You're doing nothing, aren't you?" she asked.

"The transit cop's name is Victor Gregory?"

Jark stepped between the two. "He's a sergeant."

"I'll talk to him if he's actually a cop," Roe said, writing the name in his pocket notebook.

"Find the house, the evidence and the murder axe are there," Birdie said. "Check with Joe Nagle; I told him this."

"That's another problem," Roe said. "We don't know where he is... nor does his wife."

As Roe knocked snow from his gloves, his shoe struck a low mound of snow, making a dull, hollow thud. The three stopped. A corner of a brown leather case poked from the thin snow cover. Birdie grabbed the uncovered shoulder strap, jarring the satchel free from crusted ice.

"There's a hole in the side," she said.

Roe placed a hand on hers. "Something your neighbor left behind?" Roe asked, bending over it, brushing away a light coating of snow and ice.

"He always carried it," Birdie said.

Roe unfolded a large paper bag from inside a pocket of his bulky overcoat. "How do you suppose it got here?"

Birdie stared at the satchel. She knew his words purposely jabbed at her, a sarcastic reminder she'd overlooked evidence under her feet.

"Feels heavy." Roe looked at Birdie and Jark while sliding the shoulder bag into a crumpled A&P grocery sack.

"Not looking inside?" Birdie asked.

"And give you a chance to tamper with evidence?" A slight smile played on the corners of Roe's mouth.

"It may help locate Nagle," she said.

Roe rested the sack in one arm, undid the single clasp and reached inside.

"That's why I couldn't find it," Birdie said. "He carried it with him."

Using his gloved hand, Roe gripped the smooth wood handle, removing the axe, sliding the long, tapered, blood-covered blade from the bottom of the leather satchel.

"May I," Birdie asked.

She pushed a finger into the satchel's bullet hole. Next, she reached inside, guiding her hand along its bottom.

"Now what?" Roe asked.

"This!" she said, showing Roe and Jark the flattened slug. It's a .38, and I put it here.

CHAPTER FORTY-SEVEN

After two days passed, Owen Roe met Birdie as she arrived at the midtown precinct. Her walk in the frosty morning air left her refreshed, and she greeted the detective with an air kiss on the cheek.

"You look good, and you're early," Roe said, stamping out a cigarette.

"Living on the Westside suits me."

"That was quick."

"I'm sharing Sid Breen's apartment with his son," Birdie said. "You remember him?"

"Young guy.... Sancho, your sidekick?"

"Jark... and don't be funny." Birdie smiled. "He's in over his head with Sid's death, so... I'm helping him manage Breen Productions."

Owen Roe grunted and steered her upstairs to the squad room. "Guess you plan to run Broadway."

"Lending a hand," she answered and helped herself to a chair next to Roe's desk.

"I don't have to do this. It's a courtesy because of our relationship," Roe said, pulling a chair close to his desk.

"Did Nagle's version back me?"

"That's one problem," Roe answered. "I have nothing to show you two spoke. You were here according to the desk sergeant, but Nagle didn't file a statement or a witness report."

"You think I'm poking at windmills. Victor Gregory tried to kill me after I spent an hour detailing who Breen's killer is and how I know," Birdie said. "I want Victor Gregory off the street. Hell, I incriminated myself. That's how bad I want him in jail."

"He didn't file paperwork."

"Talk to him. He'll tell you. He planned to search my neighbor's home."

"Nagle's still missing." Roe pushed a stack of gray folders across the desk. "I've gone through his current reports looking for anything. Nothing's there. His wife's shaken up... she said he's been secretive—something he wouldn't talk about."

"How long?" Birdie asked.

"Since his run-in with the Russian embassy and demotion. By the way, we found his car in an impound yard in Queens."

"You want to know what we talked about?"

"Tell me everything from the beginning. Leave nothing out."

Once again, Birdie told of her discovery of Victor Gregory's hidden stash of the victim's belongings. On this telling, she admitted removing Malda's blood-stained cape from the morgue. After covering the events several times, Roe delved into details, pulling minute facts she'd failed to recall during Nagle's interrogation.

Watching him work, probing, asking the same question repeatedly, not showing emotion, patiently waiting for an answer, she understood he'd pounce on the slightest variance, searching for particulars.

After two hours of slogging over the events of the past week, Roe sent for kosher pastrami on rye from Katz's. After the delivery man left, with no tip, Roe pushed a brown sack to her and continued his interrogation.

"We first met at Katz's," Birdie said. "I'm touched you remembered."

With a quick swallow of root beer, Roe dropped his half-eaten sandwich on the butcher wrapping he used as a plate.

"If I report you, Albany will yank your PI license, and the city will have you behind bars... but you knew that."

Birdie shook her head. "I came here to turn myself in when I spoke to Nagle."

"I want to believe that."

"I'm telling the truth."

"This arrived earlier," Roe said, opening an envelope marked private.

Birdie watched his eyes; she knew he toyed with her, enjoying the power. His eyes looked at her, although he pretended to read the paper in front of him. The slight twitch in the corner of his mouth had been a tell. He was about to speak.

"The Indian axe we found had Nagle's blood type on it for what it's worth, and the prints matched Victor Gregory's according to Transit records."

"Has he been brought in?"

"Not yet," Roe answered. "He's been a no-show for three days."

"Reznik might know something."

"He's in Russia, according to his office," Roe answered. "We'll keep trying."

"The houseboat?"

"We're running down house and boat movers. You can't transport something that size without a permit or someone seeing it. I don't care what time of day."

"Then, you believe me?"

"Doesn't hurt to check. Somebody will come forward."

Birdie pointed a finger to her chest. "What about me?"

Roe leaned back in his chair, and she saw the lines crossing his forehead disappear and the smirk she knew well appeared.

"When we locate this transit cop and his mysterious boathouse, we'll probably uncover what happened to Joe Nagle. At least, that's my hunch. Then, I'll decide what to do with you and this mess. So... be careful."

"Seems fair," Birdie said.

"I'm doing it for Nagle's family. He had a grudge and got in over his head with this Russian. It was small time and would've blown over if he'd left it alone. The Russians are harmless."

Owen Roe slapped the top of his desk and winked at Birdie.

He pulled open a bottom drawer and dropped the envelope marked private into it, locking it.

Birdie pushed against the door, leaving the precinct. Thoughts of Victor Gregory and the bizarre disappearance of his home haunted her. She'd escaped his attack—could she again? She brushed into an old man in a dirty and tattered overcoat. He stumbled, catching himself against the building. As she made an apology, the man interrupted.

"Victor Gregory is no longer of this world."

THE END

ABOUT THE AUTHOR

Robert L. Joswick grew up in the shadow of a coal mine, and is the son and grandson of coal miners. He has a MBA and retired from the business world, and is a former professional football player for the Miami Dolphins. He studied fiction writing at University of California, Riverside, California and English Literature at The University of Tulsa. Joswick has published a number of articles for a regional Southern California magazine, *Urban Living* and has written for a national publication. He enjoys archery, golf and is a former Harley Davidson rider.

NOTE FROM THE AUTHOR

Word-of-mouth is crucial for any author to succeed. If you enjoyed *Mass Transit*, please leave a review online—anywhere you are able. Even if it's just a sentence or two. It would make all the difference and would be very much appreciated.

Thanks!
Robert L. Joswick

We hope you enjoyed reading this title from:

BLACK ROSE writing™

www.blackrosewriting.com

Subscribe to our mailing list – *The Rosevine* – and receive **FREE** books, daily deals, and stay current with news about upcoming releases and our hottest authors.
Scan the QR code below to sign up.

Already a subscriber? Please accept a sincere thank you for being a fan of Black Rose Writing authors.

View other Black Rose Writing titles at www.blackrosewriting.com/books and use promo code **PRINT** to receive a **20% discount** when purchasing.

www.ingramcontent.com/pod-product-compliance
Lightning Source LLC
Chambersburg PA
CBHW010731130726
47899CB00013B/2979

9 781685 130718